Release Me

It was all very well spying on Alicia having a bit of rough, but to burst in on Tom doing what he had been doing was deeply humiliating. No handsome man should have to be horny on his own at eleven thirty in the morning! I lay in my bed thinking about Tom Hathaway. Even in that vulnerable position he had been good-looking. He had a deep, well-spoken voice – not as posh and affected as Alicia's. I don't usually go for the public schoolboy type, but he had looked quite inviting. My hand fell between my legs and my imagination built up my short meeting with him into an epic erotic event. I wanted to make the fantasy real. He would certainly get more than he bargained for with me!

Author's other Black Lace titles:

Opening Acts

Release Me
Suki Cunningham

BLACK LACE

Black Lace books contain sexual fantasies.
In real life, always practise safe sex.

First published in 2002 by
Black Lace
Thames Wharf Studios
Rainville Road
London W6 9HA

ISBN 0 352 33671 4

Printed and bound in Great Britain by Clays Ltd, St Ives PLC

1

'Not here.' Jerome pushed my hand hurriedly off his hip. We were standing face to face in his office – well, actually, I was perched on the edge of the desk in what I hoped was a seductive fashion and he was standing before me in his faded 501s and open-necked black shirt. I leant into him and put my cheek to his, smelling his woody cologne.

'Come on, nobody's looking,' I whispered, nuzzling his stubble. I glanced at the window that overlooked the open-plan office where the rest of us worked. The blinds were drawn. I could just make out the tall blond figure of Sven having his daily battle with the fax machine and Corinne chatting on the phone, but no one could have seen us unless they pressed their faces right to the glass. 'I want an action replay of last night.'

'Jo, there's no time. I've got an editorial to write . . .' He tried to pull away.

'Edited highlights then.' I am nothing if not persistent. It's one of my greatest assets and also one of my biggest faults. For my birthday my best friend Ruby bought me a copy of *The Rules* – a self-help manual for the terminally clingy, a diatribe on playing hard to get, but in my view the rules were made to be broken. What was the point of playing hard to get with a man who had already had me on many occasions, in many positions and in ways that had let him know I was very into it?

So I wrapped my bare brown legs around him,

which isn't easy to do in a leather miniskirt (our office has a casual dress code, which I like to exploit to the max). Jerome blushed. Maybe he was embarrassed, or maybe he was remembering last night's session. I brought my hand to his crotch to check. His black hair flopped over one eye as he looked down.

'You're outrageous,' he said.

'You're aroused,' I said back. I gently buried my hand under the tough waistband of his jeans, getting a skin-on-skin feel of his lovely erection. I was really fond of his cock. It gave me so much pleasure: it always waited for me to come first, it knew when I wanted it to be merciless and it knew when I wanted it to tease. In many ways it was a lot more thoughtful than its owner. At the moment I just wanted to caress it, and it rubbed its head against my palm like a contented cat.

'Jo, we can't do this here.' Jerome's voice was tightening as his hips started to grind.

'Loosen up, Jerome,' I said soothingly, gaining a rhythm. 'This is a music mag not the *Sunday Telegraph*. No one cares if we fuck in here all day. It's not like either of us is married.' That shut him up, or maybe it was my hand that did. He looked down at me with his soft brown eyes, as always shadowed by the black hair that fell over one side of his face. 'I'm sure everyone has guessed about us anyway,' I added. I didn't like the appalled look that instantly clouded his face.

'Really? I thought we'd been so careful.'

He pulled away and my hand was yanked from its warm haven. He went over to the far window and looked down over his much-prized view of the Thames. Beneath us the big grey river curled around the South Bank, heaving slowly under Waterloo Bridge, away from the Houses of Parliament. Looking at Jerome's back as he sighed, I wanted to ask him why the cloak and dagger routine was so necessary. After all, we'd been crazy about each other for three months. He was one of those men who acted full-on and intimate in the bedroom, then completely cool in the outside world. I was convinced that my bedroom-Jerome was the genuine article, and that the slightly offish work-Jerome was just an act. Ruby insisted that it was the other way round. I was about to ask why it would be so awful if people found out, but decided to keep my mouth shut. My question hung unspoken in the air. Eventually I broke the silence.

'So why did you call me into the inner sanctum then?' I asked, trying not to sound snappy. 'Didn't you like my piece on the samba clubs in Rio?' I knew full well that it was a fantastic piece; my mother being Brazilian, I'd had a lot of inside information while I was out there. I had been in Brazil for nearly three weeks writing it and getting into the heart of the samba culture. All those driving drumbeats and hot sweaty streets had got me in touch with my Latin temperament, and my days on Copacabana Beach and my nights dancing had given me that toned, tanned body I had always dreamt of. It seemed selfish not to share it with Jerome when I got back, and he had been satisfyingly appreciative.

'No, the piece was great,' Jerome replied. 'It was so good, in fact, that there's another assignment I want you to do. Quite a different piece this time.' He opened a drawer and brought out a musty old ledger covered in green velvet. I took it and opened the first page. It was inscribed in faded midnight-blue ink: *The Diary of Daphne Hathaway 1907–1908.* 'The early years,' Jerome explained, 'before she really started to write her opus. She was eighteen when she wrote this journal.'

'My God, where did you get it?' I asked, flicking

through the pages, which were thick with script. I knew Jerome was an enormous fan of this composer and that he had always wanted to do a piece on her eccentric, debauched lifestyle, but we had never come up with much in research.

'I got very very lucky,' he grinned. 'I've been mentioning my obsession to so many people something had to come out of it. You prick your arm enough, you eventually hit a vein.'

I laughed at his sex and drugs and rock 'n' roll imagery, which was typical of Jerome. He took back the book and stroked the cover possessively.

'Hang on.' I said, thinking aloud, 'if you are so into this woman's work, why are you giving me the job? Surely you'd write the definitive article on Daphne Hathaway? I don't really know that much about her. It's not really my kind of music, to be honest.' I'd never really got to grips with that classical stuff, unlike Jerome who had a taste for 'any music with quality', as he would tell me *ad nauseum*.

'Quite,' he said, almost sneering. 'If I tried to write it, it would be the biggest piece of subjective gush you'd ever find. And anyway, it needs a woman's perspective. We need it to be gripping: kiss and tell, revealing. Our sales are down. We need to spice things up a bit.'

I stared at him, flattered that he would trust me with the story. In fact, the responsibility was overwhelming. I felt like someone had just given me their favourite child to bring up. The idea was terrifying.

'No need to look like that,' he said. 'It may not be samba, but it's still sexy.' He came up to me and put his arms around me in a rare moment of affection. 'Of course it will mean you going away again.' He squeezed. For a moment it felt as if he was pleased to get rid of me. 'We have to get permission to print from her surviving family, and do some interviews with them. I want this to be as in-depth as possible.'

'I see.' I pressed my face into his neck. 'And how long am I going for this time?'

'At least two weeks, Jo.' He pulled away and handed me a starter file. I opened it up and found the address of my assignment and some dog-eared photos.

'"Hathaway Hall, Norfolk",' I read out. 'Sounds very grand.' The picture on the next page exceeded all my expectations: a fine stately home with acres of grounds, sweeping driveways, stables, the lot. 'What a time warp!'

'Exactly,' Jerome said, grinning. 'I'm thinking that if Daphne Hathaway was an eccentric aristocratic tearaway then the current Hathaways who still live in this old pile might be just as barmy. I don't know – maybe there's a story there. A new angle.'

'Who are the "current Hathaways"?' I envisaged a houseful of doddering old dears with more money than sense, but Jerome pulled a photo from the file for me. Two good-looking young people smiled out from the frame: the woman beautiful, black haired, wild eyed; the man fair, smiling shyly, green eyed. She was wearing a riding outfit and he was in an old cricket jumper.

'Alicia and Tom,' Jerome explained. 'Parents deceased, so they run the joint now. Tom is the executor of the estate. It's his permission we need to do all this. They are expecting you tomorrow.'

'Well,' I replied, gently laying my hand on his bottom. 'We'd better make the most of tonight then, hadn't we?'

Both the good and the bad thing about sleeping with your boss is that he tends to have more money than you do. In Jerome's case this meant a swish flat in

Islington with the sexiest bathroom I have ever seen. I just needed to look at the sunken bath in the middle of the room and I got excited. It was a broad oval made of white porcelain, surrounded by a crescent of candles. The walls were lined with mirrors. Jerome knew how much I liked to make love in the bath, so I gathered I was in for a good time when I got there that night and saw that he had lit all the bathroom candles and turned the lights down low.

'I thought we could eat later,' he said softly, pulling me into the bathroom and closing the door behind us.

As Jerome ran the bath, leaning down to adjust the temperature, I sank behind him and snaked my arms around him, slowly undoing his shirt. His hard broad body rippled against mine. I pulled the shirt off his back and started to kiss down his spine, just the way he liked it. His smooth skin warmed with pleasure. As he was pouring in some bath foam, I unbuckled his jeans and pulled them open, searching for the familiar hardness of his fabulous cock. He sighed as I began to play with it, both my hands fondling him until he was as big as he was going to get. He turned off the taps and turned round to me, as my hands slipped on to his buttocks.

'God, you're sexy,' he murmured as his mouth covered mine, his warm tongue tasting me possessively. His hands roamed to my breasts and he let out a moan when he realised I wasn't wearing a bra under my white cotton dress. 'Someone with big horny breasts like yours shouldn't be allowed to walk around like that.' He sighed into my neck, kissing his way down to my cleavage. His hands were exploring their way up my skirt now. I waited for the moment when he realised I wasn't wearing knickers either, my pussy moistening expectantly.

'Oh, Josephina!' he reprimanded as his hand

encountered my soft triangle. He sometimes used my full name when he got aroused; he seemed to like the exotic side of me. He was excited now, pressing up against me, his mouth moving from my cleavage to my throat to my lips and his hand gently tickling me between the legs. I hooked my thumbs under his waistband and pulled down his jeans and boxers. He kicked them off and lay naked on top of me, grinding his hardness against the flimsy white cotton of my dress.

'God, you look gorgeous.'

I smiled and rolled over, pushing him into the water. He fell with a splash into the sunken bath, sending a film of warm suds over the bathroom floor. He looked very sexy lying there naked, laughing, his black hair clinging to his neck and face. I leant over and drew my hand over his body, caressing his cock in silky slow movements, looking him in the eye.

Suddenly he grabbed my arm and pulled me in after him. I screamed and landed on top of him in the water, my white dress billowing out and becoming immediately transparent as it clung to my every curve. We struggled for a moment, wrestling until I let him win and he was on top of me, staring down at my immersed body. His eyes were intense with lust as he looked at my full breasts and dusky brown nipples, which were clearly defined beneath the wet material. He lowered his head and wrapped his lips over my breast, vigorously sucking the water out of my dress. I watched his head as it moved to my other breast. More gently this time, he lapped at the soaking fabric. His erection lay between my legs, floating slightly in the water. I pushed my hips up to meet his and held his buttocks tightly. We grated roughly against each other, his mouth still hot on my breast, my fingers digging into his buttocks, until I felt a steamy arousal pumping through my veins. He jerked himself against me faster, his cock rubbing against my clit, the water splashing around us frantically, and watched my face as my excitement grew. He kissed me deeply, his tongue sensuous and appreciative.

'Good girl,' he murmured, nuzzling my ear. 'I love it when you're turned on.'

'So do I.' I smiled and carefully rolled us over so that he was lying underneath me. My dress was saturated and heavy now. I knelt up and tried to pull it over my head, but it clung insistently to my skin, slapping wetly at me. Jerome enjoyed the spectacle, lying back and laughing. Eventually I pulled the dress over my head and chucked it across the room. It hit a mirrored wall and slid down, making a clear path in the steamy glass.

Now I could see myself naked, my olive skin gleaming against Jerome's pale body, my full breasts with nipples like berries hanging dripping wet over his face. He tenderly took a nipple in his mouth and sucked on it as if it was a sweet, his eyes fixed on me. The warm sensation of his mouth sent tiny tremors down my body and tingled in my pussy. My long brown hair made a tent around his face as I looked down at him, the ends floating in the water like seaweed around a stone. His tongue was lapping at my breast now, and he sighed with pleasure. He seemed to enjoy it even more than I did. Seeing his face like that, I was filled with an urge to make him delirious. I pulled away and slowly edged down his body, my head bent and my lips skimming across the surface of the water like a dragonfly. I could see the reflection of my face against the shape of his body, my almond-shaped black eyes travelling down his torso and coming to rest over his crotch, my hair curling underwater around him.

'What are you doing, you little nymph?' he purred, barely able to disguise the hope in his voice.

I sank my face into the water in response, closing my lips around his full prick and sucking him into the warmth of my mouth.

'Oh my God,' he said with a sigh, his hands instinctively going to the back of my head, tangling in my wet curls. 'Oh God, don't stop.'

I lifted my head out of the water with his cock still resting in my mouth and breathed in through my nose, then dived down again, sucking it deep against my throat. His skin felt smooth on my tongue and his cock tasted sweet and clean. I breathed out through my mouth, the bubbles dancing against his prick and making him squirm. Again and again I worked up and down the shaft, the bubbles tickling where I was sucking, some of them slipping around his balls like champagne around a strawberry. Soon he couldn't take any more teasing. He lifted his hips out of the water and grabbed my head roughly in his hands. The tightness of his muscles told me he would soon be coming. I concentrated on making him climax now, getting into a strong rhythm, holding his balls gently and stroking behind them. The water in my mouth made it wetter than normal, and the suds around us slapped and surged as his hips started to buck. He growled and grunted and finally held his breath as his whole body stiffened and his semen shot into my mouth. I drank it all up like a good girl, then licked my lips and gave his cock a little kiss. I crawled over him, and lay with my head on his chest, feeling the rapid rise and fall of his ribs. His face was a picture of happiness.

'You give great head,' he said, eyes still shut. 'I mean, I should know, I've had enough head in my time. But yours, it's the best.'

He pulled me to him and we lay in the lukewarm water, our bodies intertwined. I was flattered but also slightly irritated that he was comparing me to all his past conquests; probably back in the days when he was in a rock band and not just a thirty-five year old editor of an offbeat music magazine. It was something he did a lot, harping on about the past, his glory days.

'We had groupies throwing themselves at us all the time and, for some reason, they loved to suck us off,' he went on. 'We would just sit there in the bar or whatever and they would crawl under the tables and unzip us and boom, blowjob!' He kissed my forehead and pulled my body closer. I thought I could feel him harden a little at the memory. 'I mean, some of those girls were too young to know how to give a decent blowjob. They hadn't lived. They just wanted to be able to go back to their friends and say they'd sucked off a member of Black Heart. So we happily obliged.' He chuckled to himself. 'We'd play this game, the rainbow game, we'd call it. We each had to try to get sucked off by a blond, a redhead and a brunette every night we were on the road. We'd get extra points for a black chick or a Japanese girl.'

'Am I supposed to be impressed by that?' I said dryly.

'Hey, babe, are you jealous?' He rolled onto his side and cradled me in his arms, his hand slipping onto my round bottom and caressing the crack softly. 'Don't be. I'm paying you a compliment.' He kissed me and we rocked slowly in the water. 'You give the best head and you are the prettiest when you come.' He kissed me again, pushing his thigh between my legs so that with every rocking movement, my pussy pressed against him. 'And you taste the best. God, you taste like a pineapple.'

'Must be my Brazilian genes,' I mumbled, grinding against his thigh.

'Whatever it is, I'm looking forward to a taste of it tonight.' His fingers slipped between my buttocks and slid against the slick opening of my cunt. He pressed slightly so his fingertips sank in a little. 'And you have the most lovely tits. Soft and dark and delicious. Those groupies were always shoving their breasts in our mouths. God, some of them used to come just from knowing we were licking their nipples, but none of them tasted of cinnamon like yours do.'

His tongue flickered over my nipple and I shivered right down to my toes. I wrapped my leg around his hips and his fingers invaded me deeper. Now I could feel that he was erect again and my body longed to close around that big hard-on. 'And none of them were so full and round. God, I could look at your tits all day.' He began to suck at them with more passion now, the water spilling over the edge of the bath, like the moisture spilling from my pussy. I couldn't get the image of him sucking all those girl's breasts out of my head. I was filled with envy and longing, imagining them jigging about in Jerome's lap, their tops pulled up, panting and screaming and wetting themselves just because he was licking their nipples. They would go home and masturbate about it for a month, the taste of his come still tangy on their lips. I knew he had fucked some of them too, but not many. How did he choose who was allowed to get a pussyful of that supreme cock? The thought of it made me feel like a chosen one and I was ashamed at how chuffed that made me. I squirmed against him, unable to take any more.

'Please, let's make love.' I whispered. They seemed to be the magic words from the look on his face and the spring in his erection. 'Let's go to the bedroom.' He pulled me up and we stood face to face in the bath. The room was swimming in water now.

'Feeling romantic, are we?' he teased, and led me to his bedroom. He knew that I liked to do it in the bedroom whenever I needed more than just a fuck. Other times I was only too happy to have him anywhere – kitchen, stairs, desks at work, back seats of cars – but tonight I wanted intimacy.

Jerome eased me down onto my back on the bed and I dripped generously onto his duvet cover. He looked down at my shiny body and absently stroked his cock, his eyes thoroughly absorbing every inch of my nakedness. My legs were hanging over the side of the bed, my hips perched on the edge. Lying back in that position, I knew I had a super-flat stomach and my breasts were soft and pert. I pulled my arms over my head, offering myself to him. He knelt between my legs and kissed my feet, lovingly sucking on each toe. Each suck seemed to drag lust out of me. Then he kissed up my legs, and slowly arrived at my inner thighs. I was getting so excited that I was already starting to whimper, although he hadn't hit the spot yet.

'Patience,' Jerome breathed, teasingly kissing around my thighs and my trim dark triangle. I opened my legs wide, my tight pussy unfurling in his face. First he just rubbed his nose against me on my tender clit, inhaling and sighing like a hungry man about to enjoy a delicious meal. 'Josephina,' he said and drew the tip of his tongue along my slit, tasting me carefully. He licked again, harder, then again, and began to lap with a flat tongue, making me quiver for more.

I looked down and saw his mouth move greedily around my cunt, eating me up, groaning and swallowing as he went. Little cries were gathering in my throat. The pink stub of his tongue disappeared into me, his mouth pressed right up against me so he could go deeper and deeper, fucking me with his tongue, his nose pressed against my clit, his mouth stretched against me. As he groaned I felt the rumble of his voice moving up inside me and I trembled with pleasure, contracting against his tongue. My thighs on either side of his head began to quake. I wrapped them around his head to steady myself and to draw him even further in. That made him groan again and I trembled more, clamping my legs against his ears. We were locked in a vicious circle of pleasure, each groan making me crush myself against him, each crush making him groan louder.

I knew Jerome could easily make me come with his mouth, because he had done it a hundred times before, but he seemed more passionate and hungry for me tonight. Some nights he had me coming all over his face with just a few well-aimed licks on my clit, and some nights he licked me for so long that I was swept along on a roll of gooey climaxes, one after the other. This time my orgasm was coming slower than usual, but as it built up and gathered in my nerves it felt like a tidal wave was on its way. My hips started to undulate against his face, my tummy taut with anticipation. He brought his tongue from deep within me and tickled it against my clit, knowing just how fast and hard I liked it. I gasped and cried out, widening my legs now, digging my heels into the edge of the mattress and levering my groin up to his mouth. My hands were clawing and clutching at the bedclothes, my head was rolling from side to side, tendrils of hair clammy on my sweating face, caught in my mouth. Jerome was deep in concentration, but I grasped his hand and brought it up to my breast. His palm was electric against my nipple, and he grunted with desire.

I bent my head and brought the fingers to my lips, sucking on them hard as my body writhed. The feel of his fingers in my mouth made me want to suck his cock again, but it was too late, I was ready to come. His tongue pressed hard against my clit and I convulsed in a massive orgasm, my whole body wrenched with pleasure. His free hand held my hips steady against his mouth until all the tremors of my climax had passed. I felt my appreciation rush out of my pussy and bathe his face.

Jerome instantly crawled up my body and plunged his straining cock into me. I was so drenched that it slid easily all the way in, taking the breath away from both of us. His dark eyes held mine as he began to pump his hips against me. My juices from the earlier licking were dripping from his chin onto my lips. He licked them off me and lapped his tongue against mine in a mime of what he had just been doing to my grateful pussy. Soft, high-pitched moans came rhythmically from my mouth as he fucked me, my swollen clit quick to respond to the pounding of his belly. That lovely cock filled me urgently. I grabbed at his buttocks, letting my fingers dive between them so that he yelled out, losing control.

'God, Jo, you sexy bitch,' he muttered, driving faster, trying to hurt me with his thrusts. 'Oh shit!' he yelled and clenched his jaw, which told me he was about to fill me with hot come. I buried my hand between my legs and played it against my clit to catch up with him and soon we both came together, our bodies jerking against each other, my pussy and his cock pulsing in unison. The sexy swill of his seed sped hotly down my thigh, but I clung on to him, not wanting him to pull out. He was out of breath and sweaty above me, his heavy body collapsed onto mine. I was ready to go again, still twitching with pleasure, but he was well and truly spent. Eventually he rolled off me and drifted into sleep, murmuring inaudibly.

'What was that, Jerome?' I whispered.

'I said, you taste divine,' he replied sleepily and then began to snore.

2

The drive that swept up to Hathaway Hall was as long as a road, lined with ornamental bushes and well-tended birch trees. My taxi wended its way round the twisted drive and suddenly the old house came into view. It was a wide, majestic red-brick building with a domed roof. My mouth fell open.

'Pretty impressive, isn't it?' my driver said, with a hint of resentment in his voice. 'Built early 1800s for the Hathaway family,' he continued, obviously feeling obliged to give me the tourist spiel. 'They were arable farmers originally. Owned every field as far as the eye can see. Don't own a whole lot now though,' he added, smirking back at me as he parked the car in front of the steps to the grand front entrance. 'Just this pile of old bricks.'

'Looks pretty good to me,' I piped up, for some reason wanting to defend these people.

'Does it now?' He looked at me significantly. 'Don't be fooled. This building is like the people in it.'

'How do you mean?' I asked casually, rooting around for my purse.

'Well, have you ever heard the phrase "fur coat and no knickers"?' he chuckled. I asked for a receipt. I wanted to make up my own mind about Tom and Alicia Hathaway.

As I struggled up the steps with my suitcase and laptop, Alicia appeared in the doorway. Her slender willowy frame was draped in a floating blue summer dress, which seemed to illuminate her pale blue eyes. It was a baking mid-July day but she somehow looked effortlessly ice-cool.

'Darling!' she cried as if we were old friends and kissed me very lightly on the cheek. Her lips were raspberry red, I noticed. 'I'm so glad you could come and do this dear article. I do hope you won't find us all dreadfully dull.' I wondered if she was putting on her dated accent for my benefit, but I didn't think so. It just somehow seemed to fit. I assured her that I wouldn't find them dull at all, although I was sure that she knew that full well, and followed her into the house. I found myself in a large entrance hall, with deep red carpets and dark oak beams on the ceiling. A wide wooden staircase curved ahead of me, and to my right was a corridor with rooms coming off it. The mismatched furniture that filled the hall seemed to be antique or heirlooms. Two huge windows let in shafts of summer afternoon sun, but the house was chilly. 'Approve?' Alicia asked, raising a delicate black eyebrow.

'It's great,' I said. 'All authentic?'

'Oh, darling, we are nothing if not authentic.'

I made a mental note of that comment as she led me up the stairs.

'Guided tour after we've dumped those heavy bags,' she said with a smile, making no attempt to help me to carry them. The landing on the second floor was creaky and narrow, and we walked past many closed doors before turning down another corridor and up some stairs to my own room.

'What do you use all those rooms for now?' I enquired, dragging my bags slightly.

'Oh, this and that. Storage, music rooms, guest rooms. My brother's bedroom and study. Libraries. You know the kind of thing.'

I didn't have the heart to tell her that I currently resided in a one-bedroom flat in Peckham. In fact, the guest bedroom Alicia had given me was about the size of that flat. It was a beautiful old split-level room full of sun. On the higher level sat a huge four-poster bed covered in fine white linen, with a large oak cabinet, wardrobe and dresser. Down a few steps sat a writing desk complete with stationery and beyond that were two windows. I went to one window and looked out. I had a fabulous view of the grounds, rolling lawns and a distant wooded area. Climbing roses framed my window and they were alive with birdsong. My first thought was that Jerome must come down and have a good old-fashioned romp with me on that incredible bed.

'You like?' Alicia asked confidently.

'It's great.' I tried not to gush too much. 'Very atmospheric. It'll help me a great deal when writing the article.'

'Quite.' There was a little pause.

'It would be great if we could get going as soon as possible, actually,' I began. 'Is Tom available for an interview at all?' For once Alicia's glossy smile faltered slightly.

'Of course,' she said. 'I think he's a little busy now and I have to go and see the accountant about balancing the books. Tom doesn't do any of that stuff. He's useless.' She walked to the door. 'Why don't you make yourself at home? There's a bathroom next door if you want to freshen up. Dinner at eight?'

I agreed and started to unpack, feeling slightly as if I had been put in my place, and wondering what had happened to the promised guided tour. As soon as my things were in order, I pulled out my mobile and called Jerome at the office to share my news with him. He had left work, and his answerphone kicked in at home.

I called his mobile, but that was turned off. The deep vibration of his voice on his voicemail message gave me a little shiver of lust. I wondered if I should leave a message or let him miss me for a day. Before I could decide the tone went and I was talking. 'Hi, Jerome. It's me. Jo, that is. Sorry if I woke you up when I left this morning. Just wanted to let you know how gorgeous this place is. I have a four-poster bed, for fuck's sake, and I want you in it. Call me.' He'd never be able to resist that, I thought, and turned on my laptop to write up some first impressions.

When I opened my eyes, the light outside had faded slightly and the birds were giving an impressive early evening performance outside my window. My cheek was glued to the desk and, as I slowly unpeeled it and sat up, I felt an achy stiffness in my neck that only comes from a truly awful sleeping position. Last night's activities with Jerome had left me more tired than I had realised. My laptop was still on, the shooting stars screen saver making me dizzy. I sleepily shut it down and had a stretch. It was only seven o'clock, so I still had time to have a quick bath and to put on some fresh clothes for dinner.

Suddenly there was a high-pitched giggle in the gardens outside my window. I looked down and saw Alicia running across the grass, laughing. A few moments later a burly man appeared, chasing her. I knew from the photo I had seen that this wasn't Tom Hathaway. This man was stocky and dark, with shoulder-length curly hair. He was roughly attractive, a bear of a man. Alicia would be no match for him, although she was a very fast runner. She was circling a privet hedge now, ducking and diving, looking like a bluebird in her flowing dress. Finally she let him catch her and he knocked her to the ground. She was so slight that it looked as if this big man was going to crush her, but she fought back like a cat, getting the upper hand and rolling over him. She finally escaped through his legs and fled again. By now he was tired and didn't follow. I saw him brush himself down, laughing, and go the opposite way. His solid figure disappeared around the side of the building. I felt vaguely titillated by watching this encounter, although it was just a bit of rough and tumble. I decided to pass on the bath and do a bit of exploring instead. Maybe I would see where this big man had disappeared to.

The corridor was darker now. The steps were uneven, and I made my way carefully down the stairwell, listening a little at each door I passed. I could hear piano music coming from somewhere but it was distant and untraceable. It was a Daphne Hathaway piece; her trademark inverted chords, use of harmonics and unpredictable structures had been emblazoned on my memory by Jerome. He had that annoying habit of putting on a record and telling you all the wonderful things about it rather than let you enjoy it for yourself, but at least it now meant I knew a bit about her music.

I paused at the top of the stairs, trying to trace the sound. It seemed to be coming from above. I looked behind me for more stairs to another level, but there were only doors. The first one I tried was unlocked and led to a creaky wooden staircase to the next floor. It was so narrow and hidden it seemed like a secret passage. I started up the stairs furtively, feeling somehow like a naughty child. The music was getting louder. A floorboard groaned loudly under my feet and the playing stopped. I had assumed it was a record, but now I could tell it was live. I heard the scrape of the piano stool shifting backwards as whoever was playing came to investigate the noise. I was at the top of the stairs now and found myself on a broad landing with four closed doors coming off it. I felt like Alice in Wonderland. 'Curiouser and curiouser,' I thought to myself, when a cold hand clamped on my shoulder and I started. I swung round and saw Alicia smiling at me, a bit like the Cheshire cat.

'Did you get lost, darling?' she said, her steely eyes making it clear that she meant I did not belong in this part of the house.

'No, I just...' I indicated the doors. 'I was just following the music, actually. It was so beautiful.'

Her gracious smile was fixed on her face.

'Oh, do you think?' She looked at me indulgently. 'I suppose it's passable. Are you hungry? Dinner is ready.'

I obediently followed her down the stairs and on to the ground floor, listening as the music eventually started up again.

'This is the drawing room.' Alicia indicated the first door we passed. She opened it to show me a neatly arranged room with a writing desk, settees and bookshelves. 'We don't have a television, I'm afraid. So you are going to have to do without your soaps and things.' The condescending tone in her voice was quickly smoothed by her tinkly laugh. 'This next room was a ballroom – you see how big it is?' It was an immense space, with long wooden floorboards and a grand piano at the end of it. 'We only use it for parties and things. It's a bugger to heat up, as you can imagine.'

We came to the end of a corridor and I noticed another stairway leading downwards. 'They lead to the old servants' quarters. No need to go exploring down there, now,' she said pointedly. 'Of course, we don't have servants now, that would be absurd.'

I nodded in agreement.

'But we do have a cook, two maids and some cleaners. And obviously gardeners.'

I stifled a laugh and Alicia shot me a defensive look.

'I mean, I'm simply hopeless at all that stuff, and Tom wouldn't know a saucepan if it hit him on the head.' She led me into the dining room. A long oak table with matching chairs dominated the room. The walls were lined with old family portraits and there was a grand fireplace. In the corner stood a magnificent dresser laden with antique china. The table was set for two.

'Isn't Tom joining us?' I asked.

'No,' came the short reply. We sat down in silence. I looked at Alicia and for the first time really absorbed her beauty. Her black hair was long and glossy, her pale cheeks topped with a natural flush of health, and her slender lips full of colour. She had a wonderful, glowing complexion. She was the epitome of an English Rose. I felt a twinge of jealousy. I loved my olive skin and long unruly hair, but I would simply never be as glossy as this woman. She smiled up at me. 'I know what you're thinking,' she said.

'Oh?'

'You're thinking how like my great grandmother I look. Apparently I am the spit of Daphne, although she was much fuller in the figure department. Well, it was more fashionable then, wasn't it – curves and things?' I shifted uncomfortably, aware of my generous bosom and rounded bottom. Alicia was sleek as a panther. 'Anyway, I know how curious you journalists are about her lifestyle, so I have done something rather special for your first night here. Guess what?' Her eyes gleamed with childish excitement. I had no idea. I was starting to think that Alicia was capable of almost anything.

'I don't know,' I said.

'Oh, go on, guess! I hate it when people don't even guess!' she said irritably. I wracked my brains, unable to come up with anything.

'OK, er ... you've got a lot of her old recordings out for me?'

She sneered, leaning back in her chair.

'No, not even close.' She eyed me conspiratorially. 'That music stuff is all overrated anyhow, don't you think?' I decided not to answer as it felt like a trap. Instead I just smiled and decided to play the game.

'Oh, come on tell me, I'm dying to know what you've done,' I enthused, starting to emulate her tone of voice.

'Well, I've had Cook prepare Daphne's favourite meal for you!' she exclaimed triumphantly and rang a little bell, which was presumably to summon the maid. 'We are what we eat and all that.' After a while the door was opened by two young girls, both carrying silver dishes. As they began to serve, Alicia announced the menu: 'Cantaloupe Glacé, Bisque Nantua, Salade Indienne – yummy – and Asperges Vertes. And for dessert, Pêches Framboisines. What do you think?'

'It sounds delicious,' I replied, totally clueless as to what she had just said. 'Thanks for going to so much trouble.' I turned to the two girls serving us. 'Thank you so much.' They gave me an uncomfortable look and glanced at Alicia. Obviously it was bad form to talk to the servants like that.

After they had gone, Alicia raised her wineglass to me.

'Here's to an interesting fortnight,' she said.

We drank in silence and began to eat, the clinking of our cutlery illuminating the awkward pause in our conversation.

'So you can say in your article that we aren't strapped for cash,' Alicia said suddenly, indicating our meal. This non-sequitor instantly made me see why Alicia had laid this banquet on – not for my benefit, but to uphold the Hathaway family image. 'I know what people say about us – that were just hanging on by a thread and all that – but it isn't true. We Hatha-ways have always had style, and that isn't going to go away.' She smiled glamorously as she daintily ate her meal. 'Obviously we move with the times. We don't farm any more, but we have excellent income from our great grandmother's estate and we often lease parts of the Hall to film crews and the like.'

'I see,' I replied, my mouth too full to speak further.

'In fact we have a crew arriving tomorrow. They're *Americans* making a period drama set in England. Can you imagine!' She said the word 'Americans' as if it was the most outlandish thing she had ever heard. 'They're funny people but they do have money to burn.' Her eyes swept over me as if to assess my own financial position. I was wearing stone-washed denim shorts and a white Indian cotton shirt, my wild hair loosely gathered in a ponytail. She didn't seem to be able to make a judgement, unable to see my old tatty white trainers, which were firmly out of sight under the table.

'Well, that's all very exciting,' I said. 'You'll have a full house.'

'Oh yes, but don't worry dear. They are taking over the North wing, which is quite apart from your quar-ters. You won't even know they're there. Unless you want to, of course.' She gave me a little wink, which I couldn't interpret. 'Depends on your taste.'

'This food is delicious,' I said, deliberately misunder-standing her.

'Do you have a boyfriend?' she asked suddenly, her blue eyes penetrating me. 'You must do, voluptuous thing like you.' Her eyes lingered on my breasts.

'Well, I'm seeing someone,' I replied, faltering a little. Jerome always made it clear that we were in no way committed to each other. He should have 'I'm a free agent' engraved on his tombstone. 'I'm sort of playing the field,' I added, anxious to make myself sound less boring to Alicia. 'What about you?'

'Well, I'm sort of playing *in* the field,' she said with a laugh, obviously enjoying a private joke with herself. 'Good men have always been thin on the ground on this estate. But when I find one, or two, I like to make the most of it. That's the way, don't you think?' She leant in to me. 'Suck all the juice from the berry?' Her look was almost lecherous. I concentrated on my food.

'What about Tom? Did he ever marry?'

Alicia looked at me as if I was mad and then laughed heartily.

'I'll take that as a "no", shall I?' I smiled, spooning a ripe piece of peach into my mouth. 'Is he not hungry? I'd like to meet him.'

Alicia stopped laughing and looked at me coolly.

'All in good time, my dear. All in good time.'

After dinner, Alicia announced that she was going to take a walk in the grounds, but something told me she didn't want me along with her. I yawned ostentatiously and said I was going to hit the hay, I'd had a long day and various other clichés.

Back in my room, I was just drawing the curtains when I saw Alicia's slight blue shape flitting across the grass. Being curious (or nosy, as Ruby calls it) is a very useful trait in a journalist, and it's one I have in abundance. I crept silently down the corridor, acquainting myself with all the creakier floorboards, and went downstairs. The front door was open, so I made my way out into the night, staying close to the house as I followed Alicia. The moon was bright and made her look almost supernatural as she moved through the dark, like a transparent spirit or a beautiful ghost. Eventually I saw her slip into the stables and pull the heavy wooden door to behind her. I crept to the door after her and examined the hinges. They were rusty and old, and I knew it would open with a real whine, so I needed to find another way in. My old trainers came in handy now as I scaled the front wall of the stable, using ivy, wooden slats and rough bricks as my levers, until I reached an open window in the hayloft. I dragged myself through, grazing my knees as I went, and landed in the loft, which was stacked with hay. A family of wood pigeons took fright at my arrival and flew off into the night.

'What was that?' I heard a man's voice say below me, gruff and northern. I slid on my belly to the edge of the floor and peered down into the stables. Directly under me was the glossy, muscular back of a chestnut horse. In the next stable, lying in the hay with an oil lamp burning above her head, was Alicia.

'Don't be so jumpy, Harry,' she said. A man – the stocky, large man I had seen earlier – walked into view. His dark hair curled messily on his shoulders, and his arms were brown with dirt and an outdoor life. Closer to, I could tell he was in his forties, with the centred, sober confidence of a working man. Next to him Alicia looked fragile and pale and frivolous. 'Harry, I'm wearing the blue dress.' She writhed a little. 'The flimsy blue dress,' she continued, her hand playing with the plunging chiffon collar. 'Lady Alicia is here in her frilly blue dress,' she trilled girlishly, lifting the hem to expose perfect porcelain thighs. 'And she wants her slave to dirty it up a bit.'

'I told you, Miss – not slave. I hate that word.' He seemed genuinely angry, pacing the stable.

'Harry *is* Lady Alicia's slave, though.' She pouted. 'I am going to make you polish my riding boots with your tongue.'

'You're not even wearing them,' he spat. She lifted a leg up and pointed a bare foot at him.

'My feet then,' she said sharply. 'Come on, quickly. Slave!' She prodded his groin with her toes, her dress falling back to reveal that she was not wearing knickers. 'Oops!' She widened her legs invitingly so that Harry had a candid eyeful of her neat little black bush. I could see the glistening pink outline of her vulva, and so could he. He seemed mesmerised by it, his trousers bunching at the crotch. 'Slave! Don't stare at your Mistress's pussy!' Alicia scolded, but he was beyond listening. He knelt between her legs and clutched the neck of her dress with a brown fist.

'Stuck-up bitch,' he muttered, and ripped the fabric open in one muscular movement. She gasped as the dress rent in two, falling back to expose her small upright breasts. She spat in his face and started to fight him off. I wondered how much of this was play. She looked genuinely alarmed, punching him with little fists. But he was as strong as an ox and held her down with one hand while he unbuckled his breeches with the other.

'How dare you!' she gasped, kicking. He pushed his trousers down so that all I could see were his bare buttocks hovering over her, glowing golden in the lamplight. 'Get off me you brute!'

He struggled his way between her legs and manoeuvred his prick into place with his spare hand, shoving himself into her hard. She cried out and punched his back, but the blows were met by a wall of muscle. His head was at her bosom, his big mouth covering a small breast entirely, eating her up. Her expression was indecipherable. It could have been uncontrolled pleasure or just plain fear. I wondered if I should do something, but from what I had seen Alicia could take care of herself. And anyway, I was beginning to enjoy the show. His buttocks were pumping insistently. I had a perfect view of the muscles contracting and releasing in a fast, merciless rhythm. Alicia was struggling for breath beneath him, giving little helpless cries as she was taken by this massive man.

'Oh, you're too big,' she moaned. 'You're too big for me.'

'Shut up,' he said through gritted teeth, his thrusts getting more severe. She had stopped punching him now, and suddenly appeared to give up the fight. Her legs fell open to receive him and she lay, passive, her arms at her side, sighing gently. Her body jerked like a rag doll under his stabbing weight but her face was delirious, each rough sensation making her eyes roll back in her head.

'Oh, don't stop,' she whispered, her voice rising. 'Don't stop, don't stop.' His hips beat double time as he started to growl out his own excitement. 'Don't stop!' She lifted up her knees and I heard the wet friction of his cock inside her. His legs widened to push her knees further apart, and I could clearly see his full, swollen balls slap against her white bottom. A smear of her juices shone on her thigh.

'You little bitch, you deserve this,' he said, giving it to her harder still. His mouth went back to her breast. She had the reddest nipples I had ever seen, tight and puckered. He licked at one, nibbling occasionally. Now that Alicia had abandoned herself to him, he used his hands to pin her arms above her head, roughly holding them there with one fist, while his other hand snaked its way under her hips, pulling her tighter into his body. His pelvis continued its piston-like rhythm all the while.

I started to squirm, watching those even, violent thrusts, knowing what they could do to a girl. I thought of Jerome, remembering the feel of him inside me, and my panties got a drenching. But the image of this big man on Alicia was even sexier, I had to admit. He looked so heavy, so determined.

'I'm coming. I'm coming!' she was panting, as his thrusts became wilder. She cried out and whimpered and sighed as she came, her hips jerking against him. This set him off and I could see the repeated contraction of his balls as he shot off into her, each one punctuated by a grunt. As they climaxed the struggle seemed to be on again, their bodies writhing against one another.

When it was over, he got up and started pacing again. His spent cock hanging limp and dripping between his legs, but he didn't seem to care. Alicia watched him as he paced the stable, her legs sprawled in the hay, her cunt red and swollen. He looked at her and kicked straw over her.

'Little whore,' he said. I was relieved to see a slow, delicious smile grow on her face.

'Oh yes,' she purred, 'but I'm *your* little whore.' They both started to laugh, and she rolled up to standing, naked before him. 'Hurry up and get hard again, Harry. I need more fucking,' she ordered. He shrugged.

'Why don't you just get Kieran to do it?'

'Kieran's good at a lot of things, sweetie, but you are the best at fucking.' She leant against the wall and absently played with her nipples.

'Oh yeah?' He watched her closely. 'And what is Kieran best at?'

'Honestly?'

'Yeah, honestly.'

Alicia ran her hands down her body and opened herself up to Harry's gaze.

'Licking,' She replied. 'He licks like nobody I have ever known.' Her fingers started to rub softly. 'Licking . . .' she said again, obviously just to enjoy the word. A deep blush was rising again in her pale cheeks.

'I can lick,' Harry said, rather indignantly.

'Oh, darling, a girl can tell when the man doesn't enjoy it,' she chided, stimulating herself dreamily. 'It doesn't matter, Harry. You do the ravishing so well. One day I want you to pounce on me in the gardens when I don't expect it and force yourself on me.' She began to strum harder. 'Or creep into my room at night, tie me up and force your cock into my mouth.'

'I can lick,' Harry repeated and, to prove the point, he fell on his knees and buried his head between her legs, pushing her hand out of the way.

I could see what she meant. He snorted and gobbled like a pig looking for truffles, his big tongue swirling around her cunt. I could see its broad shape on her dainty mound, eagerly seeking her clit. She was watching the back of his head wiggle around her crotch, seeing what I saw. As if by accident, he seemed to hit gold and her back suddenly arched. She dug her fingers into his head to hold it still.

'There! There!' she urged. 'Oh, God, yes!' He calmed down, and now all I could see was his big mouth clamped over her pussy, sucking it all in. I was really missing Jerome now, my body burning to be touched. Alicia began to make a soft wailing noise, and the horse in the next stable became restless, blowing through its nose and stamping a foot. 'Ah, shush Tiger,' she whispered to the horse, before wailing again. Her legs were wobbling, her hips trembling, her whole body like the epicentre of an earthquake. I was so jealous, having to make do with a bundle of hay to rub against. 'There!' she cried again. 'There!' And then she came, her knees buckling, falling forward onto his face so that her whole weight rested on his mouth. He swallowed and gulped, holding her up with his hands. The horse whinnied loudly in protest. Alicia stood up abruptly and turned to the next stable.

'Tiger's jealous,' she said. 'You can't have me, Tiger.' Then she looked behind her and cheekily winked at Harry. 'Well, not without some fine lubrication, at least!' He tutted at her, unsure if she was joking. I wasn't sure that she was. From what I had already seen I could imagine her trying anything. 'I should start with a donkey and work my way up,' she continued, bending over and hanging on to the stable wall. 'Train my pussy to take a big horse's cock like that.'

'I wouldn't put it past you,' Harry said, staring at her exposed slit. 'As long as I can be there to rub your clitty as you get fucked.'

Alicia bent over further and looked round at him. From where I was, all I could see of her was the upturned crack of her perfect bottom.

'You could grease me up, Harry,' she said, excitedly. 'You could guide it into me! Like you do when we put Tiger out to stud for those lucky fillies. That's why he gets so horny, you know – he knows what we're doing. He was built for fucking. He loves it, don't you, Tiger?' She reached out and stroked the horse's shiny flank. 'Of course, he wants me, too. I'm his mistress. I really should train myself to take his girth. My God, we'd both love it.' She pushed her bottom out lewdly as if imagining the experience. 'You could help, Harry. Make me a harness to rest in while he puts his big dripping cock in me. You could make sure it gets pushed in all the way, even if I'm screaming in pain.' She opened her pussy up for him to look at as she spoke. He began to rub himself. 'You could make sure nothing slips out until I'm full of semen. Hold me still while his thrusts get harder. Play with me while I'm rammed full of cock, because you know how to turn me on like that.'

Harry was really getting off on this, his prick back to full capacity again. He walked behind Alicia as if to penetrate her again, but she stood up and turned to him.

'Is that exciting you, Harry? Would you like to see your Lady fucked by a horse?' There was suddenly a challenge in her eyes. He didn't know what to say. 'I think I deserve a little more respect, don't you?' His penis was wilting before my eyes, shrivelled by her cool stare.

'But, Miss, you were the one...'

'Shut up.' She gathered her torn clothes and wrapped herself up as best she could. 'Tell Kieran I want him next time. He doesn't have these depraved ideas.'

And with that she marched out, slamming the creaky door behind her. Harry looked baffled, and so was I. I was getting the picture that Alicia was as changeable as the weather, and that power games were her speciality. Half of me was ready to jump down and comfort him with a bit of my own special charm – goodness knows I was horny enough – but I decided not to blow my cover. Anyway, I had Jerome and, even though he wouldn't admit it yet, that was enough for both of us.

3

'Oh hi, Corinne, is Jerome there?'

'I'll just check,' she replied, and I heard her fumbling about with the telephone system. No one in that office knew how to put people on hold. I could hear her muffled voice as she finally relented and resorted to the hand over the receiver method. I thought I heard Jerome's voice, too, but was obviously mistaken. 'Sorry, Jo, he's just popped out to the printers. Can I take a message?' I couldn't think of a concise way to say all I had to say about the sex-mad Alicia and her elusive brother.

'No, nothing,' I said. 'Just checking in.'

Breakfast was laid out in the dining room, but there was no sign of anyone. I helped myself to a croissant and a strong cup of tea, wondering if I could legitimately include any of last night's revelations in my article. After all, Daphne Hathaway was herself infamous for her sexual exploits. Wasn't it interesting that her great-granddaughter not only looked like her but shagged like her, too? I thought it was fascinating, but perhaps the music freaks who made up the readership of *A Tempo* wouldn't. I hung around, hoping to catch Tom, who was surely hungry by now, but the house was silent. I got up with my cup in my hand and started to have a look at the paintings on the wall. Moustachioed men and well-dressed ladies from over two centuries peered back at me. Over the hearth I saw an excellent painting of Alicia: her black glossy hair piled on her head, her red lips curled in a smile. Those pale blue eyes twinkled with life, and her face seemed a little fuller and rosier. She looked friendlier in a painting than in real life, and I wondered if it had been painted when she was much younger. I looked for a date. The brass inscription underneath read 'Daphne Hathaway 1907'. Scanning the painting again, I could see that it wasn't Alicia. The face was warmer, more engaging, and the smile genuine. Alicia wore her smile like a mask.

Sparked by this encounter with my subject, I hurried up to my room to do some research. The velvet ledger had sat unread by my bed since I arrived, and I was determined to get to grips with it. I wasn't going to let Jerome down on this one. And until Tom Hathaway made an appearance, I didn't feel there was much else I could do.

I flung myself on the bed and opened the journal. The writing was elaborate and slanted, the capital letters especially flamboyant. I seemed to remember from a graphology quiz in some woman's magazine that this meant she had a big ego, which seemed to fit. I flicked through the pages, noting that the author did not write her diary every night. Some of the entries seemed to be gripes about servants, tutors and her older sisters Emily and Grace. Some concentrated on her father's remarriage after her mother's death. I made a mental note to ask Tom about that, if I ever saw him. I got the feeling Alicia wasn't going to give me a straight answer about anything. I fell on a page that was headed 'My Awful Birthday' and decided that was a good place to start.

February 5th 1907
It is my birthday today and my family has grown more heinous than ever. Grace is jealous because

she will never be eighteen again and no man will have her with that double chin, and Emily even more so, because she is married to that oaf Oliver, who loves the sound of his own voice so very much. I cannot wait for him to go yachting in Cowes again, then maybe we shall all be treated to some peace! Papa and his nubile young bride are, as usual, in their Mediterranean hideaway, enjoying the sun and, no doubt, each other. Mama must be turning in her grave. So, happy birthday Daphne!

I am finally eighteen and am allowed to take the ridiculous plaits out of my hair and wear full-length dresses (although frankly I will miss the freedom of those short skirts). I am to have my portrait painted next week by the very talented Sargent, in all my finery. It seems so silly. I became a woman years ago, but now I am to officially 'come out' and my calling cards have already been snapped up by many handsome young men in the area. I favour about four of them, but will enjoy as many as I can until I am locked into that cosy prison, marriage. God forbid! Papa is so distracted by his new wife, who only came out last year herself, that I am free to do what I like. And I intend to. No more dreary lessons from now on, just balls and parties and music. And men! So far a few kisses are all I have enjoyed, admittedly some of them rather illicit and exciting. But now I intend to live life to the full and that means pursuing love from wherever it comes.

Grace and her companions were off out with the hunt this morning. She asked me to come, knowing I cannot abide the sport, and I told her so, which led to another argument. She really is a sour old thing, and she has the ugliest friends. She gave me the most revolting pair of gloves for my birthday. I will use them for something scandalous. Now all the men are put on a shooting party – nothing changes. Emily came over with Oliver, who told me at length about his sore knee and invited me to feel it. Once, when Emily left the room, he placed a hand on my posterior and said, 'Now you are of age, Daphne, you may need advice on certain adult matters,' and he gave me an intimate pat. I feigned innocence and asked what he meant. He is often making sad little approaches to me. Little does he know that I have already witnessed a vast array of sexual activities: first when he and Emily were courting (my bedroom overlooks the woods) and then when Papa remarried last year. I could have told him, for example, about Papa's 'special room' that he had crafted for Julia's benefit after their honeymoon. But I didn't feel that Oliver was ready to hear about the whips and suspended chairs and strange implements of pleasure that Papa and Julia like to use. I have seen them at it and it is quite a revelation! Julia, it has to be said, is a girl after my own heart. I do not wonder that Papa married her. She is fulsome and pretty, and likes nothing more than to eat large meals and to make love to her husband. She makes the most extraordinary noises when they disappear into that chamber. You have never heard such moans and cries and howls. Anyone would think she were a werewolf.

I look forward to experimenting within those walls myself one day. In fact, I have a plan along those lines. I am allowed (with my sisters) to host my own coming-out ball here at Hathaway Hall, although Emily says it would be pointless not to go to London for it. The truth is I could not care less about finding a husband. However, I would like to explore the world of men thoroughly! What better way than to host a party and enjoy a night of pure pleasure? All I have to do is make sure Grace and Emily and all the other boring ladies are safely occupied in the ballroom, and I can have the special room all to myself!

I lay back on the bed, trying to get a picture of Daphne. I couldn't work out if she was isolated or just very independent. She seemed to be unshockable, not even shying away from spying on her own father and his new wife, or maybe she just shared my uncontrollable sense of curiosity. The writing indicated someone on the brink of unlocking all those repressed adolescent desires, and I looked forward to reading on to see where they led her. In the mean time, I was intrigued by the 'special room' she mentioned.

Alicia, who seemed to want to control all my move-ments, had not shown her face all morning, so I guessed that she was out. I opened my door and walked down the steps into the corridor. The row of closed doors greeted me, just begging to be opened. I slowly tried each handle. The first room was a small reading room, the second a music library with manu-scripts piled to the ceiling. The third room was a bedroom; a smaller version of my own. The fourth room, on the opposite side of the corridor just before the hidden stairway, was an enormous bedroom, finely furnished in turquoises and cornflower blues, with an ornate four-poster bed sitting at its centre. Above the bed was a stunning black and white enlarged photo of Alicia, her hair windswept and wild, her eyes as sharp as crystal. The photograph was cropped at her shoulders, which were bare. She looked like a model, and the shot seemed professional, probably taken out-side by the look of the light. Three wide wardrobes lined one wall, and a huge gold-framed mirror covered another. On the floor were a few discarded pairs of shoes: high heeled, expensive. The whole room had an air of stylish confidence, just as Alicia had, and the bed dominated. The urge to go in to the room and investigate was strong, but I was surprised to realise how scared I was of Alicia returning to catch me in the act. It just wasn't like me. I had walked around the slums of Rio at three in the morning hunting out street music without batting an eyelid. I had interviewed some of the most arrogant rock musicians there were and written them up warts and all. Why did this uptight, over-sexed aristo scare me? In defiance of my instincts, I crept into the room.

Once inside I could smell a delicate fragrance, a perfume I couldn't identify. Probably one I could never afford. It clung to me like a needy lover. I opened Alicia's wardrobes and stared in wonder at the array of clothes inside. The colours blue and green dominated, but there were some dazzling pieces in red and gold. Her style was feminine and individual, favouring dresses with no labels or antique clothes that looked like heirlooms. One cupboard was hung thick with furs and pelts. Some looked as old and ragged as the animal would have done were it still alive; some were new and ostentatiously glossy.

I ran my hand over a shapely gold full-length dress with a cowl neck and a mermaid tail, its tiny sequins shimmering like a fish in the sun. I felt like a poor kid rummaging through a rich kid's dressing-up box; jealous, admiring and slightly sick at the show of opulence. At the bottom of one of the cupboards was a trunk with the key in its lock. I knelt down and examined it. I had to look inside, naturally. The trunk creaked open to reveal a lining of colourful silk scarves laden with all kinds of delights: velvet gloves, a leather whip, handcuffs lined with fur, a blindfold, some candles and a selection of dildos and vibrators. I picked these up and instinctively smelt one; it had a lingering tangy aroma. There was a very large one, a double-pronged one, a small one that looked as if it might be for anal use and a couple of round ones on strings, which I recognised as Japanese love eggs. I held them in my hands and felt their inner weights moving them around. I could imagine that being an appealing, secret sensation between your legs as you went about your day.

I turned on the large vibrator and it buzzed into life. It had a strong motor, sending shivers down my arm and through my whole being at the thought of it inside me. Surely Alicia couldn't take this size? It was bigger than any man, with a painful-looking girth. I slowly lowered it to my clit, just to get a feel of it. I pressed the head against the white cotton of my shorts. The vibrations shot around my body as soon as it made contact. It was an addictive feeling. I sat back on my heels and pushed it against my vulva, feeling the shivering sensation spreading outwards, and turned it up to full speed. I had used vibrators before but none so powerful as this one. I could imagine it driving Alicia crazy. I knew how she looked when she came, the whimpering and wailing noises she made. The image of her abusing herself with this monstrous dildo turned me on. Maybe she used it on her own, or perhaps when she was having her weird sessions with Harry.

Suddenly I became aware that the buzzing was really loud and snapped out of my reverie. I turned the vibrator off and returned all the toys to the trunk. I couldn't remember if it had been locked or not. Alicia was just the sort of person who would notice if anything was different. After locking and unlocking it at least ten times trying to decide, I decided to leave the trunk locked. Feeling suddenly like a trespasser rather than just a justifiably inquisitive journalist, I backed out of the room and closed the door quietly behind me. A floorboard creaked and I swung round. Nobody was there – I had made the noise myself. I couldn't help laughing at my own jumpiness.

The elusive 'special room' still had to be found. I had a choice of going up the stairs as I had done the day before, or down into the basement, where I always imagined kinky dungeons should be. It seemed apt that people should bury the things they were guilty about deep in their cellars, like perversions lying in the subconscious. Alicia had said that the servants had lived down there – perhaps another guilty aspect of aristocratic life – although not many servants were left in Hathaway Hall. In the end I plumped for going up, if only because Alicia had so obviously not wanted me to do so the day before.

The four doors on the upper landing were all still shut. This time there was no music. I went to one door and turned the brass handle. It was locked. The next one was locked, and the one after that. By the time I came to the last door, I fully expected that to be locked too, so I turned the handle quite roughly. I was shocked when the door sprang open noisily and a wall of late-morning sunlight spilt into my eyes. The room was long and light and sparse. There was a baby grand piano at the far end and a large bed in front of me. It took me a moment to realise that someone was in that bed.

'Hello. Can I help you?'

Mortified, I looked down and saw the handsome face of Tom Hathaway framed by the crumpled white duvet and his messy blond hair. He looked equally embarrassed, leaning up on one elbow and clearing his throat. I hoped he was just having a long lie-in, and not that I was interrupting some solitary erotic moment.

'I am so sorry,' I said, smiling. 'I can't get to grips with this big old house!' I tentatively approached him and held my hand out to shake his. 'I'm Jo, by the way. Josephina Bell.' He looked at me blankly, keeping his hand firmly under the covers, which seemed to confirm that I had interrupted at a very inopportune moment. I hurriedly dropped my arm by my side. 'From *A Tempo* magazine? I'm doing a piece on Daphne Hathaway,' I went on. 'Sorry, I thought you knew. I've been speaking to Alicia...?' He rolled his eyes a bit and sank back down. Obviously there was some communication problem between the two of them. My cheeks were burning and he couldn't meet my eye. This was not a good start. There was a tense moment of silence.

'Look, I'll let you ... get on with it ... I mean, your nap or ... whatever...' I stammered, backing out of the room. 'Sorry again.'

'Nice to meet you, Josephina.' At least he seemed to be smiling now. 'Perhaps next time we can have a proper chat. About Daphne.'

'Right.' I tripped over the door-frame.

'Oh, mind that –'

'Yes, sorry.' And I was out.

I rushed to my room and buried my face in the pillow. It was all very well anonymously spying on Alicia having a bit of rough, but to burst in on a guy jerking off – because you're too damned nosy to stay out of people's bedrooms – was deeply humiliating. Jerome would kill me if I scuppered this piece. I cringed at my own behaviour and crawled into bed. I lay for a while, thinking about how bad Tom Hathaway must be feeling. Even in that vulnerable position, he had been good-looking, and he had had a nice, deep, well-spoken voice. Not as posh and affected as Alicia's. I didn't usually go for the public schoolboy type, being prone to men with more of an edge, but he had looked quite inviting lying there.

My mind began to fantasise about the situation, imagining that I hadn't floundered like a startled lamb but had taken the opportunity to sit at the edge of the bed and help him out. No handsome man should have to be horny on his own at eleven thirty in the morning, I thought, my hand falling between my legs. I envisaged my fingers sliding under the side of the duvet and curling gently around him. He would have lost a bit of his erection, of course, with the shock of being discovered, but I would soon put that right. The poor guy was cooped up with that mad sister of his all day; no wonder he needed to find some release. Once he was hard, I would crawl into bed with him and straddle his warm body, rubbing my big breasts in his face and my hungry snatch over his cock. He would get more than he bargained for with me, I thought, my hands slipping into my panties. My fingers slid about happily for a while as my imagination built up my short meeting with Tom Hathaway into an epic erotic event. But I couldn't relax into the fantasy. I knew all too well what a lie it was.

Frustrated, I tried to call Jerome again. Maybe we could have a bit of phone sex to finish me off. His voicemail clicked in again. Unsatisfied I threw the phone across the room. To my horror it flew against the window and shattered the glass.

I sat up in bed for at least five minutes with my hands over my mouth, unable to believe how stupid I was. I have inherited my temper from my mother, whose plate-smashing and vase-throwing episodes were an endless source of entertainment in our house.

But even she had the sense not to risk it in someone else's. Could my day get any worse?

Sheepishly I slunk down the stairs, reluctantly seeking out Alicia to own up to my ridiculous accident. The dining room was empty and the drawing room was locked. I went out into the grounds to find her, instinctively making for the stables. In the daylight they seemed far more innocent and wholesome and, looking at the wall I had scaled, I was pretty impressed with myself. The stable doors were open and two horses were feeding inside. I recognised Harry from the day before, bent over one horse, inspecting his back hoof. He was even bigger close up, his broad shoulders and sturdy legs giving him the air of a workhorse himself.

'It's not infected,' he was saying. 'I think it was just irritated.' He dropped the horse's leg gently and turned round to another man who was grooming the horse I had seen last night. This man was in his early twenties, with a cheeky tanned face. He was wearing old brown leathers spattered with mud, the trousers tight enough to outline a compact crotch. He saw me before Harry did, his eyes resting on me as I leant against the door frame. He smiled at me with open appreciation in his eyes, looking blatantly at my bare legs and clinging shorts.

'Hello,' he said, more to Harry than to me. Harry turned round and joined in the staring. I could instantly tell that he was more of a tit man by the way he was sizing up my chest. Alicia couldn't really compete with me in that department.

'What's your name, pretty girl?' the man continued, walking round the horse to get a better look at me.

'I'm Jo.' I could give as good as I got in the staring department and met their gaze with a steady confidence, although parts of my body were burning at the attention they were getting. I could feel the sun behind me accentuating my silhouette and slicing through the soft white cotton of my blouse. I was glad I had put on a bra today.

'Kieran,' the man said, nodding an introduction, 'and this is Harry.' The big guy smiled at me, suddenly looking a little simple.

'Well, Kieran and Harry,' I said. 'I have a favour to ask. And it might mean telling a white lie to Alicia.'

'Oh yeah?' Kieran liked the sound of that. He had a dirty mind. I liked that in a man. I smiled sweetly and explained about my little accident with the window and my phone, waiting patiently for them to finish laughing at me.

'I hate mobile phones as well,' Kieran quipped, 'but I've never actually chucked one through a window!'

'The thing is,' I said, shifting my weight onto one hip to get their attention, 'I was wondering if you knew anyone who could do repairs. Just so I can get it sorted without bothering Alicia.' They glanced at each other.

'You're in luck,' Kieran said, obviously the spokesman of the two. 'We're very good with our hands. Go and wait for us at the house and we'll be along in a minute.'

'Yeah, we just have to get the right tools,' Harry added suggestively.

I smiled and left them, wiggling my hips a bit on the way to the house. They seemed like the kind of boys who would appreciate the effort.

It didn't take long for Harry and Kieran to arrive. I noticed that they had washed a little and changed their shirts. Harry carried a sheet of glass and some tools and got to work as Kieran sat on the bed and talked to me. He had a mild Norfolk accent with a heavy tinge of London, and he was very animated, using his hands a lot when he spoke. I managed to get him round to the subject of Alicia, knowing that she used both men for sex.

'She's good to work for, you know,' he said, suddenly struggling for words. 'I mean, she's quite ... change-able, you know. Moody. You've got to get her on a good day.' Harry turned to him and they both grinned widely.

'Oh yes? And what kind of thing happens on a good day?' I asked flirtatiously, cocking my head to one side. Kieran blushed.

'You don't want to know,' he said, 'nice girl like you.'

'What makes you think I'm a nice girl?' They both looked at me and I uncrossed my legs. It was a small gesture but it drew their eyes to my crotch. I was desperate to get the story on their set-up with Alicia, and I was prepared to flirt to do it, but part of me knew that I was also enjoying turning them on. They were both fine-looking men. Real men.

'Why do you want to know?' Kieran asked guard-edly, his brown eyes searching my face. 'Did she send you to test us?'

Suddenly I saw that they were both as scared of Alicia as I was. My face must have registered my shock at the question, because Kieran suddenly felt able to open up.

'Look, she lives here on her own – no husband or anything – and she likes it that way. But she has needs and –' he looked at his friend '– we help her out with them. Simple as that.'

'Both of you?' I raised an eyebrow.

'Yeah. Why not?' Kieran looked defensive.

'Isn't one of you enough? You look like you'd be enough for any woman.' And they did. Harry especially was an ox of a man and I had seen him in action.

'She likes variety, I suppose,' Harry said gruffly. 'Spice of life.'

'Well.' I shifted on the bed. 'I'm quite jealous.' Harry stopped in his work and they both looked at me.

'You don't have to be,' Kieran said and laid a hand on my naked thigh. 'We both like you a lot.' His fingers rose until they were just playing with the frayed hem of my shorts. I watched his big hand creeping like a spider on my olive skin, ready to slip into my panties. 'I like your legs. Harry wants to suck on your tits.' He thought again. 'Actually, I want to suck on them, too.'

Harry got up and walked over to us as we sat on the bed. He stood before me, his hips at eye level, and played with my hair, cupping the back of my head. I felt the latent force in his hands as the shadow of his bulky frame fell over my face. For a moment I felt like collapsing back on the bed and just letting them do all the things they wanted to do. I had never had sex with two men at a time before, and had never had to contend with someone as big and heavy as Harry. The idea of him on top of me made my whole body sigh. But I was there to work and, anyway, I had Jerome.

'Look, boys,' I said, my voice cracking as Kieran's fingers cheekily feathered my inner thighs inside my shorts. 'God, that's a tempting offer, but . . .' Harry knelt before me and ran his fingers lightly down my throat, his eyes absorbing the swell of my breasts as if he was about to paint them. 'You see, the thing is, I'm attached.' Kieran slipped his fingers inside my panties and moaned as he encountered the slick evidence of my arousal. His eyes clouded with lust. 'I have a sort of boyfriend!' I protested, shivering as Harry's hands gently glided under my shirt and cupped my full breasts. 'Oh God,' I sighed, as his thumbs flicked over my hard nipples. Kieran was wallowing in my juices down below and I tingled all over. 'No, please, I can't!'

'Yes, you can,' Kieran breathed. 'God, Harry, she's so fucking wet. Her pussy's lovely.' He leant in to me and whispered, 'I want to lick you.' The words poured into my ear and straight into my panties, bathing his hand. 'Oh, you like that do you?' he smiled.

Harry was getting rougher, pulling on my bra, grasping my breasts, trying to push me back onto the bed.

'Harry's getting excited, Jo,' Kieran said smiling. 'Come on. Let us make you come. We're in no hurry.' I sighed and resisted. 'I want to make love to you,' he urged.

'I told you, I'm going out with someone,' I moaned.

'Yeah – what is a "sort of boyfriend" anyway?' Kieran increased the pressure on my pussy, his finger-tips rotating over my clit. Occasionally he let a finger enter me a little, teasing me. Harry pushed my bra down and played his cool wet tongue over a nipple. The sight of his big head at my breast excited me. He was like a gentle giant, but part of me knew he could lose control at any minute and crush me completely. I almost wanted him to. I couldn't help it, my legs opened for them both, I sighed, I leaned back, I melted.

'Oh no,' I murmured.

'Jo, this is nothing to what we could do for you,' Kieran said, whipping me up into a frenzy. 'This is just a taste. Come to our rooms tonight and we'll fill you up. We both want to fuck you, Jo. We want you to come all over us.'

My hands reached out to feel both their crotches. I was met with two stiff bulging shafts. How easy it would be to pull my panties down and open up for one of them. My pussy started to quiver at the thought of Harry's huge cock inside it, or Kieran's clever tongue. I whimpered quietly, pulling my knees back to invite Kieran to fill me with his fingers. He didn't, though. He just kept on teasing me. Harry was kissing my breasts, sucking them until they zinged, until my teeth tickled.

'Please,' I pleaded, wanting to come, lifting my hips to Kieran's hand. 'Please!' He pulled his hand away and unzipped my shorts.

'I want to see you,' he said urgently. 'I need to see your pussy. Otherwise I'll spend all night wondering what it looks like.' He pulled my shorts and panties down violently and flung them behind him. Both men sat back and stared at my crotch, the neat sliver of brown hair on olive skin, my moist lips. The cool air hit me, making me feel even more naked.

'Are you going to lick me?' I asked hopefully, opening myself up to him, aching for him.

'No,' he said. 'God I want to but, no – if I lick you then I'll need to fuck you. And I can tell you aren't ready for that yet.' They continued to stare at me, Kieran slipping his fingers against my wet lips and opening me up like a fig for their eyes.

'God, she's a beauty,' Harry whispered. 'I could fuck that pussy 'til my cock was numb.' Kieran got up and smiled down at me.

'Come to us when you're ready to give us it all,' he said and pressed a warm kiss on my forehead.

'But, please, I'm so frustrated,' I complained as they both adjusted themselves and went back to work on my window. Kieran lifted the new pane of glass up to the frame. 'Hey, guys, don't be like that.' I leaned back on the bed, presenting my sex to them like a bitch on heat. 'You've got to finish what you started.' They didn't respond and I wasn't going to beg. I slipped my clothes back on and sat fidgeting on the bed while they finished the job.

'Good as new.' Kieran winked at me. I came and inspected the job. Actually, I was trying to regain my status, feeling a bit like I had revealed too much of myself in every sense. I ran my finger along the frame of the window, frowning.

'No, that looks fine,' I conceded eventually. 'Thanks for mending that for me. I owe you one.' Kieran put his hand on my behind and squeezed.

'No, Jo, we owe you one,' he leered. Harry laughed. 'You know where we are if you want us.' I sniffed haughtily.

'Actually, you were right to put a stop to it,' I said. 'I'm not the unfaithful kind.' They nodded sagely, their eyes goading me.

'Of course not, of course not,' Kieran said. As they left and he turned round at the door. 'In case you are wondering, our sleeping quarters are behind the stables; the first cottage. Just in case you have any urgent requests. Any broken windows or anything.' Harry sniggered.

I smiled tightly and showed them out. When they had gone, I felt a surge of guilt. I scrambled around trying to find my phone and quickly dialled Jerome's number at work. Corinne answered again.

'How's it going in the grand Hathaway mansion, then?' she asked in her clipped, ironic New Zealand tones. I wondered if she was at all peeved that Jerome hadn't entrusted her with this assignment. After all, she had been at *A Tempo* for two years, whereas I only joined ten months ago. 'Butler being good to you, is he?'

I muttered something about finding it hard to get a decent interview and asked to speak to 'the boss', as we liked to call Jerome.

'He's in a meeting,' Corinne said. That was odd. That was the euphemism we always used when he didn't want to take a call. Jerome never had meetings, we both knew that.

'Oh? Who with?' There was a sticky silence and I suspected that Corinne was trying to block my calls. Perhaps she knew about Jerome and me. A sting of paranoia hit me and I started to imagine that maybe I wasn't the only employee of Jerome's to receive his special treatment.

'I don't know,' she said finally. Something wasn't right here. London seemed like a long way away, and Jerome even more unattainable than ever.

'Well, can you just tell him I'm having trouble pinning Tom Hathaway down to an interview,' I said in my most casually businesslike voice. 'Just to keep him posted.'

'I'll tell him,' she replied condescendingly. 'Have a good time, now!'

4

By six o'clock, hunger had set in. All my worries about Jerome, my window and my clumsy meeting with Tom were eclipsed by my need for food. In fact the day's events had given me all sorts of appetites. I pulled on a jumper and roamed around the house, trying to bump into someone who could feed me, making a mental note to buy a stash of biscuits to keep in my room in future. The dining room was sadly empty, but there was a bowl of fruit on the table. I bit into an apple and stuffed a banana in my pocket. The house was deathly quiet, but I knew that this old architecture would prevent sounds travelling from floor to floor. I decided to carry on exploring, using my hunger as an excuse this time. I was really hoping to bump into Tom Hathaway, to check him out in an upright position, but even Alicia's face would have been welcome.

As I came out of the dining room, I noticed that there was another small staircase to the right of it that I hadn't seen before. I climbed it and found myself on an unknown landing. More rooms, more doors, more twists and turns. A window in an alcove showed me that we were facing the orchard; a view I didn't recognise. I kept walking until voices emerged from the silence. Human life at last! I took another juicy bite of the apple and kept walking towards the voices. I didn't recognise them. There was a man with a slow American twang and another one, also American, with a fast nasal rhythm to his speech. I heard banging and furniture being dragged across the floor. Then there was laughter. I finally found the room they were in and listened at the door.

'Hey, who cares if the costumes are a decade out,' the nasal voice was saying. I placed it as a New York accent. 'It's only a TV movie, for Christ's sake. And let's face it, half our audience won't even know who Queen Victoria was.'

'Half our audience don't even know who *they* are,' the other voice agreed. It was a broad, mild Texan drawl, a resonant voice. 'They're all Middle American housewives on Prozac.' They laughed. 'Yeah, Ollie, you're right as usual. Guess I'm just a perfectionist.'

'Look, Ray, be a perfectionist when there's time to be, but we got a schedule here. We got actors, cameras, expensive costumes on loan. It's all set up here. Let's not blow it.' There was a pause. 'All I'm saying is, the less we spend the bigger our cut. Yeah?'

'Yeah, Ol.'

'Great.'

I took the pause to be a good time to barge in. I guessed these were going to be my fellow house guests for the next week or so, and it was only polite to introduce myself. I opened the door and smiled.

'Hope I'm not interrupting anything,' I said. They looked at me blankly. Behind them I could see a vast room with an ornate bed in the middle. Racks of costumes and wigs lined one wall, with a small bank of mirrors framed by lights for make-up. Camera and sound equipment was stacked in one corner. 'Hi, I'm Jo Bell.'

'Do you live here?' That was the New Yorker. He was short and dark with wire-rimmed glasses. I recognised his edgy, sweaty high energy from media parties. This guy had a coke habit.

'No, I don't, I'm up from London,' I explained, 'I'm

what you might call a roving reporter. Just looking for sustenance.' The New Yorker glanced nervously at his friend, who was tall and lean with a sandy moustache. They both hesitated for a moment and I realised that they thought I had come to interview them about something. I wondered what it was they had to hide. The Texan extended me his hand and smiled charmingly.

'Ray Hobbs,' he said calmly, shaking my hand and pressing his card into it in one suave move. 'And this is Ollie Mangel. Can we help you in any way?'

'What is it you're actually shooting here, Mr Hobbs?' I asked, playing a little on their paranoia.

'Just a little movie for TV: *Fallen Angels* we're calling it,' he replied slowly, watching me with a sharpness in his steely eyes. 'All above board and kosher, of course. A run-of-the-mill costume tele-drama for the folks back home.'

'There's no story here,' the other guy piped up, which instantly led me to believe that there was. His taller friend glanced at him impatiently, aware of how guilty he looked. I feigned complete innocence and laughed.

'Oh! Of course not, sorry. I'm not here to report on *you*. Did I give that impression?' I saw their shoulders fall as the tension drained out of them. 'No, no, I'm just a music journalist doing a piece on Daphne Hathaway.'

'Who?' Ollie Mangel shrugged at me.

'She was just a composer who used to live here,' I said dismissively, trying to make him feel better about not having heard of her, not that he looked particularly embarrassed. 'So I just thought I'd say hello. We'll be seeing a lot of each other about the place.'

'I hope so,' Ray Hobbs said, obviously warming to me. Now he knew I wasn't on to him for something, he was looking at me in a new light. 'You've got great skin, you know,' he remarked. 'Perfect for screen work. Have you ever done any?'

I shook my head, my sense of flattery vying with my sense of suspicion.

'Isn't she photogenic, Ollie?' he continued. 'Ollie does all my photography and cinematography, Jo. The best in the business.'

'Yeah, for what you're paying,' Ollie jibed, squinting at me. 'You're right, Ray. What a peach. Nice figure, too.'

'Have you ever thought of going into movies, honey?' Ray drawled. I had the distinct feeling that I was being beguiled with compliments to keep me sweet.

'Well, you're both very charming, gentlemen,' I answered wryly. 'But you can save all that flannel for your actresses. We journalists don't really go for that stuff. Honestly, I thought they talked straight down in the Deep South, Mr Hobbs.'

He laughed, throwing his head back, his eyes twinkling. It was the first genuine reaction I'd had from either of them.

'We've got a lot of frisky fillies down there, too,' he chuckled, 'and they need a firm hand to keep them in line. So you'd better watch it, young lady!'

'Point taken.' I took another bite of my apple, which was browning slightly now. 'Well, it was lovely to meet you both but I'm hungry. Have you seen our hostess anywhere?'

'Yeah, she said she wouldn't be around this evening. She said she'd leave food for us in the dining room at eight. If you want any, help yourself.'

'I will.' I was a bit annoyed that she hadn't let me know about this arrangement. 'Thanks.' Ray put his hand on my arm as I turned to go.

'And it's Ray. Not Mr Hobbs.' Charm poured out of him as he beamed down at me. 'Don't go making me feel old, now.'

'Alright, then. See you around, Ray.' I turned to his little friend, who seemed baffled by me for some reason, his eyes still cool and suspicious. 'See you again too, Mr Mangel,' I said pointedly. I could still feel his eyes on me as I walked down the corridor, and I heard him mutter something to Ray. I was going to have to keep my eyes on that one.

Jerome finally called the next morning. It was 10 a.m. and I had overslept, engrossed in a strange dream in which Daphne Hathaway was running around a maze in search of the special room. The piercing ring of my mobile woke me up and I answered with my voice cracking with sleep.

'Jo?' My heart leapt to hear Jerome's voice. It had been three days since we last spoke and I was beginning to think he was avoiding me.

'Jerome, hi. Where've you been?' I asked, stretching out in my bed.

'It's ten in the morning, Jo. I haven't sent you there to lie about all day.' The hardness of his voice woke me up. 'What's the deal? Corinne says you're getting nowhere with Tom Hathaway.'

'Well, hello to you, too,' I snapped. Even if he was in the office and in work mode, that was no way to speak to me.

'Do I have to come down there?' he continued. 'Can you cope?'

'Yes, I can sodding cope.' His tone enraged me. He had given me this important assignment and now it sounded like he didn't trust his own judgement. 'What is this, Jerome?' There was a pause. I heard him sigh a little.

'Sorry, just under a bit of pressure that's all. The parent company is pressing me for a quick increase in sales or we're going to get the chop.' Against my better judgement, I started to feel sorry for him. 'And you can't call me three times a day, Jo. It's too much.'

All my excitement about sharing the eccentricities of the Hathaway family with him drained out of my body. For over two days I had been dying to talk to him, and now I couldn't wait to get off the phone. I should have taken Harry and Kieran up on their offer when I had the chance.

'I'll tell you what, Jerome,' I said, feeling my temper rise. 'Why don't I wait for you to call me?'

'Jo, don't be like that –' he began, but I took great pleasure in cutting him off. I stomped into the bathroom and ran a hot bath. I was going to start this day again. As I soaked in the tub, I decided that I would pin Tom Hathaway down to an interview as soon as possible. Only then could I really begin to write up the notes I had already started, and to tie in the past with the present day.

Back in my room, I decided to dress to impress. I pulled on my favourite lilac trouser suit, the plunging jacket accentuating my cleavage nicely. It would appeal to both the conservative and the salacious; I had yet to discover which category Tom Hathaway fitted into. I sat on the bed to paint my toenails a matching shade, and noticed that I had missed a call on the mobile. It was Jerome's number. He had left a message. This would be interesting, I thought, and carefully painted my toenails as I listened to it: 'Yeah, Jo, sorry about that. You sounded a bit pissed off with me, so I thought I'd better call you back ... but you're not picking up. Maybe you are pissed off.' There was a pause, then his voice dropped a little. 'Look, I do miss you. Ring me tonight and we'll have a little phone session. Yeah? OK, talk later.'

I listened to it a few times, then erased it. Something about his voice had turned me on. I had heard it groaning into my ear at so many sexy moments that it instantly sent my nerves tingling. I was a victim of association, like an erotic Pavlov's dog, and I realised that only now was I in the perfect environment to retrain myself not to fall for him so easily. Here I was, in the middle of nowhere, in a house full of nice-looking men and beds the size of boats. This could be an adventure playground for me if I wanted it to be. And Tom Hathaway could be my first playmate. After all, I was a free agent.

This time I knocked very politely on Tom's door. I knew he was there because I could hear him playing the piano. This time the piece was not one of Daphne's, it was too modern, too jazzy, but it certainly had some of her influences. He stopped playing and a moment later the door opened. He was taller than I had imagined, and fully dressed this time. His style was casual and understated, his shirt hanging out of his trousers, his feet bare. His fair hair was streaked with blond and needed a cut, but it suited him that way.

'Hi,' I said, feeling a bit overdressed. I indicated my notebook and pen. 'Nice to meet you again. Any chance of a chat? My editor is getting a bit jumpy.'

He smiled and showed me in. Once inside, I could feel the difference in character between Tom and Alicia. Her room had been indulgent and stylish and colourful, but Tom's had a bare, unpretentious air to it, with just a couple of paintings on the wall and the only personal items being his piano, guitar and a teddy that lay on his bed. He saw me looking at it, bemused.

'Oh, Christ, why did I leave that there?' he mumbled,

shoving it under the duvet as if it was a porn mag. 'Just an old toy. We didn't have many when we were little so it has extra sentimental value. Sorry about that.'

We sat by the windows, the morning sun warming our backs and shining in a golden halo about his head.

'Sorry I haven't been around much,' he said. 'To tell you the truth, Alicia organises everything and she didn't mention you were coming. Otherwise I would have made more of an effort before.' He hesitated. 'It's not that I don't want to talk to you. I like talking about Daphne. Let's just say I'm a bigger fan of her music than Alicia is.'

'Then why didn't she set us up for a chat earlier?' I asked. He looked uncomfortable.

'Have you got any brothers or sisters, Miss Bell?'

'It's Jo,' I said, wondering where this was leading. 'And I have three brothers.'

'Well, then you know that it's a complicated relationship.' I looked at him blankly. 'I mean, it's competitive. And it's ... possessive.'

'Well, I can identify with that!' I laughed, remembering my brothers' overprotective ways of keeping my admirers at a distance when I was a teenager. But I got the feeling that this was a little more complex than that. 'Does Alicia play the piano like you do, Tom?'

'No.' He looked at me as if that explained everything. 'She doesn't get music. It's hard for her. She doesn't have that passion in her life like I do. And like Daphne did.' Having seen her with Harry in the stables, I begged to differ, but I kept my mouth shut. There was an awkward silence.

'What was that you were just playing?' I asked eventually. He looked bashful and shrugged it off. 'I liked it. A lot.'

'Really?' He had a lovely shy smile, with laugh lines creasing his cheeks. 'Well, it's one of mine, actually. I do a bit of writing – just for fun.'

'I recognised a few phrases of your great-grandmother's in there,' I said. He looked impressed. He had obviously had me down as an ignoramus, and he wouldn't have been far wrong. My knowledge loosened him up a bit.

'That's right. I'm doing some variations on a theme around her Sonata in A minor,' he said animatedly, 'using jazz chords under some of her original melodies. Her writing lends itself to interpretation like that. Particularly the fast movements.' He was obviously more relaxed talking about music than discussing his sister, which perversely made me want to return to the subject of Alicia. 'I'm just mucking around – it's nothing serious. Just playing with the fusion of jazz and classical –'

'What does Alicia make of your pieces?' I asked, a little abruptly.

He stopped in his tracks.

'Does she encourage you?'

He smiled ruefully.

'She doesn't really appreciate music generally.' He had a natural sense of diplomacy, I noticed. 'So I don't play them to her. In fact, please don't mention that I'm composing. It just irritates her.' I was intrigued. No wonder Alicia had tried to keep me from Tom, if she was so threatened by his talent.

'And is she proud to be associated with Daphne?'

'Yes, of course. She moulds herself on Daphne,' Tom enthused. 'They have such similarities, you see. They're both vivacious, independent young women, both motherless, both convention breakers, both social butterflies,' he began, his admiration for his sister shining in his eyes. 'They are both beautiful and sought after, with a touch of madness in there somewhere, I'm sure. Alicia knows that. She feels it's all part of her genetic destiny or something.'

'But Daphne had music as the centre of her life,' I interrupted. 'That was the most important thing for her. She knew what she cared about. What does Alicia have?' He thought about this for a moment, looking at his piano.

'I don't think she knows yet,' he replied quietly.

'It's a tough thing, not having that grounding talent or passion, don't you think?' I asked. 'Isn't she a bit lost?' He nodded regretfully.

'I think it explains her, really,' he said. 'Everything's a game with Alicia, because nothing seems real.' Then he got up and went back to his piano stool. 'But you should really talk to her if you want to know what makes her tick.'

'But I like talking to you,' I smiled, following him. I leaned against the piano and listened while he played around with some chords. 'I asked her if you were married and she laughed at me. Why did she find that so funny?' I was wondering if he was gay. It was more than a professional interest I was developing.

He sighed a long-suffering sigh.

'God, she's embarrassing. She found that so funny because ... I'm terrible with women,' he replied candidly. 'Absolutely awful. It's always a disaster and she's always the one who has to pick up the pieces.'

'Perhaps you are going after the wrong sort of women?' I suggested. 'You seem perfectly fine to me.' His eyes met mine properly for the first time, and for a moment I was locked into their green-gold stare.

'Well, you're not like the girls I usually get to meet, to be honest.'

'Oh no?' I sat on the edge of his piano stool, slipping into gossip mode now. 'And what would they be like?'

He shrugged and took his hands off the keys.

'I don't know. They're usually friends of Alicia's.' I could just picture them. 'They always start out alright but become a bit highly strung and offish.' He played a few bars on the piano, his head bent over the keys, and I felt suddenly as if I was outstaying my welcome. I got up and stepped back.

'I'll let you get on with it,' I said. 'I hope we can chat more later.' He turned to me, still playing.

'Alicia's putting on a big meal tonight for all the house guests,' he said. 'I'll see you there.' I looked forward to it. Finally, in this house full of masks and games, I had found the genuine article.

When I was at the door, he stopped playing for a minute.

'You never told me if you were married,' he called after me.

'No, Tom,' I answered, holding out my naked ring finger, 'I am very much single.'

5

We were summoned to the dining room at eight-thirty for Alicia's special welcome evening. She obviously liked a sense of occasion, dropping a little invitation card into my room that afternoon, indicating that dress was 'smart'. In my world, my lilac suit was smart but I was suddenly insecure about how it would measure up to Alicia's idea of formality. I searched my cupboard for alternatives, eventually choosing my favourite little red dress for the evening. After all, I had taken quite a shine to Tom and he was going to be there, so looking good wouldn't go to waste. I never really wore make-up, but decided to apply a bit of gloss to my lips and some shimmer to my eyes, accentuating them with a slick of mascara. I scraped my hair up into a stylish bun and put in some butterfly combs that had been passed down to me by my Brazilian grandmother, their red and gold wings matching the red chiffon of my dress perfectly.

I looked at myself in the mirror and approved. The dress was in a baby-doll style, scooping my breasts up and supporting the golden swell of my cleavage nicely. The skirt was short and diaphanous, showing a lot of leg. I finished it all off with a pair of red kitten heels and prepared to meet the others. As I left the room, I felt like a soldier who had just put on his battle gear and war paint, and I realised that I was making all this effort not to impress Tom, but to compete with Alicia. Her subtly snide comments had put me on the defensive, and now I was going to show her who was the better woman.

My walk was ultra-confident as I strode into the dining room, fashionably late. All heads turned to me as I came in, and I was greeted by admiring smiles and compliments. Ray and Ollie were there, sizing me up again, and Tom sat at the far end of the table, smiling warmly. His eyes had lit up when I came in, but I guessed this might just be because everyone had run out of conversation. A man in his late fifties sat next to Tom, good-looking for his age, in the archetypal country gentleman tweeds. Only Alicia had yet to arrive.

'Who's this beauty?' the older man asked Tom, looking me up and down. 'You finally got yourself a woman?'

'She's a reporter from a music magazine, Mr Wootten,' Tom explained, patiently. 'Jo, this is Rory Wootten, a friend of the family. Rory, this is Josephina Bell.' I smiled politely at the man and sat next to him.

'Josephina?' He repeated my name as if it were the Latin term for herpes. 'What kind of name's that?'

'A very beautiful one,' Tom replied, apologising to me with his eyes. 'Jo, Rory was our tutor when we were growing up. Well, when we were doing our O and A levels. I went away to school after a while but he taught Alicia all she knows. He still comes to visit us. Can't seem to get rid of him.'

Mr Wootten leant back in this chair, looking at his former pupil with amused disapproval.

'Insubordination,' he growled, and turned his eyes on me. 'I hope you're a bit more obedient than these two,' he said, turning into a real old flirt. 'You're none of you too old to be put over my knee.'

'Can we Americans be excused from that?' Ray laughed and Mr Wootten looked a little embarrassed. He had obviously forgotten that they were there.

'I don't think so, do you?' I interjected and grinned

at Ray and Ollie, who were watching Mr Wootten as if he were entertainment laid on by their host. Ollie was looking particularly edgy and restless. Either he had just had a fix or he needed one. Ray, however, was still swathed in an aura of calm self-composure and flashed me one of his charming smiles.

'Can I say how beautiful you look in that red dress,' he said softly. 'Not every woman can wear red, but you have that passion and colouring.'

I looked at Tom, amused by Ray's endless capacity for smarm.

'Really, I mean it.'

'Why, thank you, Mr Hobbs,' I simpered in a Southern drawl. 'Should I be in the a movies, do you think?' He dismissed me with his hand.

'You don't know how to take a compliment,' he grouched good-naturedly, and he reached out and tickled the back of my neck for a second.

It was a tiny gesture, but all the hairs on my arms suddenly sprang up, as did my nipples. I gave a little shudder. The thin, clingy chiffon of my dress rose over the little peaks and I attempted to cross my arms over them until they calmed down. Ray had a keen eye for such detail, though, and his gaze was loaded as he eyed my breasts.

'Oh, you are a pretty thing,' he said softly. I glanced at Tom and he quickly looked away.

Alicia saved us by choosing that moment to make her entrance. As soon as I saw her I knew I couldn't compete. She was wearing a turquoise silk full-length dress, with a delicate halter neck. She draped herself in the doorway for a moment.

'Have you been waiting long?' she asked graciously. As she came into the room, I could see that her dress was totally backless, skimming her bottom so low that she could not possibly have been wearing panties. It rested on the curve of her bottom and the fishtail skirt clung to her slender legs. I was well and truly beaten. I felt like a sugary glacé cherry floating on a luminous exotic cocktail.

'My God, you look stunning,' Ray breathed, forgetting all about my sightly nipples. All the men around the table stood up, as if in awe of her beauty.

'Alicia, what a pretty dress,' I agreed, determined not to appear too jealous. She flashed me a dazzling smile and sat down at the head of the table.

'Oh, do sit down, honestly, what a fuss,' she said to the guys, flicking her glossy black hair over a perfectly toned white shoulder. 'Josephina, I think you look sensational, darling.' She glanced at Tom. 'Isn't she delicious?'

Tom didn't know how to reply. There was an awkward silence while he tried to get the right words. I could see his problem. He didn't want to say I was delicious, because that wouldn't be his style, but he didn't want to disagree and offend me. He faltered and spluttered for a moment.

'You both look great,' he said eventually and Alicia smiled meanly at his ineptness.

'Well, *I* think she looks splendid,' she countered patronizingly, as if Tom had said he didn't. 'Don't you boys?' Ray looked from one of us to the other.

'Like fire and ice, ladies,' he said. 'Every man's fantasy. Wouldn't you say, Mr Wootten?'

'They're both very naughty girls. We won't be able to concentrate on our food.'

'Don't worry, Rory,' Alicia's tone was indulgent. 'I promise you'll have a good evening. Now let's eat up and stop talking about silly shallow things like dresses.' She rang her bell and the maids arrived with the soup. 'Ray and Ollie, I want to know all about the movie business!'

'Well, there's nothing deep and meaningful about our line of work, Alicia,' Ray laughed. 'Not the stuff we do anyhow.' He shot her a significant look and she caught it with a twinkle in her eye.

'I look forward to seeing your work, Ray,' she said, enchantingly. 'It sounds fascinating.'

'What the hell does he do again?' Mr Wootten interrupted, and we spent the whole of the soup course trying to explain to him what a tele-drama was. Their movie was a period drama set in the Victorian age, although they didn't seem too fussed about historical accuracy. Ray spoke with charming modesty on the subject, self-effacing in the extreme, while Ollie sat eating hurriedly and only interjecting when invited to by his colleague.

Alicia was in her element as hostess, fielding the conversation with great aplomb and always managing to bring it back to herself. She expressed a desire to see herself on screen, much to Ray's delight. When she apparently felt her other guests were out in the cold, she invited them into the conversation. Her attitude to her old tutor sparked my interest. She was indulgent, affectionate and flirtatious with him. His gruff manner seemed to appeal to her, and she was always promising him 'treats' if he behaved himself, although we were never told what those treats would be.

'Did you have a favourite teacher, Josephina?' she asked, seeing me watching Mr Wootten. 'I was so lucky with Rory. He taught me so much.'

Mr Wootten smiled over at her, a secret smile.

'Well, I didn't have many I could ask over for dinner,' I said. 'I was a bit of a tearaway at school, I'm afraid. Always in trouble.'

'I can imagine,' Ray grinned.

'Needed a firm hand,' Mr Wootten agreed. Wanting

to test Alicia's reaction, I decided to flirt with him a little.

'Well, you know what they say, Rory: it's never too late.' I let my eyes catch his for a moment too long. 'I never had the benefits of a private education. Perhaps you can tell me what I've been missing?'

'Perhaps I could, my dear,' he replied intimately.

His fat hand crept onto my knee, caressing the tender underside. I tried not to jolt with the sensation.

'Well,' Alicia said tightly, 'I think I'm ready for the main course. Where's that blasted servant?' she spat, losing her cool for a moment, ringing her bell impatiently.

Mr Wootten's hand was creeping upwards in slow motion, the rough skin scratchy on my leg. My flimsy dress flowed over his hand and soon his fingers made contact with the hot apex between my thighs. I wanted to giggle, barely able to believe what he was doing. I felt like I was being molested by a friend's dad. I tried to keep still, the pressure making me want to squirm in shame and excitement. Glancing down I could see the eager tenting in his trousers.

The doors opened and the maids brought in silver platters of fish and vegetables. As they served us, Mr Wootten's hand stayed firmly on my panties. The staff must have been able to see when they stood behind our chairs to pour the wine but he clearly didn't care.

'I had this real hot teacher at school,' Ray said. 'Miss Klein. God, she was sexy. It was a boy's school and she used to come in every day dressed in these little tops that weren't quite big enough for her, and tight trousers. Nothing was left to the imagination. She'd bend over in class so twenty-five boys got a clear view of her tits. Man, she was something else.'

'Teenage boys are very easy targets,' Alicia commented.

'Teenage girls are just as excitable,' Mr Wootten said pointedly, his thumb pressing against me. 'In fact, they're worse. Because they know they can get a man to do anything they want.'

'That's true,' Ray said. 'Teenage boys don't have that possibility. It's all fantasy.'

The conversation got a little blurry as Mr Wootten's fingers caressed me in subtle circles. I wondered if I should stop him. After all, my flirtatiousness had started just as a way to annoy my hostess and it had done the trick. The melting sensation in my groin pulled me on, though, and instead I curled my pelvis up slightly to meet his fingers. I heard his loud breathing quicken a little.

'At least teenagers have some energy,' Alicia was saying, 'I'd try one.'

'Me too,' Ray grinned. 'I'll bet you were a naughty teenager.' Alicia nodded and Mr Wootten let out a wry laugh.

'She was devilish,' he said. 'An absolute little tease.'

'It's a wonder I ever learnt anything, isn't it Rory? Too many distractions.' She smiled deliciously at him and he started to frig me harder in response. I imagined Alicia as a teenager in the study seducing him. I was sure she had been irresistible. Maybe he had touched her like this at family dinners, I thought, blood rushing to my cheeks. I could imagine her creaming all over his hand while passing the salt. I swallowed hard.

'Don't you like your fish?' Tom's voice seemed very far away. After a moment I realised he was talking to me.

'Oh, sorry.' I saw that I hadn't touched my food. 'I was miles away.'

'We can see that, darlin',' Ray winked. I wondered if he could see Mr Wootten's arm bending between my legs, but he was just talking about my flushed cheeks. 'All this talk of teenagers got you hot and horny, has it?'

I laughed and took a large bite of potato so I didn't have to answer.

'It has!' Ray goaded.

I brushed the schoolmaster's hand from my pussy, feeling suddenly disgusted with myself.

'No, no, no. I was just shocked at all of you!' I said in mock outrage.

'So, what turns you on then?' he persisted. 'Older guys?' I noticed Mr Wootten bring his fingers to his nose and inhale my scent lasciviously.

'Maybe,' I replied. 'All kinds of things, actually. Too many to go into now.' I was aware of Tom in the room, and it made me uncharacteristically cagey. I didn't want to scare him off.

'Oh, come on!' Alicia chided. 'Don't be square.'

'I don't have a little list of things that turn me on,' I retorted. 'I just like to suck it and see.' There was a pause while the men in the room enjoyed the figure of speech.

'Well,' Ray said finally. 'That's a girl after my own heart.'

After the meal, we were all glued drunkenly to our chairs. Even Tom was looking merry, although I could see this wasn't his type of evening. Ray went to the record player and dug out some sexy jazz music, dancing his way back to the head of the table. He stood behind Alicia, stroking her hair and jigging his hips.

'I think we should play a game,' he said, a naughty grin telling me it wasn't going to be Monopoly. Alicia leant back against him, her shoulders pressing on his crotch.

'Oh yes, what a fabulous idea,' she drawled. 'What are the rules?'

'There are no rules!' Ray declared and everyone laughed for some drunken reason. Only Tom sat quietly, listening hard to the music.

'Oh, let me go first!' Alicia demanded, 'I do so want to play. Will I get a prize?'

'Yeah, baby.' Ray caressed her neck and slipped his fingers over her collarbone. She shivered in delight. 'It's truth or dare.' She clapped her hands with glee.

'Ladies first, I think, don't you gentlemen?'

Tom got up.

'I think I'm going to turn in,' he said, running his hand through his hair.

I was disappointed. I was hoping things were about to get interesting.

'Are you sure?' I asked. 'The night is young.'

'I think I'd better.' He shot Alicia a look of regret and disapproval. 'This isn't really my scene. Goodnight everybody.'

I watched his attractive figure leave the room and felt a little dejected myself. The room fell quiet for a moment.

'Oh, ignore him,' Alicia said, shouting after him, 'party pooper!'

Ray sat back down and leaned on the table.

'Right, ladies, truth or dare?' he asked, his eyes glinting cheekily. 'Jo?'

'You have to ask the question first,' I said, 'then I'll decide.'

'Alrighty.' Ray thought for a moment. 'Hey, this is good. You ready for this?' I nodded nervously. 'Jo. Is there – or was there – anyone at this table tonight whom you would like to fuck?' I laughed in shock at his question. 'And if so, who was it?'

'You can't ask that!' I protested.

'It's me isn't it?' he jibed, winking. Alicia was intrigued.

'Jo, darling, who is it?' she purred, watching me squirm, like a cat about to kill a mouse.

'Nobody!' I shouted. They all looked at me reproachfully. 'OK, dare,' I conceded. I had never been able to resist a dare anyway. 'But it doesn't mean anything, OK? What do I have to do?'

All eyes were on Ray, and he sat back in deep contemplation, his fingers playing at the edge of his moustache. I started to giggle nervously.

'I think we'll go easy on you,' he said eventually. Mr Wootten made to protest, but Ray raised his hand. 'No, she's a sweet thing, far away from home.'

He went to the record player and rifled through the vinyl, finally choosing a song to put on. As soon as the needle hit the groove I recognised it as Peggy Lee singing Black Coffee, her creamy voice melting into the sexy groove underneath.

'Right, Miss Bell, up on the table!' Ray ordered.

I clattered unsteadily up. My skirt was so short that I was aware that everybody was now able to see right up it. Mr Wootten's eyes lingered hungrily at my crotch, blatantly examining the scanty material of my black thong.

'Very nice,' Ray commented, sitting back down to get better view. 'Now, give us a striptease.' The table erupted into laughter.

'Can't I just do a song or something?' I asked shakily, although part of me was dying to give a strip a go. It had always been one of my fantasies. Jerome had often talked about taking me to a strip club and watching as I bared myself to the punters.

'Not on your life, lady,' Ray replied and lit a cigar. The rising smoke gave the room a bit more atmosphere, and I began to sway a little to the music. It was sexy but slow, and my hips gyrated naturally, toned and flexible from their samba holiday.

'That's good.' Ray's voice was mellow.

I sunk along the table to Alicia and shimmied down to meet her face with my cleavage. Mr Wootten behind me got a candid view of my round bottom and I could hear him sigh his approval. Then I knelt before Ray and slowly bent backwards into an arc, presenting his mouth with my crotch, and ground my hips in slow circles in time to the music.

'Christ,' I heard him say, his breath hot against me. I gyrated nastily in his face, knowing we both wanted him to put his mouth on me but not able to see his expression. I wondered if he could smell my arousal. I could see Ollie from my upside-down position; he was sweating, his narrow eyes fixed on my cleavage. The sight of him put me off my stride for a moment and I collapsed back down, much to Ray's disappointment.

The sleazy brass section kicked in and I rolled down the table until I was lying on my stomach, facing Mr Wootten. He had an approving smile on his face, and I could see his hand pressing against his trousers. He suddenly looked so helpless, just a dirty old man reduced to leering at a young girl way out of his league. I decided to give him a treat, as Alicia had put it, and licked my lips slowly. His hand pressed harder and I crawled up onto all fours, still looking him in the eye, still rotating my hips as if being fucked doggy-style by an invisible man. I could almost feel the creaminess of my cunt as I moved.

'God help me.' I heard Ray's voice behind me. 'Look at that beautiful butt. Jesus, she's hot.'

I knelt up, glancing back at Ray over my shoulder, and slowly unhooked the straps of my dress, sliding them down to reveal my full, golden breasts and dark, engorged nipples. Only Mr Wootten and Ollie could see them full on, and I heard Ray groan for me to turn round. The music poured through me like a dream and, when I guided Mr Wootten's mouth to my breast, it hardly seemed real. His tongue was hot and very wet, slurping on me as if he couldn't believe his luck. I remembered his skilful, subtle fingers under the table and the sexual tension between him and Alicia and a slow fire began to burn in my pussy. I wondered if he had sucked on her like he was sucking on me, whether this had been her extra tuition. I imagined having him suckle on my young breasts when I was a wayward, curious teenager. I sighed, knowing how I would have loved it.

Peggy Lee broke out into a sleazy middle eight as I felt tingles rush over my body: 'A man is born to go a-lovin'', she crooned as Mr Wootten was getting into his element. He grabbed my shoulders to pull me into him. His tongue flicked and lapped, sending a gooey rush into my thong. He was making soft, guttural noises, and his hands began to explore my body, clutching my bottom and pulling the cheeks apart. I pushed him back. I was the one in control and I liked it that way.

I got up, rocking my body faster, wriggling out of my dress so it lay in a red puddle around my ankles. Now I stood only in my thong and heels and the song was coming to an end. I turned to Ray and he moaned at the sight of me, banging the table in rhythm to the music. My breasts bobbed slightly as I danced, and I scraped my hands up them, sending blood to my nipples. I took the butterflies from my hair and unpinned it so it cascaded down my shoulders and back. It tickled, brushing my already tingling skin.

'God, show us your pussy,' Ray breathed, his eyes shining with lust. 'Come on. I'll bet it's a beauty.'

I could hear the last phrase coming up – 'It's drivin''

me crazy, this waiting for my baby...' and I stopped moving. I looked him coolly in the eye and began to pull my thong down inch by inch, feeling it slide over the curve of my hip. I could feel Mr Wootten breathe out as the thong unpeeled itself from the globes of my buttocks. I finally revealed the top of my triangle when the song ended.

'Sorry, boys,' I smiled, snapping the thong back up smartly. 'Perhaps some other time.'

'Oh, come on!' Ray protested, getting up.

I could see his erection straining in his trousers. It made me want to touch him, or let him touch me. I stepped off the table, my tits bouncing as I jumped down.

'Christ, this isn't fair,' he groaned.

I went up to him, my palm tingling at the idea of rubbing his cock. When I was inches away, I smiled up at him, my breasts pointing perkily towards his face.

'Should have chosen a longer song,' I said with a grin.

He looked dejectedly at my body.

'The other guy got to suck your tits,' he grumbled.

I took pity on him, and my own restless arousal, and cupped a bosom in my hand.

'Be my guest, Mr Hobbs,' I said.

His eyes lit up again. The room went awfully silent as he lowered his mouth to my heavy breast, gently stimulating the nipple with his tongue. The wave of pleasure that rose in me knocked me off my balance, and I leant back against the table. It seemed amazing that only yesterday I was having my first stilted conversation with this man, and now his lips were at my naked bosom, his hands resting lightly on my hips. I could feel his thumbs pointing inwards, gently stroking between my legs, tantalisingly close to my bud.

The room was quiet but for the wet, secret sound of his mouth on me and the little sighs of pleasure I was making.

He manoeuvred himself into a chair, licking me all the time, so that his head was at waist height. Now that he had to look up at me to suck my breasts I could clearly see the delirious expression on his face. I had one leg on either side of his legs, and I sank onto his lap, straddling him. I so wanted to shuffle forward onto his cock and rub us both to climax, but something stopped me. I gently took his head in my hands and brought it up to look at me. His eyes were bleary and his cheeks flushed.

'Thanks, Ray,' I said. 'That was really great.' For a moment he looked like he was going to persuade me to carry on, but instead he just smiled.

'Any time, darlin'.'

'Quite, it's my turn!' Alicia cried petulantly, snapping me out of the moment. I got up and shakily pulled my dress back on. 'I am all fired up now, thanks to our pretty little guest, and I'm ready to go.' She fidgeted about in her chair.

I found myself slightly jealous as Ray turned his attention on her.

'OK, beautiful, truth or dare?' he asked.

'What's the question?' she demanded quickly. It was clear she wanted to do the dare but she was going to play by the rules.

'OK, let's think.' Ray tried to get his head straight.

'I've got one,' Mr Wootten piped up.

'Shoot,' Ray said, giving me a wink. 'And better make it a good 'un.'

'It is,' he replied, his face a picture of dirty anticipation. 'What is your most perverted fantasy? What's the lowest, most shocking sexual desire you have?'

Alicia ran her hand over her hair coyly.

'Don't you know this, Rory?' she flirted. 'I'm sure I've shared it with you.'

'Well, share it with the rest of us,' Ray said, intrigued. 'I'd sure like to know that.'

Alicia thought for a moment.

'You know, I would like to tell you, just to shock you all. But I won't!' she pouted. 'It is really very naughty and taboo and perverted.'

'And immoral,' Mr Wootten chuckled, taking a long sip of red wine.

'Well, darling, all the best things are,' she smiled. 'So I am afraid I must undergo one of your beastly dares, Mr Hobbs.'

'Make it a dirty one,' Mr Wootten added. 'She's unshockable, this one.'

Ray considered for a moment, then smiled to himself.

'Alright, get up on the table,' he started.

'Oh no, not another striptease,' Alicia sulked, climbing up elegantly.

Ray shook his head.

'Nothing so tame, young lady. You want it dirty, you got it dirty.' The fire in Alicia's eyes told us she wanted it as dirty as it got. 'Take all your clothes off. We wouldn't want to spoil that dress now.'

A naughty smile crept across Alicia's face.

'Ooh, I do like the sound of that,' she said, stepping out of her dress. She had nothing on underneath. Her pale body was lean and faultless, her tiny nipples crimson with anticipation. The black hair between her legs pointed like a glossy arrow to her sex. I felt a zing of envy – it could even have been desire – at the way she looked. She stood boldly above me, her body an open book. 'What now?' she demanded.

'Lie down on your back, knees apart,' Ray ordered, 'and keep the heels on, baby. You look sexy like that.'

She obeyed, seeming to relish all the attention, her black hair spread out behind her in a glossy mane. We watched her primed body in silence.

'Ooh, I feel like I'm lying on the altar and the priest is about to fuck all the sin out of me,' she breathed. 'I'm like a virgin sacrifice!'

Mr Wootten laughed throatily.

'Hardly,' he muttered, leaning in to examine Alicia's naked body more closely. His eyes lingered over her legs and he bent down to peer at her pussy. 'Pretty,' he said to himself, his hands back under the table.

I almost wished I was still next to him, enjoying the urgency of his fingers.

Ray was over by the sideboard, holding up a bowl.

'Some naughty girl didn't eat her dessert,' he teased, lifting a spoonful of chocolate mousse mixture into the air.

'A girl doesn't look like this by eating chocolate and cream all day,' Alicia smiled back, her slender body arching to show off her flat tummy.

'Well, it's a waste, sweetheart,' Ray grinned, 'and we're going to finish it all up for you, how about that?' He turned to Mr Wootten. 'What was your favourite part, sir: the cream, the chocolate mousse or the raspberry coulis?'

The old tutor licked his lips.

'I was rather fond of the raspberry,' he said.

Ray came up to the table and spread coulis all over Alicia's naked breasts, swirling the mixture over her nipples. She flinched as the cool liquid hit her body.

'What about you, Ollie?' Ray looked at his friend, who had been quietly watchful all night.

'The mousse, I guess,' Ollie replied.

Ray smiled and dropped dollops of the stuff on her feet and toes.

'Don't worry, honey, that's his favourite fetish,' he reassured Alicia, although I was sure she had no qualms about getting people to lick her feet.

'What about you, Josephina?'

All eyes turned on me, Alicia's sharp with interest. I had assumed I would be let out of this game.

'I've done my forfeit,' I said lamely. 'I want to watch.'

'Oh no, no, no,' Ray smiled. 'We want to watch *you*.' I realised I couldn't get out of the game without spoiling the party, just when it was getting really hot.

'Well, I'm a fan of chocolate,' I said, 'but not of feet. So –'

'No worries,' Ray interrupted, dripping a line of the dessert across Alicia's lips. She shivered with excitement. I could imagine her tasting the cool sweetness, anticipating all the mouths that would soon be on her.

Now Ray spooned up a scoop of whipped cream and looked intensely at Alicia's prone body. 'I'm a cream man, myself,' he whispered, and carefully applied it to her pussy, smearing it all over her mound and letting it slide between her legs. 'In fact, I can't get enough of the stuff,' he continued, dabbing another generous helping over her. We stared at her greedily, her body a decorated mess of cream and chocolate and syrup. Her lips were open and her pelvis rocking softly.

'Oh, please hurry,' she murmured.

'Very well,' Ray answered, climbing up on to the long table and kneeling between her legs. 'Bon appetite, everybody.'

Mr Wootten was the next to move, standing over the table and falling hungrily on her small sticky breasts. I saw his greying head bowed over her, his mouth sliding through the coulis from one nipple to the other, her young body responding instantly to his skilful touch. She sighed and took his head in her hands, guiding it over her pert bosom.

'That's it, Rory,' she moaned, her body churning harder now.

We were all entranced by the sight of Alicia being lapped up by the older man. My pussy gushed in sympathy as his tongue moved over her. I was intrigued by their relationship. They were obviously sexual with each other and I wondered when it all began. Looking at her nubile body gyrating under his ageing face, I felt as if I was watching the tutor take liberties with his teenage pupil in the classroom. I wished I had had some A level coaching along those lines.

As if reading my fantasies, Alicia started a little show of her own.

'Oh, Mr Wootten,' she panted. 'My father might come in at any minute.'

This talk obviously excited him and he started to suck furiously and noisily on one of her nipples. She stretched out with delight at his passion, like a cat being stroked.

'Mr Wootten, you're a very bad man,' she breathed. 'You shouldn't be sucking me like that! I'm going to tell my daddy.'

'Shut up and behave,' he growled into her skin. 'Or I'll give you a good smacking.'

'Oh!' She positively shuddered with delight at this threat, and my thong got a fresh drizzle of excitement. Ollie was excited too, I noticed, as he made his way to her feet, his black trousers straining slightly against his compact erection. He began slow, deliberate licks all over her feet, sucking each toe deliriously. I didn't fancy him, but his foot job looked amazing and, from the strange sounds Alicia was making, it was. The mousse hung around his lips as his fat tongue bathed her soles and tasted her delicate feet. He groaned like an animal.

Ray caught my eye, registering my interest.

'Stand up,' he mouthed. I obeyed and he reached out to my breast and caressed my hard nipple gently. I was desperate for him to touch me between the legs, but instead he dropped his hand altogether and bent between Alicia's splayed legs to start his sensuous lapping of her cunt. I saw his moustache sink into the deep layer of cream, his eyes shut with pleasure, as he tasted Alicia. As soon as his tongue touched her she let out a deep sigh, and her hips met his face rhythmically. The cream was dissolving into his mouth, clearing my view of his sexy tongue licking her pussy in long, thorough strokes. I trembled with jealousy as I saw him speed up, faster and faster, until his tongue was flapping as fast as a hummingbird against her clit.

I felt left out at the sight of the three men dining on Alicia's body, and I gently rubbed myself between the legs as I watched. She started to shake and cry out and soon she came in frenzied, helpless jerks, but that didn't stop any of them. They powered on relentlessly, their mouths sliding over her gooey body, making her come again and again. I bent over her face and tenderly licked the chocolate from her lips, desperate to be a part of this mass of lust. Her mouth was so sweet, I had to taste it again. She pushed her sharp tongue against mine and I was suddenly locked in a deep kiss with her. She clasped the back of my head and pulled me into her. I could feel her moans of lust vibrating into my mouth and I masturbated fast, trying to catch up with her, my fingers buried in the red chiffon of my dress. I sensed Mr Wootten pulling away from her breast to watch our hungry kiss and heard Ray's voice saying, 'Damn, that's horny.' I glanced up and all three men were watching us, their cocks in their hands.

'Don't stop, honey,' Ray whispered, 'keep it up.' Alicia engaged me in another hot battle of tongues, almost bruising my mouth with her hard lips. Her fingers hurt as they dug into my scalp. I took my hand away from my sex to steady myself on the side of the table. Suddenly Ray was behind me, his fingers slipping inside my thong, slithering in my wetness.

'Jesus, what a juicy pussy you got there,' he said, his voice hard and urgent. 'I can't wait to fuck that pussy.' He pressed his cock against my bottom and I swooned at the idea of it inside me. I'd had enough teasing: I wanted some action. I wished Jerome was there to fuck me. I knew I couldn't give myself to this stranger. It would change things too much for me in the house, and I would probably lose my job. But as his fingers gently fluttered on my clit, I instinctively pressed back into his groin.

'Oh, man,' he grunted, frigging me harder. I jolted against his hand, screaming my climax into Alicia's mouth.

Once I had come, clarity came back to me and I stumbled away from the group. Ray, Ollie and Mr Wootten all had their cocks out like boys playing with guns, hovering over Alicia's smeared body. Ray started to jerk himself off again, leaning over her torso, and Ollie was at her feet, his fist frantically moving up and down his small shaft. Only Mr Wootten couldn't really get into his stride. He was huffing and puffing, pulling on himself. Alicia noticed his frustration and turned her head to him. She opened her lips and pulled him to her, guiding his shaft into her chocolatey mouth. He groaned as his cock sank into the warm haven.

'Yes, my dear,' he sighed. 'That's a good girl. Suck it nicely, there's a sweet thing.' She was fixed onto it like a lollipop, and soon his hips were thrusting into her. She seemed to love sucking this man's cock, her legs falling open again, her hips starting their gyrations.

'Oh, that's good, Alicia,' he breathed. 'Oh, suck harder, there's a good girl.' Her head jerked at his crotch, a sight too much for Ray, who groaned and shot a spray of come over her belly. Ollie followed suit, his sticky seed covering her foot. She flinched as she felt the hot liquid on her, then rolled on to her side to concentrate on her blowjob, her head bobbing frantically backward and forwards. I had never seen her so submissive and obedient. Her tutor had obviously taught her how to please him; his expression was one of unadulterated joy. The closer he was to coming, the more excited she seemed to become, her hips dry fucking the air, her body quivering. When finally he did climax, she gulped it all down hungrily and licked him dry afterwards. Then she sat up on the table and did up his trousers for him. He kissed her forehead. 'Very good, my dear,' he praised her. 'It gets better every year.'

The room was subdued after this erotic game, and we all agreed to abandon Truth or Dare for the night. My body was still electric from what I had seen, and the wetness in my thong made me uncomfortable. Alicia was still playing the charming hostess, as if not noticing that her bare body was splattered with semen and chocolate. I left her and Ray lighting up a cigar and made my way to bed.

Alone in my bedroom I was so aroused that I gave in to my desire to call Jerome. He had, after all, asked me to do it. I would let him give me the phone session he had promised and listen to him trickle sexy words into my ear. It was after midnight, so I called him at home. His answerphone was on. Maybe he had gone to bed, I thought, kicking off my shoes dejectedly. I chucked ·my dress in a pile and crawled naked into bed, stroking myself to sleep.

6

My laptop kept exploding into stars, the insistent screen saver reminding me that I had terrible writer's block. I glanced at my watch for the fourteenth time. Eleven o'clock. How was I going to write up yesterday's events? I could just hear Jerome chastising me, using that stern voice he saved for when he was really cross with me (usually when I accidentally referred to him as my boyfriend). Annoyed with myself I got up and decided to go out and do some serious interviewing. I had to remind myself – and every one around me – that I was there to work, not to get sucked into all kinds of sexy games. I was a respected music journalist.

I found myself wondering around the corridors, looking for inspiration, eventually approaching the wing where I had met Ray and Ollie the day before. The sun was shining aggressively through the windows and I was occasionally blinded, squinting and shielding my face with my arm. Soon, I heard voices again. I must have reached the rooms where they were filming. I knew better than to go inside, and instead perched myself on a window seat, my back soaking up the heat. I shut my eyes and tried to think of a strategy to get this article done. It had all been too distracting so far.

Suddenly the voices in the room stopped. I head Ray say 'Action'. At first I thought it must have been a silent scene, because for ages I could hear nothing.

Then it came: a weird low moan. Perhaps it was an emotional moment, I thought, getting up and sticking my ear to the door. The moan came again and then a whipping sound and a shriek of delight. All thoughts of serious journalism fell from my intrigued mind. I bent down to peer through the keyhole, but could only make out shapes and colours. This was the weirdest Victorian tele-drama I had ever encountered. The woman was bent over, her black hair trailing on the back of a plush Victorian chair. Behind her all I could see was the bronzed shape of a man's thigh and an unfeasibly large erection. A leather crop fell across the woman's buttocks and she cried out again. I knew that voice. It instantly took me back to the previous night. This woman was Alicia.

The man positioned himself behind her and began to stroke her with the crop handle, letting it slide into her. She whispered something and he pushed it further, wiggling it around. Then Ray moved and obscured my view and I was left with the tantalising sounds of Alicia's moans and cries. Soon the man began to grunt in rhythm and I guessed that he was inside her. I shut my eyes tight, savouring the naughty sounds.

When I looked again, Ray had moved and I could see the man fucking Alicia wildly from behind, shaking her pale body with each thrust. He held the crop against her neck and applied pressure a couple of times, making her gasp and come at the same time. She obviously liked it rough. When he couldn't bear it anymore, the man pulled his huge shining member out of her and shot off generously over her smooth buttocks. I saw Ollie with the camera looming in to get a close-up. The sight of him suddenly took the edge off my arousal and I realised how compromised Alicia was. At least last night she had seemed to hold some power, holding court in her own sexual arena, but here she just seemed used. I got up and walked away. I needed to see Tom. He'd get me back on track.

Back downstairs I ventured out into the grounds, looking for Tom. I felt my body instantly respond to the heat of summer and kicked off my shoes and walked barefoot on the soft lawn, closing my eyes and throwing my head back. All I could hear now was the buzzing of a few lazy bees and the birds singing to each other. I didn't like to think of what Alicia was getting herself in to upstairs. I didn't like to think of what Jerome was getting up to in London, or what he would say if he knew how I was behaving down here. I didn't want to think about anything. Instead, I emptied my mind and found a stretch of dappled shade to lie in, convincing myself I just needed a rest. The sweet scent of freshly cut grass was heady and I soon drifted off to sleep. I started to have vague dreams about Alicia, her mouth as red as a poppy, her skin made of glass. People were laughing at her, and then I realised that the laughter was real, and opened my eyes.

Kieran stood over me, his gaze lowered frankly to my crotch. In my sleep my skirt had ridden up to reveal my panties. Glancing down I was relieved to see I had chosen a sexy pair that day: lilac satin and lace.

'Nice,' he remarked, his face locked in a stupid grin.

'Hello, Kieran,' I responded coolly, pulling my skirt down and sitting up a little too fast. I felt giddy and fell back on to my wrist. He was instantly by my side, helping me sit up, half gentleman, half lecher. His hands lingered too long on my waist and arm.

'I'm OK, just a head rush,' I said, defensively.

'Yeah, I get that way around you, too,' he said, giving me what he obviously hoped was a charming smile.

'Really? I thought the blood would rush to some

other part of you,' I teased. His eyes sparked with humour.

'Why haven't you come to visit us?' he asked, stroking my forearm.

My skin shivered where he touched me, the hairs standing up.

'We're waiting for you. We can't wait much longer.'

'I told you, I'm attached.'

He let out a snort of laughter and took my hand.

'Why is that so funny?'

'Nothing,' he said, in a way that made it clear I was supposed to ask further.

'What?' I shrugged his hand off me. 'There's nothing wrong with being faithful, you know. You should try it.'

He gazed toward the house, his eyes full of amusement.

'It's just that Miss told Harry that your so-called boyfriend was flirting up a storm with her on the phone, that's all.'

Now it was my turn to laugh. This country bumpkin obviously couldn't tell the difference between being charming and flirting. Jerome often used his social skills to butter up a subject before an interview.

'Yeah, he's been pestering her with little calls almost every night, she says.'

My blood ran cold. Every night? I pictured myself making all those desperate calls to him, just hoping for a chat, when all the time he had the nerve to be calling her.

'Yeah.' Kieran smiled, warming to his theme as he saw the effect it had on me. 'He's become quite an admirer. Says he wants to take her out some time. Got an open relationship, have you?'

A cloud must have drifted over the sun, because I felt suddenly chilly.

'Course, she's up for anything, is Miss Alicia,' he continued. 'Me and Harry can hardly keep up. She's insatiable, that one.' He said this almost as a challenge to me. 'No prude.' He was rubbing it in, making me feel frigid for not having leapt into bed with them. 'I can't wait to give you a taste of what she loves so much. Why don't you come down tonight? We'll make you feel better.'

He laid his hands on my breasts and gently fondled my nipples that had hardened with cold under my white top. I felt my body start to heat up again, warmth slowly radiating out from my breasts. I tried to shift away from him but he pushed me firmly down onto my back and lowered his hot mouth onto mine. It tasted of tobacco, his insolent tongue pushing uninvited between my lips. Before I knew it he was pushing my thighs apart with his knee, pressing a muscular leg hard against my lilac panties. I somehow let it happen, still digesting the news about Jerome and Alicia. I opened my legs to him involuntarily and sighed into his mouth as the stiff thickness of his cock pressed against me. I felt like a teenager having her first tumble in the school playing fields. His wet, inexpert kisses were urgent and oddly arousing, his erection insistent and hopeful. I remembered the boys at school being just as clumsy and sure of themselves, just as excited as they fumbled around in my school uniform, accidentally fondling me just where I wanted it and surprising both of us.

Kieran was grinding against me now, his hips mimicking the act of fucking. I knew then that I would love to have him inside me. My lilac panties were getting wet, my face red. He took his mouth away from mine to watch me, smiling smugly when he saw my flushed cheeks.

'God, you have to let me fuck you,' he whispered,

panting. 'You have to let me lick you until you can't take any more, then fuck you.' I remembered what Alicia had said about his wonderful tongue and swooned slightly. 'That guy's mad if he prefers her to you,' he breathed, his hands scraping over my breasts. 'Look at you!' His hips started to jolt now, and I knew he was coming. He didn't take his eyes off me all the time, his pelvis glued to mine, thrusting and shuddering against me. My pussy was getting sore with the friction of his hardness, but it was a lovely pain. I opened my legs even further and flooded my panties as his face contorted with a long, draining orgasm. I shuddered underneath him, suddenly wanting to come. 'You see how you turn me on?' he said when he was done. 'Next time we do it for real. And I'll make sure you have a good time.' And I believed him.

My legs were still a bit wobbly when I got to Tom's room. I hadn't changed my panties either, feeling strangely turned on at the thought that I was standing there with gooey knickers. I hoped that some primeval part of him would smell my sexy scent and respond instinctively to me although, looking at his shy face as he opened the door, that didn't seem all that likely. He indicated for me to come in. I saw that he had laid some lunch out for himself: cheeses, French bread and tomatoes.

'Sorry, are you eating?' I suddenly realised that I was hungry and my tummy let out a big hint of a rumble.

'You're welcome to join me, of course. Just hiding from the house guests!' He grimaced then realised his faux pas. 'Well, not you, obviously. Sorry. Christ, I told you I was bad with women.'

I begged to differ, noticing for the first time how broad his shoulders were as he sat down at the table and split open the French stick. I sat opposite him and took a bite of a tomato. Unfortunately the juice spurted out and splashed my white top, little orange seeds trickling onto my right breast. He burst out laughing and handed me a cloth, just stopping himself from dabbing it himself. I felt my cheeks burning. I had hoped my enthusiastic bite into a tomato would conjure up an image of myself as an earthy, natural woman with healthy appetites, not a dribbling fool.

'I don't believe it,' I muttered. 'What an idiot.'

He smiled at me and took a tomato, deliberately biting messily into it so its juice emptied generously all over his shirt. We laughed and I saw again how genuine Tom was. The juice glistened a little on his neck. I found myself licking my lips at the thought of leaning over to kiss it off him.

'It's a new trend,' he joked. 'They're all wearing tomato stains in Paris apparently. It's the new black.' He chuckled to himself as he cut a hunk of cheddar and popped it into his mouth.

'I'll probably give that one a miss,' I said, eyeing my ruined top. 'You know it stains, don't you?'

'Really?'

I laughed at his horrified face. He got up and pulled the shirt over his head. That shut me up. He had a lightly sun-kissed torso, naturally broad and firm. Dark golden hairs curled on his chest. He saw me look at him and blushed.

'Oh, sorry, didn't think . . .' he stammered, walking to the other end of the room and pulling on a T-shirt. He chucked the shirt in his basin and turned on the tap.

'I don't mind,' I said, belatedly. 'I mean, I'm not a prude about that sort of thing. I'm half Brazilian, and they don't really believe in clothes at all. Smallest bikinis in the world! Dental floss, really.'

'Remind me to put Brazil on my holiday list,' he

said, coming back to the table and tucking into his lunch again. 'Especially if they all look like you.' He didn't look up when he said this, which was a good thing because I was gob-smacked and sat there with my mouth open. If Kieran or Ray or even Jerome had said that it wouldn't have meant much, but I knew that Tom wasn't just using it as a line. Tom eventually noticed that I had stopped eating.

'What?' Then a look of realisation dawned on his face. 'Oh, Christ, I'm sorry. I am so rude. Your top – do you want to soak it along with mine?' He got up and rummaged through a drawer. 'I can offer you a fine selection of T-shirts, all clean. Well, mostly.' He picked out a black one and sniffed it. 'Lovely and fresh.'

'Well . . .' I wasn't sure about just pulling off my top with him standing there but realised I couldn't get out of it for reasons of modesty, not after giving him my 'I'm half Brazilian' speech. As if to prove a point I got up and pulled my top unashamedly over my head. Tom didn't expect that and turned away a touch too late. I was wearing my best bra, a push-up lacy lilac number that accentuated the fullness of my bosoms. I wasn't in any hurry to put them away, but he was being the perfect gentleman and had turned to the wall. 'It's OK, Tom,' I said, laughing and taking the T-shirt out of his hand. 'I know you're not leering at me.'

'Do you?' His voice was a little tight. I craned to see his face, but couldn't.

'Tom?' I giggled at his formality. 'I got a good look at you, you know. Don't be all proper and make me feel like a dirty old woman.'

'Is it on yet?' he asked.

'Yes,' I lied. He turned round and I stood there, hands on hips, grinning at his suddenly aghast face as his eyes fell to my full breasts. 'Sorry, sorry. Couldn't resist it!' I said and finally pulled on the T-shirt. He was blushing and smiling.

'Don't apologise,' he muttered, quickly taking a bite of bread. We ate in silence for a while, then I remembered that today I was going to be the serious journalist.

'So,' I said, a propos of nothing. 'Daphne Hathaway. Genius?'

He laughed at me, then realised I was serious.

'You want to do an interview now?' he asked incredulously.

'Yes.'

'But – forgive me – but I've just seen your breasts.' He looked bashful and lustful at the same time. 'How the hell am I supposed to concentrate?'

'There's much more to me than that!' I teased. 'Come on, tell me what you think of your great grandmother. How did she fit into the whole Bloomsbury set thing?'

He laughed again, shaking his head.

'OK. She had that bohemian streak, I suppose,' he replied. 'Wayward. Just like my bloody sister.'

'That's a good word for her.' I pictured Alicia on the dining room table, being licked to a frenzy by her tutor, or being fucked senseless with a whip around her neck in a porn film. Then an unwelcome image of her having sex with Jerome popped into my head. I shuddered.

'What?' Tom asked.

I had conveniently neglected to mention my romantic attachment, and I wasn't about to tell him now.

'Is Alicia ... Does she know when to stop?' I wondered how much Tom knew of her exploits.

'Probably not.' He sat back and ran his fingers through his hair in irritation. 'She drives me mad sometimes. I mean, I'm sure you've got the measure of her by now. She's got a destructive streak.'

'Self-destructive, you mean,' I corrected.

'No, both, actually,' he said. 'I mean, any relationship I've managed to strike up with a woman has always suffered some well-aimed blow by her. She's good at finding your Achilles' heel.'

I thought about what my own weakness might be, realising that Jerome was probably it. Alicia had certainly managed to hit me where it hurt there.

'Be careful of her, anyway. I mean, I love her, she's my sis and all that, but she isn't all sweetness and light.'

'Not like you,' I observed. He didn't know whether or not I was joking and eyed me questioningly. 'I mean it. Chalk and cheese, you two.' I got a strange tingle as his eyes locked into mine and a tense moment of silence pulled between us. 'Anyway, interview. I'm interested in the parallels between Alicia and Daphne.' I sounded a little flustered even to my own ears.

'OK,' Tom replied and thought for a moment. 'Well, it isn't all coincidental, you know. Don't let her fool you. She thinks she has some spiritual bond with Daphne. She does things to mirror her.'

'Like?'

'Like her party.' He saw the blank look on my face. 'Surely she's told you about her big thirty-third birthday party? She's been planning it for months. Going to be in the great hall next week.'

I smiled. I liked parties, especially ones in stately homes. I had a romantic image of myself swirling about the dance floor in a big pink ballgown in Tom's arms. He must have noticed my dreamy expression.

'Don't get ideas,' he smirked. 'God knows what she'll come up with. And her friends are the most horrifying bunch of snobs and perverts.'

'So, it won't be like the ball scene in *The Sound of Music* then?' I asked, disappointed.

'No, more like that scene where the Nazis come to the convent to capture the family. Nasty.' He was obviously dreading it.

'So, how does that tie up with Daphne?' I asked, back to being the serious reporter.

'Well, you know, she loved to throw parties. And she had her coming-out ball here, in the great hall. It's all in the diaries, I think.' He gave me an intimate look. 'Apparently it's where she lost her virginity.'

'Ooh my.' I smiled, suddenly wondering about Tom's virginity but stopping myself from asking. 'So Alicia will finally lose her virginity next week.' My voice dripped irony.

'Oh, it's long gone.' He looked rueful. 'A fleeting thing, my sister's innocence.'

'Mr Wootten?' I remembered the old man's many insinuations last night. I loved the idea that he had taken her virginity in the schoolroom. It all seemed so decadent and aristocratic.

'No comment.' He suddenly looked at me sharply. 'Hey, I forgot, you're the enemy. You're not going to write lots of scandalous things about my family in your article, are you?'

'Hmm, I don't know,' I teased. 'Depends how nice you are to me.' Before he had time to ask what I meant, I got up and brushed the crumbs from his black T-shirt. 'Better get my nose to the grindstone.'

'What about your top?'

'Give it to me later.' I smiled. 'And don't go trying it on and stretching it.' I flashed him one of my killer Latin looks and went straight to my room to bury myself in the diary.

March 31st 1907
What a glorious, glorious night! Everyone should be allowed to throw their own coming-out party and

not have fussy parents and relatives ruining it for them. If only I could come out every year, with the same celebration as I did tonight. The evening took a most exquisite and forbidden turn – but enough of that. Later! I will recount it as it happened. I am always too impatient to cut to the quick and, as I learnt tonight, the quick is not always the most pleasurable part.

Well, Emily and Grace arrived at five to help organise the staff, who were milling about making the great hall look wonderful and making beautiful dishes for the guests to eat. Of course, Grace immediately took over and started bossing people about (made Mary the chambermaid cry!). Grace was wearing the most revolting yellow gown you have ever seen, with some meagre fur collar that looked like a rat had expired around her shoulders. Emily looked tired. Oliver is a demanding spouse, I am sure. I do not envy her.

By seven o'clock people started to arrive. Some local well-connected families came, Reverend Hartley, some bright young things from London, some eligible bachelors from Cambridge invited by Oliver (he does have some uses). I was pleased to see how few girls arrived. I have no need for female companionship (two sisters is quite enough). I greeted everyone in the great hall and my gown was avidly admired. I chose the white one in the end; very feminine and soft. I looked like a snowflake on the dance floor, so light and dazzling. I stood next to Grace as much as was possible to get the full effect of my beauty compared with her lack of it. Within an hour we had all eaten, and drunk deeply of some of Father's excellent red wines, and the hall was full of laughter and music. I enjoyed a number of dances with local boys and then an undergraduate from

Cambridge called Nathan, who had an endearingly bushy moustache. By now I was quite intoxicated and ready to put my plan into action.

I could see that Emily was busy looking after Oliver (who cannot take his drink) and Grace was hopelessly trying to charm some poor American gentleman, so the coast was clear. I pulled Nathan out of the room and into the dining room, where the secret passage is. Soon we were at my father's special room. Before we went in I looked up at Nathan with sparkly eyes and said: 'Are you ready for this, young man? They don't teach you this at Cambridge.' Then I swung the door open and I laughed as I saw his jaw drop and his eyes cruise over the plush red velvet walls. He went in and slowly investigated the whips, chairs, braces, buckles, chains and – to my certain knowledge, Julia's favourite – the waterbed. I could see that it was arousing him from the swelling in his trousers. He turned his handsome face to me and gently told me to close the door. Then he beckoned me over and sat me in the special chair. This is a soft, fur-lined contraption that hangs from the ceiling. With a pulley you can lever the chair higher or lower. It has weights in it to allow it to sway once you have set up the momentum, a little like a child's swing. He sat me so that my face was level with his chest. My heart was beating madly; I wonder if his was. He knelt before me and whispered: 'You are so beautiful, Daphne. And very virginal in that dress.' He had a wicked voice, the sort of voice you might expect a fox to have if it could speak.

'Of course I am virginal,' I said back. I knew he liked the idea that I was untouched, so I used my sweetest face and voice. 'I need an educated man of the world to show me the ways of love.'

'Oh, let me, let me,' he sighed and pressed his mouth to mine. His lips were hot and tasted of wine; his moustache tickled my cheeks and nose. It made me want to giggle. Then his fat tongue pushed in to my mouth. That shocked me at first, but I soon grew to love the sensation of it writhing with mine like two angry snakes having a fight. He was making little noises in his throat, grunts or groans. It was then that I felt his hand slip under the base of my gown and rest on my ankle. It rose under my skirts, encountering the white bloomers I was wearing, tugging at them. 'Damn,' he muttered and began urgently to try to pull them off. I hadn't thought that my undergarments might cause a man bother. I quickly stood and freed myself of them, settling back down on the soft chair and opening my lips to his again. This time his rough hands slipped easily up my legs and rested on my thigh. His tongue forced its way far in to my mouth and I felt strangely excited at his ardour. His fingers were making little tantalising circles on my skin. I was eagerly anticipating that he might touch me in the most secret forbidden place.

I began to make odd noises myself now, like a baby about to cry. How strange! His moustache scorched my soft skin, and I was sure I would be raw there. Finally – oh finally – he tenderly dipped his finger inside my warm private place and I quivered all around it. 'You are as slippery as an oyster,' he said admiringly. I hoped this was a good thing. I think it was, because his finger explored happily in the wetness, causing me to sigh and jolt. 'Do you know of the wonderful things a man can do to a woman?' he asked, his bushy lip pressed to my ear. I couldn't reply, I was crying out. 'A man can take her breast in his mouth and suckle her like a baby,' he said. I was amazed. 'A man can kiss her all over. He can probe her secret place with his tongue.' With that his fingers flickered against me so fast that a strange fit overtook my body. 'And a woman can taste a man, too. Would you like to taste me, Daphne?' I nodded furiously. I wanted to taste everything that life and love had to offer.

He sprang up and stood before me, lowering the chair so that my face was at hip height. He swiftly unbuckled his trousers and out sprang the most extraordinary-looking thing I have ever seen. I had seen one from a distance obviously, or through keyholes, but never like this, so close to my face that its pungent odour invaded my very being. It had a thick purple head and was surrounded by wiry hair that brought his moustache very much to mind.

'Taste it,' he urged. It was more of an order. I took a tentative lick at it. He chuckled, grabbed my hair and forced it into my mouth. I gagged, which made him laugh more. 'You'll get used to it,' he said, and began to push it and pull it in and out very fast. He growled like a bear and started to mutter things I couldn't hear because my ears were full of a thundering noise. Suddenly, with no warning, my mouth was filled with a creamy, sour liquid. I swallowed instinctively, which seemed to please him. He buttoned himself up and smiled broadly. 'Thank you, my dear.' And with that he was off. I have to confess, I was slightly disappointed. Although I had enjoyed Nathan's excitement, I expected there to be more. (There was! And from a most unlikely source!)

I went back to the party, a little unsteady on my feet. Grace was now dancing with the unfortunate American, boring him senseless from the look on his face. Emily and Oliver had gone home. Nathan, I noticed with an odd twinge, was talking to Annabel Jameson, the rather plain girl who lives in Blythe House, the lawyer's daughter. I have never liked her, and she looked particularly smug and annoying tonight, which she has no right to with eyebrows like that. I hope she and Nathan do marry and have the most hairy children. After a while I consoled myself that a bore like Nathan could never make a real connection with a butterfly like me; he needs someone plainer. I have no doubt they will announce their engagement within the month.

As I watched jealously, Reverend Hartley came over to me. He has been our vicar for ever, a stern, unforgiving man (which always seemed somewhat unchristian in my eyes, but Grace says I don't understand the church). He eyed me with a particularly steely look, his grey eyes scouring my body. Could he tell? My heart missed a beat. Beads of sweat collected at the neck of his dog collar. His greying hair and bony hands made me think of my grandfather.

'Yes, Father?' I asked eventually, as he was obviously not going to speak.

'Have you looked at yourself?' he asked quietly. I shook my head and he grasped my arm hard and pulled me into the hallway, where there hangs a tall mirror. I was shocked to see that my face was red where Nathan had kissed me. 'Evidence of sin is always hard to hide,' he muttered into my ear. 'I fear your lack of moral guidance will lead you into all kinds of trouble. It must be corrected.' I looked at his face behind me in the mirror. No trace of kindness sat in its lines, only determination and rectitude. I confess, he scared me.

'Yes, Father, I will come to church in the

morning –' I began but he took my arm again, pulling me roughly into the dining room.

'Now. You will show me the place of your sins and we will absolve them together,' he ordered. 'I saw you go in here, Daphne.' I hesitated to show him Father's private room. I didn't want to get him into trouble, too. But I was more scared of Reverend Hartley, so I obeyed. Soon we were standing in the room. Reverend Hartley's face was set in an angry mask as he took it in. I have to admit, it seemed more depraved than ever in his presence. I felt a weird gush between my legs; somehow fear and horror and embarrassment had become arousing to me. I saw my white bloomers discarded on the floor, and he followed my eyes.

'Sorry, Father,' I said meekly as he picked them up. To my surprise he brought them to his face and took a long deep sniff at the gusset. His eyes closed in a kind of ecstasy.

'You must be corrected,' he said into the material. 'Tell me what you have done.' I falteringly told him of Nathan: how I had sucked on him and he had touched me intimately. He nodded as he listened. I suddenly noticed a twitching under his black robes. When I had finished he sighed and told me to approach him. 'You must be as naked as a baby to find your innocence again,' he said. 'Disrobe.' I obeyed nervously, taking some time to unlace my bodice. He watched me thoroughly. I am not stupid; I knew that this was not a normal religious practice, but I was too curious and frightened to disobey. He sat at the edge of the waterbed and beckoned me to come closer, which I did. His face showed no emotion. His eyes slipped down my body, lingering first on my breasts (my little nipples had become quite red and stiff under his gaze) and then at the silky hair between my legs. He looked at me for a very long time. 'What else did you do with this student?' he asked.

'Nothing, Father,' I said. 'He told me of other practices, but we didn't do them.'

'Such as, my child?'

I hesitated. The words stuck in my mouth. Blushing fiercely I admitted: 'He told me that a man can suckle at a woman like a baby, Father.'

Reverend Hartley nodded grimly and lifted his hand to my breast. He toyed with me thoughtfully and then pulled me to him. To my astonishment he lifted his face and began to suckle me. His mouth was surprisingly wet as it closed around my nipple, his tongue slithering over me, leaving streaks of zinging pleasure wherever it went. It wound in tight circles over my livid bud, sometimes flickering like a candle about to go out. Then he moved across to my other breast and repeated his actions, sometimes sucking noisily. I watched him, his eyes closed, as my legs grew weak and a heavy sense of lust filled my loins.

'Oh, Father,' I murmured. 'Oh, Father!'

He pulled his head back and slapped me lightly across the face.

'No, my child,' he snapped. 'You must not enjoy this. I am pulling the devil out of you.' I found it hard to believe him especially as his penis was clearly erect under his cassock, but was sobered by the slap.

'Sorry, Father,' I whispered.

'What else did this heathen tell you?' he demanded.

I began to get excited at the mere thought of it.

'He said, Father, that a man can taste a woman with his tongue.'

The Reverend's grey eyes sparked with rage. He reached out to my secret place and gently stroked along the silky crack, his fingers sliding quickly through the wetness.

'You bad girl, you must not enjoy it.'

'Sorry, Father!'

With both hands he softly prized apart my lips and peered at me closely. He brought his face to my groin and inhaled. I hoped, I wished, I prayed that he was about to punish me with his tongue. My whole body craved for that severe face to be buried lasciviously between my legs. Surely then his mask would crack and he would have to show his lust! His stern face lingered at my fur. Then, like a lizard, he licked me quickly. I trembled. I yearned for more.

'Lie down, my child. This is a severe case.' I obeyed, lying next to him on the waterbed. It undulated underneath me. 'You have been a bad girl,' he repeated.

'Yes, Father.' I opened my legs subtly, to invite him to lick at me. I couldn't bear it if he stopped now.

'We must not taste the forbidden fruit!' he exclaimed as he bent his head between my legs and slurped at my aching cunny with the hunger of a starving animal.

'Yes, Father!' I looked down to see his grey head bobbing up and down at my mound, feeling with delirious happiness the hot pleasure of a tongue snaking inside me and lapping insistently against me, like an angry sea against the rocks. 'Yes, Father!' I cried again.

He was feeling himself through his cassock, I noticed, and I could hear his muffled groans climbing inside me. They grew louder and more exciting by the minute. The room was filled with wet noises, like when my cat Tosca licks up his cream, quick, greedy licks and oh, how I loved to be the cream! I was quivering and sighing. The bed bounced us around like two little boats on a stormy sea, but he never took his mouth from me. Over and over again, I felt myself convulse with peaks of pleasure, but he would not stop. Maybe he was trying to cure me, I thought, using excess as a deterrent. But on he went, for almost an hour, licking and licking. His face was shiny when he did finally look up at me. By that time I was exhausted and limp, barely able to open my eyes. I could feel only numbness and lust.

'You are almost cured, my child,' His voice shook a little and a most weird sticky substance spilt from his mouth as he spoke. Then he crawled up the bed, pulled up his robes and speared me with his mighty erection. Oh! He was merciless and as hard as a rock. My tired sex soon woke up and started to quiver again as he pounded into me. It was pain and burning and joy and delight all in one. 'Come, my child,' he moaned into my ear. 'Come, bad, sinful girl.'

His voice excited me beyond reason and I called out 'Oh, yes, Father! Yes, Father!' over and over again, so loudly that I am sure the servants must have heard. Soon I was delirious again, quaking, thrashing. When eventually the final fit came, I was so overcome, I fear I lost control of my bladder and bathed Reverend Hartley's cassock in urine! And he squirted something into me as well. Far from being disgusted at my shameful loss of bodily control, he seemed pleased and told me it was the evil pus of the devil seeping out of me!

I let him out of the manor by the back entrance. Then (fully clothed) I rejoined my party, feeling very much a woman, and not at all a girl. If the good

Reverend cured me of anything, it was the burden of innocence. Now I know what pleasures await me in the world, I mean to sample them fully! I will taste many men, I hope. And I desperately hope I will one day finally meet one who can fulfil all my passions. Does such a man exist? If he does, any woman would be mad to let him go.

As for my deflowerer, my only regret is that I will have to face him in church every Sunday and listen to his droning sermons knowing full well the extent of his hypocrisy. After all, however much he insisted it was for my moral welfare he performed those acts on me, I know full well it was for his own pleasure, although it somehow pleased me at the time to believe he was 'correcting' me, as he said. So you could say I learnt two lessons tonight. The first is the lesson of the arts of love, and the second is that sometimes believing in a fantasy makes the reality all the sweeter. I feel quite inspired to compose. A fantasia, perhaps?

I lay flushed on my bed, the green velvet diary rising and falling on my stomach. Of course, my fingers had been gently sliding around in my panties while I read the diary and, now that I had climaxed, many questions whirled through my mind. Was Tom worried that Alicia had something like this planned for her birthday? Had he read the diary himself? I was aroused and restless, more impatient than ever to find the special room. My body craved male attention. Daphne had written of finding a man who could fulfil all her passions. I wondered doubtfully if I had found one to fulfil mine. Jerome certainly had his moments. Knowing full well I shouldn't, I called him. I'd give him one last chance. I was surprised when he picked up his home phone almost before it had rung.

'Hi,' he murmured sweetly, as if he was expecting the call. His voice was particularly soft and gravelly. It was his intimate voice. His making-love voice. I recognised it instantly.

'Hey,' I replied.

'Jo?' There was a pause, just long enough for me to wonder who he'd thought it was. 'Jo, babe! Hi, gorgeous. Long time no speak.'

He was gushing now to cover his embarrassment. I realised with a cold heart that he might have been expecting Alicia on the phone. My face started to burn and I prepared to launch into a full-scale Latino fury, but I managed to quench the fire. I was going to play this one cool. After all, I only had Kieran's word to go on about Jerome and Alicia. And if it was true, knowledge was power. He didn't know that I knew, which gave me some form of advantage.

'So, what's up?' he asked, cheerily. 'Progress?'

'Oh, yes,' I replied, my voice oozing confidence. 'This is going to be a great story. You were right, Jerome, these aristos are totally barmy. I mean, off the scale!'

'Yeah?' I detected an element of denial in his voice.

'Believe me. I mean, Daphne was a saint compared to Alicia.'

'Really?' He warmed to this theme. 'Tell me about her, is she a real goer?'

I paused. I didn't want to turn him on.

'Well, she's a cold-hearted, manipulative, depraved, jealous little rich girl, who will sleep with anybody. I mean *anybody*, Jez, it's sad.'

'Mhm.'

'And the guys that take advantage are so desperate.' I ironed the note of warning out of my voice.

'Right.' He paused. 'Jo, I don't know if you can write this article if you're going to be so biased against her.'

'What?' The fury started to rise again.

'I mean, she seems delightful to me.' He searched for the word. 'Enchanting, even.'

'Enchanting?' I had never heard him use a word like that before. He sounded like he was talking about the fairies at the bottom of his garden. 'Enchanting?!'

'Yes,' he was defensive now. 'It's just that class thing, I suppose. The difference between a lady and a woman.'.

'A lady who fucks her stable hands and her tutor and anybody else with a cock?' I raged.

'Jo, your mouth!' he chastised, sounding so much like my mother that my stomach turned. 'Christ, a healthy sexual appetite never hurt anybody.'

Even his accent had changed, I suddenly noticed. Gone the rock star transatlantic-cum-East End twang. He had picked up his aitches and polished up his vowels. Obviously these daily conversations with my hostess had made an impression. The urge to chuck the phone at the window again was unbearable.

'You know what, Jerome?' I yelled. 'You can take your *enchanting* country lady with her alabaster skin and her cut-glass vowels and her "healthy sexual appetite" and shove her up your arse!' I realised I could have thought of a more eloquent put down, but continued. I was on a roll. 'And you can fucking well forget about me, with my coarse language and my flat in Peckham, you prick!' That was when I chose to throw the phone, which thankfully landed against the wall this time. I was livid. I paced about the room like a tiger in a zoo that had just been struck on the head with a coke can. I knew that if I saw Alicia now I would deck her, and that would be the end of it: the end of the story, the end of my career, the end of my friendship with Tom. I had to get out.

By seven o'clock I had packed a small bag and written a quick note to Tom explaining that I had been called away to London for a few days. By ten o'clock I was sitting in a wine bar in Covent Garden with a Bloody Mary, laughing my head off with Ruby.

'So let me get this straight,' she said, shovelling a handful of peanuts in her mouth. 'You're pissed off with Jerome – who, by the way, has never even let you call him your boyfriend because he is a complete wanker – because he's been having phone sex or something with this stuck-up bitch Alicia?'

'Yes.'

'But, at the same time, you've been cavorting around this posh guy Tom's bedroom in your bra –'

'My lilac bra.'

'Yes, your favourite lilac bra, flirting and wanting to kiss him?'

'Yes.'

'And in the meantime, two – I can't fucking believe this – two "stable hands" have been coming on to you? Even though the bitch is also sleeping with them?'

'Yes.'

'Girl, that's one mess you're in!' She cackled, throwing back her head, which this week was covered in long braids. She changed her hairstyle as often as she changed her men. The last time I had seen her she had been labouring under an impressive seventies-style afro. 'OK, let's sort it out.'

'Yes.'

'OK, so Jerome. Girl, what are you still doing with him? He is the dirt on the bottom of my shoe.' She wrinkled up her face. She genuinely hated Jerome. 'No, he's the worm squashed in the dirt on the bottom of my shoe. Just some washed-up has-been rock star with no respect for you. Bring him here and let me sort him out!'

I believed her. She was tiny and slim, but I could well imagine her beating Jerome up. I loved her for wanting to fight my corner like that. 'You gonna dump him?'

I hesitated.

'Josephina!'

'Yes.' I said, my voice full of regret. I had dumped guys before and it had been easy. But for some reason the fact that Jerome had never really been *mine* made it hard to leave him. It was like giving up the hike without ever getting to the top of the mountain. And I was the sort of person who had to get to the top of the mountain. 'It's just that I want to see the top of the mountain,' I said lamely.

'You what?' She looked like I had gone mad. 'Listen, hon. Plenty more fish in the sea.' I knew she was right, but something about Jerome's indifference tantalised me.

'It's just ... you can't throw a fish back in the water till you've caught it,' I explained. Her face was now a picture of bemused puzzlement. With Ruby everything was black or white.

'The only thing you're going to catch from him is a nasty rash,' she said. 'Give up, Jo.' She had worn me down.

'Yes.' I said. 'OK.'

'Good. I need a drink. I'll get another round,' Ruby grinned, hopping off the bar stool, which was far too high for her. 'Then you can tell me which one of them other lovelies you're gonna fuck first.'

7

The second time I swept up the impressive drive of Hathaway Hall in a taxi it had lost some of its intimidating grandeur. Now I knew what went on inside it had the air of some erotic Victorian lunatic asylum and I felt nervous at getting caught up in its crazy world again. One night with Ruby was all I had needed to ground me, though, and now I felt more in control. If things were going to get out of hand this time, it would be because I wanted them to. And part of me did.

I had had time for my feelings about Jerome to turn from hurt to jealousy to anger to disgust to pity. Ruby saw him as a sad old rocker who couldn't commit to anybody, and she'd convinced me to think the same. My newfound sense of freedom must have shown in my walk, because I heard Kieran call out after me:

'Dump him then?' I swung round and saw him following me towards the house. His rubbery grin and cheeky flashing eyes made me giggle. 'You look as if you haven't a care in the world,' he commented. 'Just like me.'

'I haven't,' I smiled back. 'And yes, he is history.'

'We'll be seeing you tonight, then?' he asked hopefully.

I thought about it. I hadn't honestly decided about those two, but I did know that a night of passion with them would exact some kind of revenge on both Jerome and Alicia, and that was a tempting thought. I wasn't so over him that I had forgiven what he'd done with her.

'Hesitation!' Kieran shouted as if he had nailed me. 'You want to!'

'Maybe I do.' I turned to go. 'Maybe I don't.' And with that I disappeared into the house.

'But maybe you do!' I heard him call after me and laughed.

Once I had unpacked, I sat and typed up all my impressions so far, focusing on the links between Daphne and the Hathaways of today. To start with I had seen Alicia as the most interesting subject, but the more I wrote the more I realised that Tom was the fascinating one, with his quiet, hidden talents and his submission to his sister's wishes. If I had an instinct for anything it was for musical talent and innovation. I had seen it in all its forms, on the streets of Rio, at rock stadiums, in smoky student union rooms, at classical concerts. And Tom had it, I knew that. Maybe I could find a way to profile him along with his ancestor, the past with the future. Armed with a note-pad and lots of ideas, I marched to his room. This time I was determined I wouldn't be distracted by tomato juice or torsos or flirting.

I could hear him playing the piano as I approached his door. It was a beautiful, sensuous piece, with thick jazz chords and a haunting melody. I listened for a while until he stopped and started experimenting with different endings. He was writing as I stood there! I knew I should have left him alone with what I had now convinced myself was his genius, but I couldn't resist. I knocked on the door. I heard the scrape of his piano stool and then the door opened. I had forgotten how tall he was. His hair was unruly, as if he had been running his fingers through it obsessively. Obviously the writing hadn't come easy.

'Tom, you've inspired me,' I announced as I barged into his room, slapping my notepad on the table.

'That's funny, you've inspired me,' he retorted.

It wasn't the reply I had anticipated.

'What?' Was he taking the piss? 'No, I mean it,' I continued. 'I want my article to be about you just as much as it is about Daphne.'

'I started writing this piece just after you left the other day. It's great, because I was suffering a bit of writer's block ...'

'Me too!'

'And then it all started flowing.' He was talking excitedly, like a little boy describing Christmas. 'I couldn't stop it. All thanks to you, Jo. It's never been so thrilling to write music.' I wasn't quite sure what I had done to facilitate his writing but I wasn't going to argue. 'I have to say, it's one of my better pieces. Want to hear it?' He went to the piano stool and sat down.

'Of course!'

'It's not finished.' He played a few chords just to get a feel for the keys. 'Christ, what's the matter with me, I'm nervous,' he said with a laugh. 'My hand's shaking.'

It was so endearing that I had to start scribbling down notes just to avoid flinging myself across the room and hugging him.

'Oh no, missy. No note taking. That's not fair,' he said.

'I'm just recording what you've said,' I protested. 'It's my job!'

'No, no, no. Put it down.' He pointed to my pen. 'Put the pen down. Come over here.' He patted the space beside him on the piano stool. He didn't have to ask twice. 'You can just shut your eyes and listen.'

I settled beside him, surprised by the warmth of his bare forearm against mine. I was aware of the softness of my body pressed up against his firm side as we sat there. I was wearing a flimsy cotton summer slip dress. I noticed him glance down at my body before he started playing, taking in the generous swell of my breasts beneath the fabric. And then he started.

The music was slow at first, dreamy and low. I watched his big hands moving sexily over the keys. 'Shut your eyes,' he whispered, and I obeyed. The vibration of the music travelled through his body and into mine. Whenever he hit a high note, his arm would gently brush against my chest until I felt my nipples harden in anticipation. He must have felt that, because he apologised the first time, then seemed to brush against them more and more (or maybe it was arrogant to think that – maybe it was just that the music was rising in pitch). My heart quickened as the music sped up, became forceful and passionate, like a dance. And then I recognised the refrain I had heard from outside the door. I leant against him and the music got slower and wistful again. My long black curls tumbled over his arm.

When he got to the point where there was no more music left he stopped. I didn't want to open my eyes. I was quite happy pressed up against him, our skin touching, my body yearning to turn towards him for more contact. Maybe he would think I was sleeping, or in a trance. I almost was, the echo of the music still winding around my head. I felt his breathing quicken slightly as the silence became heavy. Then his hand gently brushed my hair off my face, soft against my skin. I could feel his warm breath on my forehead and knew that he was looking at me. I tilted my face up towards the warmth, my eyes still shut, like a flower looking for the sun. And then I felt his lips press against mine, tenderly. I sighed into him and kissed him back, twisting my body to him and putting my hands to his face. I had never had a kiss like it, so gentle and exquisite, almost like it was still part of the music. Then he put his arms around me and the kiss grew deeper and sexier. I opened my mouth more to him and felt his tongue push against mine. A hiccup of pleasure escaped from my throat and he broke away, laughing.

'What was that?' he teased, but I could see from his bleary green eyes and flushed face that he had been as affected as I was by the kiss.

'It wasn't me, it must have been you,' I protested.

He put his arms around my neck and held my hair back off my face, searching it with his eyes.

'You are so beautiful,' he said, simply. This filled my eyes with tears. It wasn't that I hadn't heard the line before; maybe when a man wanted to fuck me, or if he knew I was about to dump him. Jerome had said it himself on occasion, although it always seemed to imply a 'but' in his case. Maybe I was still getting over being effectively ditched by Jerome in favour of Alicia, I thought, as a tear plopped onto Tom's forearm.

'Hey,' Tom said, and kissed me again.

Although I knew that he probably did that just because – like all men – he didn't quite know what to say, I enjoyed it deeply. My breasts pressed themselves into him needily, wanting attention, but to my frustration he didn't touch. I ran my hands down his body, but he pulled away and smiled in a way that told me that was all I was going to get. I was confused. Surely preserving one's modesty was the woman's prerogative?

'Aren't you going to make some notes now?' he teased. 'On your serious journalist notepad?'

Although he was joking, I felt that he was

effectively asking me to get off his stool. I went back to the table and wrote 'not a bad kisser'. I tried not to sulk, but my face obviously showed some hurt that he had pulled away first.

'Hey, Jo, I told you I was bad with women,' he said.

'Are you trying to tell me you're gay?' I quipped defensively, still jotting down some notes on my pad as a diversion.

'No. I'm not gay.'

'Definitely not gay,' I wrote.

'Anyway,' I said, 'I came here to work and that's what I will do.' However sorted I tried to sound, I was aware that there was a petulance in my voice. 'How do you incorporate Daphne's music into your own?' I looked up at him in a clear, cool way.

'It's just that, when things get that hot, I start to get nervous,' he said. 'It's not that I don't want you. God, I do want you.'

My pussy tingled when he said that.

'It's just – I know I shouldn't listen to her but it's hard to ignore it.'

'What? You've lost me?' I wanted him to go back to the bit about wanting me.

'Alicia.'

This was taking an odd turn.

'Your sister? I don't get it.'

'It's just that she's always made me think I would be hopeless at anything – you know – sexual. She mocked me about how useless I was even before I knew what sex was. And she's such a sexual person herself, it's almost as if there wasn't room for both of us to be that way.'

I was trying to catch up.

'I'm not a psychologist, but isn't that just a bit ... fucked up?' I asked.

He laughed.

'Yes, definitely.'

I scribbled on my pad. He leant forward, trying to get me to understand.

'You know how, in a family,' he went on, 'you get your roles. You might be the quiet one or the funny one or the clever one?'

I nodded.

'Well, Alicia is the sexual one. I'm the shy one who's terrible with women.'

'I see.'

'What are you in your family?' he asked.

I thought about this.

'The nosy one,' I guessed. 'The one that gets into trouble, I suppose.' I still wasn't convinced. 'You know, you say you are terrible with women, but that was one amazing kiss you gave me.'

'Really?' He seemed genuinely surprised and chuffed.

'Yes,' I insisted, then felt a flicker of doubt flare up in me. 'Didn't you like it?'

'Christ, I loved it.'

We sat looking at each other, both remembering the kiss.

'You've got to remember how important Alicia is to me,' he continued.

I wished he would shut up about his sister.

'I mean, our parents are dead. She's all I've got. But to her, that's power.' He shrugged. 'I guess she's used it to make me think I can't ... perform.'

I'd had enough of all this talk. I moved over to his bed, which was messily made up with white sheets. I pulled them back and picked out his teddy, holding it to my breast. I sat on the edge of the bed, kicked off my shoes and looked him in the eye.

'You know, I can't play an instrument,' I said. 'But I always imagine it must be a bit like making love. You just have to feel the moment, Tom.'

'But –'

'You know, I bet you're a fabulous lover. You've got the timing, the rhythm, the sensitivity. Most men get to the finale before they've even finished the slow movement!' I persuaded.

He laughed a little nervously. 'Come here.' He walked towards me. 'Now do as I say or the bear gets it. Sit down.' He sat. His eyes soaked up my curvy figure and I was pleased to see a rapid rise in his shorts. At least the basics were working. 'Why don't you just pretend I'm a piano keyboard,' I improvised. 'Touch me.'

He gently caressed the curve of my left breast through my dress, his thumb brushing my nipple to attention. He looked at me as if he wanted to memorise me, as if he wanted to see every pore. His other hand began to stimulate my right breast, sending starry tingling sensations dancing around my nipples. He had wonderful, soft, sensitive fingers. 'That's lovely,' I breathed. His confidence grew and he kissed me, still stroking me, and we fell back onto the mattress. My hand wandered curiously to his crotch and lightly felt his erection. It was sturdy and long and my pussy began to melt at the thought of him inside me. His hands were moving over me now, taking in each curve and hollow. He was taking control.

'Is that OK?' he asked.

'It's gorgeous,' I whispered and guided his hand under my skirt to the moist fabric between my legs. I yearned to have him touch me there, to feel how aroused he had made me. But he resisted, returning it to the safety of my breast. 'You can touch me, Tom. I want you to.' I was imagining those long fingers slipping inside me, those fingers that had been so clever at the piano. If they could tease such beauty out of the piano, what could they do to me?

He pulled away and lay back on the pillow. 'Can I ask you a question?' I said eventually.

'Have I ever slept with a woman?' he interrupted quickly.

I hesitated. In fact it hadn't occurred to me that he might still be a virgin. I was actually going to ask him if he found me attractive, but this line of questioning was far more intriguing.

'Go on,' I said.

'Well, I am ashamed to say that in my thirty years, I've only had a couple of lovers. Alicia has a way of putting a stop to things. Of bursting in, or warning a girl off.' He rolled onto his side and looked at me. 'Jo, I'm no use to you, am I?'

'Oh, shut up,' I said. 'And don't tell me again that you're terrible with women or I'll hit you.' He laughed and I rolled on top of him, loving the heavy pressure of our bodies so close together. 'You can't get a girl all wet then make her go back to her room on her own.' I kissed him again, opening my legs so I was straddling him. He groaned into the kiss, relaxing. By now my panties were drenched and I was ready to come as soon as he touched me.

Right on cue, the door swung open and Alicia stood there, hands on hips. Her cool eyes were flashing with annoyance.

'What the hell's this?' she demanded.

I decided not to scramble off him. Instead I sat up defiantly and met her stare.

'Haven't you heard of knocking?' I asked.

She let out a derisory laugh.

'That's rich. Whose house is this anyway?'

Tom sat up awkwardly.

'Look, Alicia, this is between me and Jo –'

'She's supposed to be here on business,' she spat.

'Now come on,' Tom began.

'Get out, you little slut.'

I could see that Tom couldn't handle the situation, and I wasn't going to sit around and be insulted. Feeling let down by his spinelessness I got to my feet and grabbed my notepad. Just as I was leaving she turned the knife.

'Oh, and your *boyfriend* called. Wants to speak with you, urgently.'

'Boyfriend?' Tom looked bewildered. He stared at me as if he had never seen me before. Of course, I hadn't officially dumped Jerome, but I wasn't with him either. We were free agents, as he liked to repeat endlessly.

'Thanks,' I muttered and tore off the top sheet of my pad, shoving it in her hands.

'What's this? "Not a bad kisser, definitely not gay, fucked up over sister"?' she read quizzically. 'What the hell . . .?'

But by then I was through the door, leaving them to sort out their own mess. My body buzzed with irritation and sexual frustration. I thought about rushing to ring Jerome back, but decided that Ruby was right. I had lots of options and I was going to try them all out. Now.

By the time I got to the stables, my blood was on fire. I had paced there with anger growing with each step, and now I was a seething mass of passion. Jerome, Alicia, Tom: all of them had let me down, and now I was going to take some control.

Harry was bent over the horse's back leg, scraping dirt from his hoof. He looked up with instant knowingness at me and dropped the leg.

'There you go now, Tiger,' he said in his rich Northern voice, patting the horse's shining flank. 'That's all for today.'

The horse blew out a snort of protest, but Harry was already approaching me. I had forgotten how tall and broad he was. His body was like a thickly built clay sculpture, brown and solid. Wordlessly he took my arm, his big hand encircling it completely, and led me to his lodgings. His powerful physical presence almost scared me, along with the memory of the vicious fucking he had given Alicia in the stables. My heart pounded as I wondered what I was letting myself in for. I was almost running to keep up with his long strides.

When we got to his lodgings, he flung the door open and I went in. It was a basic room with two beds: one double, one single. There were few possessions. A door was open into the bathroom and I could hear the shower running. Steam was escaping into the bedroom, giving it an aromatic humidity.

Harry led me to the bed and pushed me down unceremoniously. He slowly went round the room, closing curtains and locking the door. I could hear Kieran singing in the shower, utterly tuneless in total contrast to Tom's musical skills.

'You don't seem surprised I came,' I said eventually to Harry.

He fixed me with his brown eyes and smiled. It wasn't too late to escape, I thought. We stared at each other. 'Look, maybe this was a mistake . . .' I began, but then the shower stopped and I was distracted.

After a moment Kieran walked in, loosely covered with a yellow towel. His torso was compact and very muscular, his neat body contrasting with Harry's big frame. The steam seemed to cling to him as he came in and stood in the doorway, grinning.

'I was just thinking about you,' he said suggestively. 'In the shower,' he added, as if I didn't get it. 'Wished I'd saved myself up now, though. Look at you.' He walked towards me. I found his cheeky insinuations much less menacing than Harry's silence and started to relax. 'Look at her little white dress, Harry. Sweet!' He stood over me, a slow rise obvious under his towel. 'Well, things certainly are looking up,' he joked.

Part of me still wanted to leave, but another part was very curious. I wanted to know what Alicia saw in this odd double act.

'So, you've intrigued me,' I said. 'I hope you live up to your own hype.'

Kieran sat on one side of me while Harry stood leaning against the fireplace, watching us. Kieran placed a hot hand on my thigh and moved it upwards, bunching my dress around my crotch.

'I hope you live up to my fantasies,' he smirked. 'Nice legs, by the way. Fucking nice.'

I laughed at his lack of subtlety.

'I hope you come up with better than that for Alicia,' I commented.

'She's not choosy,' Harry said gruffly. 'She likes the rough stuff.'

'What do you like, eh?' Kieran leant into my neck and whispered in my ear, his hot breath peppermint sweet.

'I like to keep my options open,' I retorted, leaning away from him a little. For some reason I couldn't get my mind off Alicia. What was it about her that made Jerome want her, Tom obey her and these two guys fall at her feet? I realised, rather belatedly, that I was intensely jealous. Something in me wanted to try out being her for a while; being this sex-crazed, haughty woman. Kieran's cheeky hand was snaking its way up my dress now, landing on my breast and kneading it firmly.

'Fuck, her tits are huge,' he said to Harry, who shifted, still gazing at us. 'Can't wait to come all over them.' Kieran pulled my dress off over my head and I sat there in my bra and panties while they examined my body. Kieran's hands smoothed over my skin, getting to know each curve and swell, and Harry's eyes followed, somehow more invasively.

'Do you just stand there watching with Alicia?' I asked him, my voice quite breathy. 'Or do you join in?' Kieran unhooked my bra and slowly revealed my heavy breasts. Both men looked hungrily at me.

'Jesus,' Kieran whispered. 'Beautiful.' His tongue was now sliding around my hard nipple, leaving wet trails of pleasure over my cinnamon skin. I watched him enjoy me, seeing my stomach tighten with anticipation when he flicked his tongue against me. He fell on to the floor, kneeling in front of me, and cupped both breasts as he made a feast of it. I tingled with delight.

'Does Alicia like that?' I asked. He looked at me strangely.

'Why do you keep going on about her?' he said. His blue eyes were misty with desire and he looked really sexy crouching between my legs, my tits spilling out of his hands. I shrugged. It was a good question but my mental faculties were blurred by lust.

'Just curious,' I replied.

'Just curious?' A slow grin crept across Kieran's face. 'Do you want us to show you what she likes?' he asked. My pussy burned. 'Do you want to be Alicia just for one night? Shall we show you all the things that make her go wild?'

'Yes,' I whispered. 'Yes, please.'

For the first time, my arousal overtook me and I completely surrendered. Kieran pushed me back onto the bed and exchanged triumphant glances with Harry as I complied willingly, letting my knees fall open.

'You asked for it,' Kieran said, yanking down my panties. 'Oh, Miss Alicia, you look like you need a good fucking. You look like you want it bad.' He threw the panties across the bed and stared at my naked groin. I widened my legs and felt myself open up to his gaze. 'Look at that pussy. It's steaming.' He crouched between my legs and stroked me, his face inches away from my cunt. I had already been wet when I came back from Tom's and now I was positively dripping. I felt Kieran's breath as he peered closer. 'You naughty little bitch.' He dipped his finger in the juice and tasted it. 'Christ, she's fucking delicious,' he said to Harry, who had a hand stuffed down his trousers and was stroking himself slowly.

'Miss Alicia, not a peep out of you while I clean you up,' he said to me and then trailed a hot tongue along my slit. I moaned as he reached my swollen clit and circled it languidly. 'Not a word,' he said and continued his slow, tantalising exploration of my pussy with his tongue. I bit my lip and tried to be silent, opening my legs wide and lifting my hips up to meet his face. Looking down I could see his expression of ecstasy as he tasted me and I began to tremble. His tongue strokes got faster and deeper and after a while I started to whimper. I couldn't help it. I buried my hands in his hair and gasped as he started to play his nimble tongue across my clit again. Suddenly Harry was on the bed behind me, stuffing my knickers in my mouth.

'Shut up, bitch,' he hissed.

He removed his leather belt and tied it round my mouth to gag me. I let out a muffled cry of protest, but my mouth was full of material stained with my own tangy juices. I kicked and bucked, but Kieran's mouth was steady on me and his tongue never lost its rhythm. Now that Harry was on the bed, he had started to play with my tits, fondling and licking and brushing his stubble against them. He growled like a brown bear as he started to suck on me. My arousal crept hotly over my skin like a nettle rash. I put a hand on each head and sighed deliriously as I felt them bob and swirl over me, two hot mouths drawing pleasure from all my nerve endings, two hot tongues smearing my most intimate parts with lust. My breath started to quicken and I struggled to fill my lungs, breathing noisily through my nose. I started to feel dizzy, not getting enough oxygen and struggled against both men, pulling at their hair, wanting to be released from the gag. They just laughed at me and continued to work on my body, Kieran's tongue teasing out such pleasure from me that I screamed through my gag. He lifted my hips and threw my legs over his shoulders, his face squelching against me. I stopped kicking so much, feeling weak and dizzy, and released myself to a giddy, confused, intense climax. When I had stopped thrashing around, Harry removed the belt and pulled my panties out of my mouth. I breathed hard in relief.

'You're a naughty girl, Miss,' he said, wiping the sweat from my brow with the panties. I took great gulps of air and lay exhausted, my legs unashamedly open. Both men were looking at my pussy now, sliding their fingers through the tide of wetness.

'Look at that cunt,' Kieran smiled, his face shining. 'I'm going to fuck that cunt till it cries out for mercy. Then Harry's going to fuck it even harder. Taste it, Harry, it's like a fruit.'

Harry bent between my legs and started to gobble away at me, just like I had seen him do to Alicia. My spent pussy twitched and wriggled under his over-eager administrations, the feeling returning slowly. Kieran lay beside me and kissed my cheek.

'You OK?' he whispered.

He was obviously the less severe of the two. I nodded and he kissed me on the lips, gentle at first, then deeper, his tongue still tasting of my juices. While Harry lapped away at me, Kieran held me tight and French-kissed me until my whole body felt hot again. Harry was beginning to grunt between my legs, humping the mattress as he went down on me, and the deep vibration of his voice sent shivers through me.

'He's like an animal, isn't he?' Kieran whispered against my ear. 'A beast.' The grunting got louder. 'Would you like that, Miss? A big beast licking you, a big hairy animal grunting between your legs?' I shut my eyes and let his words fill me with perverse, delicious images. 'When it's finished licking you, it's going to mount you and fuck you with its huge, monstrous prick. It's going to fuck you for hours, hard, before it fills you with its come.' Harry's tongue went faster now, snuffling against my clit. 'It's going to hurt, because it's got a huge cock. Big and black and hairy, with a massive head that tears you apart.' I started to climax, letting out little sighs. 'You're going to come and come on its big animal prick until you're so faint you can't take any more. It's going to stretch you so wide, you'll scream.'

My legs were splayed open as Harry fucked me with his tongue, his face pressed up against me. The image in my head was disgustingly erotic. 'And when it's finished, it'll start all over again, licking you and fucking you. You can't escape it. Licking you and fucking you . . .' My body braced itself for another big orgasm, shuddering against Harry's face. My cunt felt empty and ached to be filled and I moaned in frustration. Even as I came, I wanted more. All Kieran's talk of well-endowed beasts had me dying to be fucked.

'You're a dirty bitch, aren't you, Miss,' said Kieran with a grin. 'Shall we do your favourite, Miss Alicia?'

I nodded furiously, both terrified and excited. God only knew what Alicia's favourite was. Kieran lay on his back, finally taking off his towel to reveal a modestly sized, proudly erect cock. He intimated to me to crawl on top of him, and I did. With a sigh of relief, I lowered myself onto him. I was so drenched, he slipped in far too easily. I ground my hips against him, urgently wanting to be filled to the hilt. But he slowed me down, laughing at my enthusiasm.

'Now, now, Miss. You know you have to wait for Harry to climb on board before the train goes!' he chided, steadying my hips. I felt the bed dip behind me and Harry was there, caressing my shoulders and kissing the back of my neck. 'We're going to make a little Miss sandwich.'

Harry's breath was hot and wet in my hair, his rough hands scratching the soft skin around my neck. I hadn't even seen him undress, but I felt from the tickle of his pubes against my buttocks that he was naked. He pressed his big, hairy torso against my back, his hands reaching around to cover my breasts. I could feel the big fat rod of his erection press against my bottom, and I yearned to have it fill me up. I had been teased and titillated for too long. I gyrated impatiently on Kieran's cock, making him jerk with lust.

'Hey, stop, slow down. I'm ready to explode here,' he protested, watching Harry's hands crawl across my breasts and pinch at my swollen nipples. Harry's fingers stroked down my flat brown belly, sending butterflies of delight across my skin, and finally landed in the moist haven of my pussy. I was sure I felt him lightly caress the root of Kieran's erection before he began to play with me, sliding his forefinger across my clit over and over again. All my desire seemed suddenly to burn unbearably in that one spot and I groaned in ecstasy, bearing down on Kieran's small cock for relief.

'Oh, please, you have to fuck me,' I moaned, hot sweat collecting in all my pores. 'Please,' I begged, as my legs trembled out of control. I was starting to unravel. Harry's fingers were persistent and merciless. 'Oh, God! Oh, oh God!' Another little climax shuddered through me and I fell forward over Kieran, whipping his face with my hair. I panted and sighed, but the orgasm hadn't satisfied me. It only served to make me hunger for more. My sex ached for a pounding. I had seen Harry in the stables and I needed some of that aggressive attention. I remembered his round, golden buttocks rising and falling, his hips thrusting like a piston, his huge prick – how I wanted that prick inside me now! Petulantly I raised my hips and Kieran slipped out of me with a whine of protest.

'Hey, bitch,' he said and tried to force himself up me again, but I wanted Harry. I presented him shamelessly with my open pussy, lifting my buttocks to him and trying to sit back on his big cock. Its bulbous head slid inside me for a moment, forcing me open, but he pulled away. I moaned.

'Behave,' he growled at me and I suddenly felt the searing flash of his leather belt across my bottom. I yelped in pain and surprise. He hit me again, the cushion of my buttocks absorbing the pain. The leather made a sharp whipping noise as it met my skin.

'I think she needs punishing,' Kieran said, and pushed my head down to his crotch. 'Suck on me, you naughty girl. Bad girls have to suck cock, you know that!' I nodded and sucked him hungrily into my mouth. He had the perfect prick for blowjobs, small enough and smooth.

As I lapped him up, Harry knelt behind me and began to spank my upturned bottom. My skin started to burn as he slapped me over and over again. Each blow pushed Kieran's cock deeper and deeper down my throat and he groaned.

'Oh, you bad girl, you're enjoying it,' he murmured, grabbing my hair. 'Oh, you dirty tart!' he cried and my mouth was soon filled with his creamy come.

Harry continued to spank away, occasionally slipping a finger into my pussy to remind us both how turned on I was. 'Now Harry's going to have his way with you, you bad girl,' Kieran said to me, and pulled me up by my hair so I was on all fours over his body. I shut my eyes in delirious anticipations, waiting for him to fill me up. 'He's going to fuck you,' he whispered making me groan in anticipation, 'up the arse.' I opened my eyes. 'He's going to stuff you until you're sore.' He laughed at my face. 'Yes, he is a big boy, isn't he,' he said, reading my mind. 'But it is your favourite. Isn't it, Miss?'

So that was Alicia's thing. Harry smeared my copious juices around the entrance of my anus and lathered his prick with lubrication. I tried to relax as I felt the huge head of his penis push through my tight rosebud. Cramping pain shot through me as he forced his way up. He grunted.

'Fuck, she's tight,' he muttered in his thick Northern voice. My face was a grimace of pain, and Kieran gently stroked my cheek as Harry began to fuck me. I tried to pull away but they were too powerful for me.

'You asked for it,' Kieran said. Harry pushed in another inch and took my breath away. 'You love it.' Harry began to thrust very slowly. My cunt felt emptier than ever as he filled my arse with his huge erection, but somehow I felt like I had never been fucked so thoroughly before. Harry was nearly all the way in now, thrusting a little harder. My muscles relaxed and I began to enjoy the degrading sensation, a deep moan escaping from my throat. He responded by speeding up his strokes, pushing further, until I felt his heavy balls slap against my bottom with every thrust. I was impaled and helpless as he fucked me harder. This was a new feeling, raw and violent. I almost blacked out as I got into the pleasure of it, barely catching my breath, and Harry pushed me down so I was lying on my stomach on top of Kieran. Kieran slipped his hand between our bodies and gently guided his newly erect cock to my pussy. The men had a moment of complicity between them and Harry paused, panting into my ear, as Kieran pushed himself into my cunt. The two pricks seemed to be vying for space inside me, and I sighed in delight as I was filled to the hilt front and back. We let Harry do all the work, each of his thrusts also sending me sliding back and forth on Kieran's erection. I was helpless between them, used, degraded. I gave up all control and enjoyed being just an open vessel for their desires, my body full of them. My clit was rubbing vigorously against Kieran's groin with each movement and I felt another climax start to vibrate within me.

'Yes, come on,' Kieran urged, seeing me begin to lose it. 'Come on, good girl, come for us. Let Uncle Harry and Uncle Kieran fill you up.' Harry started to pump me faster, his hips wild and merciless. Pain and pleasure rippled through me, and I couldn't get enough of either.

'Oh, yes,' I moaned. 'Oh, fuck me, please.'

They both stepped up a gear. Everything started to go blurry again as the pressure mounted in my pussy and arse. Harry was grunting above me, making me think of the beast Kieran had talked about. He certainly did feel unnaturally large inside me, and his whole weight was heavy on my back. 'Oh God!' My pussy squelched loudly under all the pressure, pouring hot juice over Kieran's cock. 'Oh, I'm coming, I'm coming!' I cried. Kieran shouted out and started to climax too, jerking his spunk into me over and over again. 'Oh, God!' I was getting there, still being fucked hard by Harry and sliding about on Kieran's wilting shaft. 'Oh yes!' My orgasm took me over, contractions pulling on both cocks as I came and came. Soon Harry unloaded himself into me, and all our bodies were joined in a sweaty, exhausted mess. We lay there for a while until eventually Harry pulled out.

'That's how she likes it,' Kieran said. 'Miss Alicia. That satisfied your curiosity?'

I rolled off him and lay there panting, so jealous that Alicia could have that kind of a fucking whenever she desired.

'Or do you want more?'

More? The man was crazy. I felt as if I had run a marathon and fucked a football team. I laughed and wiped the sweat off my face.

'Maybe another day, then?' Kieran asked hopefully.

Harry was up now, pulling on his pants.

'You enjoy that?' I asked him, determined to break through his taciturn exterior. He grunted. 'Was I better than your mistress?' He paused, which didn't fill me with confidence. Maybe Alicia had some tricks I didn't know about.

'Much better,' Kieran said. 'For a start, you don't start abusing us just after you've come.'

Harry laughed gruffly.

'And you've got tits. Such tits!'

I don't know what it was – the sex or the reassurance

– but I fell asleep after that, splayed out on Kieran's bed, naked, my pussy smeared with the evidence of our adventures. Ruby would have been proud of me.

It was pitch black. For a second I forgot where I was. My heart pounded and a man's voice hissed at me to get up. I was pulled to my feet, my dress stuffed in my hands.

'Go through the window,' Kieran pushed me as I sleepily pulled the dress on and staggered into my shoes, suddenly remembering. Then there was banging.

'Open the door, morons!' It was Alicia's voice, shrill and hard. 'What's going on in there?'

'Nothing.' Even Harry looked panicky, straightening the room out. 'Is it locked, Miss?' Kieran hoisted me up to the window.

'She'll kill you if she finds you in here,' he whispered.

I jumped through, landing on a flowerbed. I sat there, dazed in the moonlight. I could hear the sound of Alicia being let in and slapping someone out of frustration. I heard frantic apologies and excuses; they had accidentally locked the door, they'd had too much to drink and were sleeping too deeply to hear her knocking. Soon silence came, then moaning and whispers and I knew she was being pacified in her favourite way. I listened for a while, leaning against the wall of the cottage and looking up at the clear night sky. The cool air was calming on my sore pussy and I opened my legs a little. It was then that I realised that my panties were somewhere in that room. Almost simultaneously Alicia let out a screech of indignation.

'That hussy!' she yelled. 'Her dirty knickers in your bed!'

Then there was a medley of screaming and denials.

I couldn't help but feel a little smug. It was almost as if I had left a calling card for her to find, a little note that said, 'anything you can do I can do better.' God knows why she brought out that competitive streak in me, but I was determined to come out on top. Smiling to myself I got up, brushed myself down and meandered back to the house, the cries of her fury still carrying across the wind.

8

Over the next few days I kept my head down and my nose to the grindstone. I wasn't going to get into a catfight with my hostess, or a steamy session with her staff. I even avoided Tom, not sure how to play it with him. Whenever I passed one of them in the corridors or in the gardens I just said a polite hello and hurried on. I read, wrote and researched in the extensive library at Hathaway Hall, which was conveniently stocked with memoirs of Daphne's friends and books of the period. I ate furtively in my room, only occasionally bumping into Ray and exchanging pleasantries. Life was simpler that way.

Luckily the house was in a state of utter distraction, as Alicia was planning her big party. Whenever I caught sight of her she was swanning around importantly, making lists and giving orders.

One sunny afternoon I was holed up in the library with my head buried in a book about Elgar when a shadow fell over the page. I looked up and Tom was standing sheepishly over me, wearing tennis gear. He looked flushed from a game, as if he had really given himself a workout. I waited for him to say something but he just stood there.

'You win?' I asked coolly.

'What?' He looked momentarily confused, perhaps thinking I was referring to his power struggle with his sister.

'The game.' I indicated his tennis gear.

'Oh!' He instantly relaxed. 'Yes I did, actually. Which

hasn't helped Alicia's mood. I think she was hoping to beat the crap out of me. Make her feel better.'

I shifted in my leather armchair, wondering if she had told him about the knickers-in-the-bed incident.

'Oh?'

'Tense about the big do, I think,' he explained, pulling up a chair opposite me. 'Tense about ... well, us. Me and you.'

'What us?' I asked, a little sharper than I meant to. He was so darned handsome sitting there, but I still hadn't quite forgiven him for not standing up to his sister. I had had enough of complicated males, especially gorgeous ones.

'Sorry, presumptuous, I know.' He looked around him. 'Tell me, your ... boyfriend?' He grimaced as he said the word.

'History.'

He looked at me with interest, obviously as unsure of our relationship as I was.

'Couldn't be more over.' I really ought to get around to telling Jerome that, I thought. I still hadn't returned his 'urgent' phone call, choosing rather to make him sweat it out. Besides, he had my mobile number.

A smiled creased Tom's cheeks.

'Good. Well, not good for him, obviously,' he said falteringly. We sat in silence for a while. 'Look, I just wanted to say sorry,' he said eventually. 'I'm sorry I'm such an idiot.'

'That's OK,' I said. 'You can't help it. You're a bloke. It's DNA.'

He laughed nervously at my weak joke, playing with the handle of his racket.

'I wish I was a man of action,' he said. 'I'm more a man of talking and ruminating and bloody botching things up.' I laughed. 'More a Hamlet than a Romeo, I'm afraid,' he added, smiling apologetically at me.

'Romeo botched things up as well,' I pointed out. 'Ended up dead, I seem to remember.'

'Yeah, I suppose,' he nodded, 'but at least he got laid.'

His understated humour started to win me over again. I was just deciding to give him another chance when suddenly the door swung open and Alicia came in. My heart missed a beat. Tom and I were getting on so well, I didn't want to spoil it all with talk of threesomes with stable hands. I searched her face for signs of vengeance, but it was as calm and unruffled as a frozen lake, a charming smile illuminating her blue eyes. She looked neat and stylish in a pretty designer tennis dress, her long pale legs perfectly toned.

'There you are, my darlings!' she said generously.

I sat up. I had expected her to attack me or expose me, but this was somehow more unnerving.

'Jo, sweetheart, I haven't seen you for days. Where have you been hiding yourself away?' she asked. 'I miss your funny comments at dinner.' She wrinkled her nose a little as she said this. She came in and perched prettily on a stool. I could just see the frill of her white tennis knickers.

'Just working,' I said nervously.

'Work work work! You London girls are all the same,' she laughed. 'My dear, you are too young and beautiful to be scribbling away all the time. You should be doing something fun! Like helping me prepare the party. It's going to be a hoot.' I couldn't think of anything worse, but just smiled. She turned to Tom and tutted at him. 'And you, you had better behave, Thomas. All your old flames are going to be there and I don't want you going to pieces like a little boy. Honestly, Jo,' – she turned to me conspiratorially and Tom rolled his eyes – 'he had the choice of four lovely girls and did he blow it? Yes he did.'

'They were not "lovely",' he protested, 'and I recall that *you* were the one who ruined everything –'

'First there was Fenella,' Alicia ploughed on, turning to me in a gossipy all-girls-together mode. 'Very pretty. Very rich.'

'She was such a bigot,' Tom said. 'A total prig –'

'Then there was Juliana Harker.'

'Spoilt. Rich, spoilt brat,' Tom interjected. 'Cocaine-addled, too.'

'No! Lovely girl, Tom, you little prude.' Tom grimaced at me and I couldn't help but giggle. 'Then Thomasina.'

'Need I say more?'

'Thomasina is one of the most eligible bachelorettes in Norfolk,' Alicia said. 'Not a natural beauty, but an excellent horsewoman.'

I could just picture her.

'Looks like a bloody horse as well,' Tom muttered to me.

'And then that village girl. What was her name?'

Tom blushed. I could see this one was different.

'Anyway, she won't be coming – a bit common,' she confided in me as if I was suddenly landed gentry.

'She was OK. You were just jealous,' Tom objected, steering into dangerously familiar waters. 'Saw her off in a hurry.'

Alicia bristled for a second then laughed falsely.

'Jealous? What an idea!' she cried, winking at me.

I summoned a smile.

'Anyway, the party is going to be just smashing. You must come and pick out a dress from my collection, dear,' she said to me, 'if we can find one to fit.' She couldn't resist a dig. 'I have a gold number that will suit you magnificently.'

My eyes lit up as I remembered spotting it in her wardrobe when I was having a snoop. How could she know that one had been my favourite? 'Yes,' she said. 'You are going to look a million dollars.'

I turned dreamily in front of the full-length mirror in my room. Every inch of my body was coated in a clinging shimmer of gold. The dress hugged my hips and breasts like a needy lover, being designed for the svelte figure of Alicia, but I liked the effect. I felt more shapely than an hourglass, and more golden than Midas himself could muster. The cowl neck of the dress and its tiny straps made me feel feminine, and the low back barely skimmed the dimples at the top of my bottom. This was definitely a no-underwear creation. The tanned colour of my naked arms, back and cleavage was illuminated by the gold of the dress. I carefully applied a light sheen of make-up and scooped my long curls into a tousled bun. Alicia had given me a pair of her shoes, elegant golden kitten heels with tiny straps. As I put them on I felt like Cinderella, with Alicia as the not-so-ugly sister who for some reason had become incredibly magnanimous. Then I put on the gold choker and bracelets she had given me, and a ruby-encrusted gold tiara that clipped into my hair. Again I did a twirl and sighed.

So far I had resisted the affluent, arrogant charm of Hathaway Hall with its old money, but this dress had totally won me over. I felt uncomfortably as if Alicia had named my price and I had fallen for it, sold my soul to the devil. Could I be so shallow that my price was a pretty princess dress and an extortionately expensive pair of shoes?

As I watched my reflection, I could hear from downstairs the laughter and elaborate greetings – all just a bit too jolly and forced – that always accompany the start of a party. There were admiring gasps at Alicia's frock, and I wondered what she could have chosen to wear. Presumably she would save her best outfit for herself, but what could be better than this glitzy thing? Alicia had insisted on keeping her own outfit a secret from me, so I expected something truly stupendous. Taking a deep breath, I slowly emerged from my room and proudly walked to the staircase. As I descended the stairs I spotted her in the hallway surrounded by friends. Then it all suddenly jolted into focus.

The group of assembled women were dressed in skimpy, modern designer numbers or ultra-cool street gear. They looked sleek, funky and feminine. None of them had gone for the full-length dress. Some wore little strappy dresses, others were dressed for clubbing in snakeskin bikini tops and hipsters, denim hot pants and knee boots. They looked like any other gathering of hip young women on a fun night out, and I had come as the queen of the bloody Nile. I stood on the stairs like the fairy on a Christmas tree, watching as they slowly clocked me. Their mouths fell open. One girl stifled a little laugh. The group parted like the red sea to admit Alicia, who waded through to take a look at me.

'Darling, you're a picture!' she declared.

I had never seen her look so funky. She was clad in a skin-tight white cat suit with huge 70s lapels and cobra skin cowboy boots. She wore a white Stetson with a silver chain around it and a low-slung diamond chain hung around her hips. My instinct was to run back up the stairs to change – God, I could *do* funky. All those media parties I'd been to and pop stars I'd mixed with meant I was well equipped with a killer wardrobe. But I had fallen in love with the idea of a ball – like the one in Daphne's diary – and Alicia had seen right through me. Suddenly I was the yokel and these country aristos were the trendy elite.

'I didn't know it was fancy dress,' a toothy girl quipped bitchily.

'Shh, Thomasina!' Alicia scolded her.

I knew that my only option was to join the party and not lose face. If I ran back up to change now Alicia would have a mini victory and I couldn't allow that. Anyhow, I was pretty sure I looked shit hot in this dress, even if it was hideously inappropriate. I walked gracefully down the stairs, smiling.

'Happy Birthday, Alicia,' I said, although I had seen her a lot that day. I kissed her coolly on the cheek and walked past the group toward the big hall. A dj was at the far end of the room, mixing his own blend of dance and bhangra beat. In the flashing lights I could see a few people were already dancing, looking a little stoned, swigging beer from the bottle. I knew dancing would be a little tricky in this gown, especially minus the bra, so I leant up against a wall in a dark corner and watched the room heat up. Alicia walked past at one point with two girls and they all giggled.

'She looks like Alexis Carrington in *Dynasty*, for God's sake,' one of them said loudly enough for me to hear. I watched as Alicia started to sway to the beat, her lithe body letting go to the music. The ultraviolet lights picked up her white outfit and she glowed in the dark as she moved. The group laughed and drank and hugged. Various men kept coming over to her and kissing her, running their hands over her body. She was like a beacon; always charming, always cool, always sexy. As the room filled up I saw Ray and Ollie come in and was glad to see they had dressed in tuxedos. Ollie looked as sweaty and beady eyed as ever and I noticed that while Ray was getting the drinks in, Ollie subtly handed a little parcel to Alicia, which she tucked into her top. I picked a flute of champagne from a passing waiter and watched Ray greet Alicia with a deep kiss and an intimate squeeze on her pretty little rump. She introduced him to the group, and they carried on dancing. The actor I had seen fucking Alicia came in with another man and two women. The other man had a square-jawed, perma-tanned beefiness and the women were scantily clad, their breast implants buoyantly on display, their collagen-puffed lips in a permanent pout of pink gloss. No prizes for guessing what they all do for a living, I thought, slurping down my second glass of bubbly.

The dj suddenly changed the mood and put on a Madonna song. The floor filled with people and everyone started to groove. I skulked further into the darkness of my corner, trying to become invisible, which wasn't easy in a luminous gold floor-length dress. Alicia's strappy sandals were starting to cut into my feet, and a draft blew down my back, giving me goose bumps. I felt my nipples harden in the cold and I covered them with my hands, trying to calm them down.

'Can I help with that?'

I heard Ray's Southern drawl before I looked up and saw him. Could this evening get any more embarrassing, I wondered.

'No, just ... adjusting myself,' I said and smiled up at him. He scrubbed up well, cutting a dashing figure in his tux. There was something comforting about his old Southern chivalry and his red-blooded appreciation of the female form.

'You look incredible,' he said. 'Just beautiful. Why are you hiding yourself away here? You're the prettiest thing in the room.'

I was grateful for the kind words, and no doubt I would have been belle of the ball down in Tennessee, but my face must have shown that I felt like a great big golden goose.

'Oh, don't worry about them in their little tops and trouser-suits. What do they know? You know what a real man wants out of a girl?'

'Blowjobs?' I suggested.

He cracked up.

'No,' he drawled. 'Well, yes, actually.' He looked me up and down. 'Don't give me ideas, young lady.'

'OK, so what does a real man want, Mr Hobbs?' I asked, gaining the confidence to stand up straight.

'Just what you got, babe. Titties he can lose himself in, a butt he can grab hold of and a beautiful face.'

I mused on his words of wisdom.

'I see,' I said eventually. 'Is that Oscar Wilde, or did you come up with it yourself?' I grabbed another glass of champagne from a passing waiter and felt my body heat up as the liquid slipped down.

'It's a truth as old as Adam,' he replied. 'It's practically in the bible.'

'Oh.' I drained my glass. 'I must have missed that day in Sunday school.'

'Too bad.' He took the empty glass from me and put it down. 'You're going to dance with me,' he said and pulled me on to the dance floor. Some 80s disco tune was playing, but Ray still held me in a ballroom pose and we slow-danced across the floor. His tall, lanky frame was easy to hang on to and he knew some great moves, twirling me around in a firm grip.

'So,' he said, when I was starting to feel dizzy. 'When can I have my way with you?'

I groaned. Just when I had started to enjoy myself, he went and spoilt it.

'I'm here for work,' I reminded him, 'and so are you.'

'I know. I did mean work,' he protested.

'You want me to do one of your "tele-dramas"?' I asked, my voice loaded with irony. He looked into my eyes.

'That'd be great, honey, but I don't think you're ready for that yet,' he said, and dipped me into a backbend. 'But I sure would like to take your picture.' His breath, mingling with mine, was heady with tobacco. His hand on my bare back was hot. He pulled me up and smiled. 'Of course, I would want to see the whole you. The real you. Everything.'

I suddenly got what he meant.

'Ah, you mean like for a porn mag?' I asked. 'I don't think so.'

'No, no,' he laughed. 'Just for you. For you and me. Beautiful shots. Black and white. I'm quite an artist, you know.'

I thought about it. Vanity and curiosity fizzed with the champagne in my head to make the idea tempting.

'You're a beautiful woman, Jo. And a real woman. I could just eat you up. And I know the camera would too.' He twirled me for a while and the champagne whooshed around my head. 'Your skin, your eyes. Your shape.' He sighed, pulling me closer. There was a little firmness in his trousers that actually felt quite nice against my belly. 'Just think: you could have these subtle, beautiful, tasteful shots of yourself to send all your exes. Show them what they've given up.'

My mind instantly shot to Jerome and before I knew it I was nodding.

'OK, Mr Hobbs,' I said. 'You got yourself a model.'

'Good stuff. Listen,' he said confidentially, 'don't tell Ollie about it. He gets kinda ... carried away when he knows a pretty girl likes to be photographed. OK? He's not as nice as me.' He smiled broadly and whirled me so fast that I collapsed in a giggling heap at his feet. He pulled me up. 'Alright, young lady. Hang here – I'm going to get you a glass of water.'

I nodded and watched him leave, suddenly alone and conspicuous again. The gold dress had twisted on my body, leaving one breast almost bare. I adjusted myself furtively. A couple of drunken toffs grabbed at me as they danced by, their beery breath sobering me up. I staggered to the wall and leant on it, seeing the room sway. The actors were gyrating against each other, taking their work home with them.

I thought about Jerome, wondering where he was. We hadn't spoken for nearly a week and, although I had let him go, I still couldn't help but bristle at the fact he hadn't called. After all, he didn't know I had chucked him, and he had the perfect excuse to call me: to check up on the article. I started to feel miserable and picked up a cocktail from a passing tray. It was pink and creamy with a huge kick to it.

As I drank I scoured the room for Tom. He hadn't made an appearance all night, and I had planned to keep my dance card empty just for him.

I decided to go and look for him, stumbling between the dancing bodies, avoiding elbows and feet, until I came out into the hallway. It had been candlelit and the red walls glowed with a kind of gothic lusciousness. I came to the big mirror at the bottom of the stairs and caught my reflection, gold and voluptuous and a little blurry. I suddenly realised that this must have been the mirror that Daphne had been dragged to by her naughty vicar, stubble burns on her face. That set me thinking about the 'special room', the venue of Daphne's defloweringlng.

In the spirit of journalistic thoroughness – and inebriation – I decided I had to go and visit the room, to soak up its atmosphere. I staggered into the darkened dining room and started to push away at the wall panels, desperate to find the hidden entrance. I knocked the walls to listen for the hollow sound of a door, but nothing happened. Carefully I began to lift up the portraits on the walls in search of a key, a special lever or something; I beginning to feel a lot like Thelma in *Scooby Doo*. Suddenly I felt a cool breath on my shoulder and swung round. Alicia's eyes glinted at my in the half-light. I started to stammer out some feeble protestation, but she just smiled.

'Don't worry, darling. I expected nothing less of you,' she said ambiguously. 'You are a curious little thing, aren't you?' She handed me another pink cocktail and I drank it, noting that Alicia seemed remarkably sober. 'Are you in search of Daphne's Daddy's special chamber of delights?' she inquired. I nodded. 'Come on then,' she whispered, and took me to the far corner of the room.

There was a tall dresser covered in china, with a cupboard underneath it, which came up to shoulder height. Alicia reached up and took a small key from inside a teacup and opened the cupboard door. It was full of linen and tablecloths. She reached down and switched a latch inside the cupboard, then closed the doors again. As she did so, the cupboard started to pivot on its central axis, swinging into the wall to reveal a secret passage. The tall shelves stocked with delicate china remained fixed to the wall above.

'Ooh, you look all starry eyed,' Alicia mocked as I stepped with trepidation through the opening into the darkness. 'Just like the children going into Narnia.'

She followed me through and led me along the musty corridor until we reached a big oak door. She pushed it open and my eyes dazzled at the light. Hundreds of candles lined the room and sat in the corners, reflecting off the deep red velvet of the walls. Someone had obviously prepared the room for the party.

It was just as I had pictured, an erotic fairground. Some of the rides looked cosy and soft, others intimidating and painful. Bridles, handcuffs, strange chairs, whips, chains, harnesses all intrigued me, and I went around the room taking it all in, sipping on my pink cocktail.

'It could be heaven or it could be hell,' Alicia said, coming up behind me. I looked at her and she wiped a delicate finger across my lips and then sucked it. 'That's the name of the cocktail,' she explained languidly, then laid a gentle warm kiss on my lips. 'Sweet,' she said. She moved about the room in her white cat suit, playing with the toys carelessly, finally arriving at some handcuffs attached to the wall. They were lined with velvet. 'These were Daphne's favourites,' she said. I hadn't picked that up from the diary, but I wasn't surprised. 'Want to have a go?' Alicia said it to me like a dare, and I could never refuse a dare, although I didn't trust her one inch.

'Why?' I asked.

'Oh, come on, where's your sense of fun? Just try them on,' she cajoled, waving me over. I approached her and leant in position against the wall, feeling its warm soft velvet against my back. She pulled one hand up above my head and clicked it into a cuff, letting her lithe body press against me as she did so. It was comfortable but constraining. 'Other hand,' she said. I held on to my glass and shook my head.

'Oh no,' I said. 'One's enough. You can let me go now.'

'Oh, you are a killjoy,' she said sulkily and started to tickle me under my cuffed arm. I buckled and writhed, weakened with the giggles, pushing her hands away with my free one. In all the tussle she managed to take the glass away from me. 'Naughty thing.' She smiled and wrestled my hand up to the other cuff.

'Alicia!' I protested, still giggling nervously. 'Stop it!'

She smiled and clicked my hand into place. I stood there, arms above my head, wriggling around.

'You look like a little golden fish,' she laughed. 'A golden fish on a hook.'

'Come on, that's enough.' I was starting to sober up again and attempted to give her a firm stare. 'Let me down.'

She pouted at me.

'Let me down,' she said in a baby voice and giggled. She leant into me again and kissed me deeply, her hot little tongue probing me sensuously. She lowered her hand to my crotch and tickled me gently, and I began to respond, against all my better instincts.

Suddenly I heard voices coming from the corridor and soon a group of her friends came in. I recognised them as her inner sanctum, the people she had been dancing and flirting with all night. They carried whole bottles of champagne and whisky and beer and were laughing drunkenly.

'Has the show started yet?' asked a red-faced boy with the poshest voice I had ever heard.

'Not yet,' Alicia replied, winking at me.

The group started to investigate the room, each finding a spot to sit in, or something to lean on. I stopped writhing, my blood running cold. What was she going to do to me? 'But it's going to be good.'

'Jesus, your family's fucked up,' another bloke commented, holding up a whip and chain. 'Are you all sex mad?'

'Of course,' Alicia said simply.

The trendy clubby girls sprawled themselves on the waterbed, their legs all entangled, and started to roll a joint. The room was filling even more. Ray and Ollie came in, along with the four porn stars. Someone flipped on a trance CD, which curled hypnotically around my head. Alicia leant into me.

'This will teach you,' she whispered, her voice cut-crystal cool. 'Little slut.' And with that I saw her pull on a cord and I was hoisted up the wall, rising higher and higher. The velvet burned my back as I was pulled up, until I was left dangling.

'What the fuck are you doing?' I protested, but she ignored me.

'Henry, come and give me a hand,' she said to one of the men. He came over and they secured my legs wide apart in ankle-cuffs, giving me very little room for manoeuvre.

'OK, joke's over,' I hissed, my body starting to ache from the suspension and the struggle.

'What'll we do about the dress?' Henry asked.

'What do you mean?' I demanded.

The room started to gather round me like tourists at a zoo when the chimps are being particularly playful. I jerked my chains. 'What's going on, Alicia?' She took a hatpin out of her Stetson and reached up, lifting my dress above my hips with Henry's help and pinning it to the wall behind me. I gasped and struggled as she exposed my naked crotch to the room and left me helpless to cover myself up. The more I writhed, the more exposed I felt.

'Ah, look at the little golden fish,' she mocked. 'All helpless on the line.' The girls laughed. 'Now let's have some fun,' Alicia whispered, pulling out the parcel Ollie had given her, which was unsurprisingly packed with white powder.

I saw Ray watching me, his hungry eyes exploring every inch of my bare pussy. No more the Southern gentleman, I thought. I spied Mr Wootten coming in, totally out of place in his tweeds. He eyed the scene with great interest, taking a ringside seat. The room started to go quiet as Alicia dipped her finger in the cocaine and smeared it inside me. My pussy was in line with her face, and she leant into me as she left traces of the drug inside me and fluffed it through my silky pubes. I could feel its sweet narcotic buzz starting to soak into my skin, but I resisted. I needed to keep my wits about me. The room was silent except for the strange music as Alicia leant into me and gave a little sharp lick to my clit. I winced. She rolled her tongue around her gums and took another lick. This time, the taste seemed to appeal to her and she cupped my buttocks in her hands and let her tongue trail lasciviously around. Her pretty face was intent on my privates, her mouth glued to me. I tried to jerk my hips away and she pouted up at me.

'What a yummy little pussy you have,' she murmured, before smearing me with more coke. Some of the powder slipped down my inner thighs and clung to my skin like talc.

'OK, that's enough now,' I warned.

Alicia staggered back to the group, landing on her old tutor's lap. His hands closed over her body with trembling enthusiasm. She laughed wildly.

'Oh no it isn't!' she cried, and pushed the red-faced toff forward, handing him a banknote. She let Mr Wootten stroke her as she watched the proceedings.

My new suitor leered as he approached me and noisily snorted the coke from my inner thighs and mound. He then licked me messily with his cold beery tongue. Despite being pretty numb down there by now, it felt as if a slimy slug was crawling through my pubes and slithering on my clit. I gagged at the feel of him, yanking my hips back.

'Let me down, you bastards,' I spat, struggling.

Another man came up and started to lick at me, dispensing with the banknote altogether. He was tall and gangly with long ginger hair. He looked no older than eighteen, and his technique was eager and amateurish. His hot, unwelcome tongue snaked invasively into me and lapped at me incessantly. By chance he mashed his mouth into me at my most sensitive spot and my anger began to give way to a tingling sense of helpless arousal.

'Come on, everybody,' Alicia called out. 'You all have to have a lick of my horny little house guest. She loves it. She's got the wettest little pussy in London, haven't you, my dear?'

I moaned and scowled in response.

'All of you have to have a go,' Alicia cried. 'She isn't choosy. And the first one to make her come gets a prize.' The man at my crotch lifted up his flushed face for a moment.

'What prize?' he slurred.

'Me!' Alicia exclaimed and laughed.

'Oh, you bitch,' I muttered, my breath quickening.

Another man pushed away my current admirer and started to flick his long tongue against me like a lizard on speed. This one was older and more sober, and he worked away at me like a true expert. His greying hair was tied back in a ponytail. I looked down to see a look of serious intensity on his face as his tongue flapped away against me, going so fast that it blurred to the eye. My muscles started to tremble reluctantly, my body instinctively responding despite everything. I felt the hot moisture of arousal fill my cunt.

I looked around the room. The girls were staring at me jealously, their hands crushed down their knickers, lazily masturbating. There were little whimpers and groans of pleasure emanating from their glossed mouths. The men were leaning forward, craning to see, lining up to have a go. A few couples had started to make out, caressing each other, watching the show as they did so. Alicia wriggled around on Mr Wootten's lap as his hand stroked at her. Her eyes gleamed with the triumph of the situation.

After a few minutes, Ray came and politely asked the greying man to move on. He looked up at me.

'I can't pass up an opportunity like this,' he said huskily. 'The thought of doing this to you has been keeping me warm at nights.'

It was a kind of apology, but by now I had abandoned all resistance and was more interested in getting a good licking.

'You look kinda turned on,' he uttered, noting my flushed cheeks. Then he looked straight into my pussy and sighed deeply. 'Oh God, you're wet,' he murmured before plunging his big tongue inside me and fucking me slowly with it.

I felt his deep voice groan into me and creamed copiously on his face as he continued to lick in and out, in and out. He grasped my round buttocks in his big hands and pulled my crotch on to his face. His moustache tickled and rubbed my clit so wonderfully that I instantly gave up my initial aversion to it. From now on all my boyfriends will have to grow moustaches, I thought feverishly. I gyrated softly on its bristles as Ray licked me thoroughly. His tongue crept round to my anus and tickled my rosebud there, making me cry out. The girls were frigging faster now, I noticed, their hands going crazy down their panties. They were coming like dominos, cries relaying around the room. The boys were stroking themselves. Soon one came over to usurp Ray. He was a handsome youth with a full beard. I itched to have him go down on me; if a moustache could feel that good, what could a beard do to a girl? Ray stepped gallantly aside and my new lover licked his lips at the sight of my glistening pussy.

'Jesus, I can't wait to lick your cunt,' he crooned giddily and then lapped at me eagerly as he wanked himself off. Ray watched calmly as the boy slavered all over me. The beard was pleasantly itchy against my bottom and his tongue was wonderfully eager. He grunted rhythmically as his hand jerked away at his cock. I began to come but the boy beat me to it, spurting hot semen onto my foot and screaming into my pussy. His girlfriend petulantly pushed him away.

'That's typical of you, Gerald,' she scolded. 'The poor girl's bursting to come. Look at her mushy little pussy. Let me!'

And she had a go, licking at me like I was an expensive ice-cream, her blond head bobbing around between my legs. The sight of that was too much for some of the guys around us and I heard grunting orgasms echo across the room as they started to relieve themselves. Alicia was enjoying a series of climaxes of her own, courtesy of her old tutor. I saw his plump digits working away at her as she jolted and trembled in his lap.

Some of the other girls decided to get on the bandwagon and hurried, giggling, up to me, taking it in turns to trace their silky tongues through my pussy. They were subtler than the guys, and knew how to tickle my clit so that I wanted to wet myself. My legs were shaking like leaves on a tree and I was crying out for mercy. They had to hold me still with their sharp-nailed hands as they buried their faces in me. One girl in blond pigtails attached her pink mouth to my cunt and licked at my clit so cleverly that I soon was humping her face, crying out, moaning, writhing and screaming. She never lost her concentration and, as I watched her sweet pigtails bob between my thighs, I finally came. Her immaculately made-up face was treated to a bath of my grateful juices. She turned triumphantly to the room, her rosy cheeks smeared and sticky, her lips more glossed than ever.

'I win!' she announced, as I panted in my shackles, recovering slowly. My muscles were limp now, and my arousal trickled down my legs. 'She came on my face! I'm better at it than any of you!'

'Ooh, a winner,' Alicia cooed, and hooked arms with the girl. 'You want to claim your prize, Dixie?'

Soon they were kissing deeply, their hands roaming over each other's bodies. The men gathered around to watch while I hung, helplessly suspended. Surely she had had her fun now, I thought, and I could get down. Alicia had her hand in the girl's panties and was finger-fucking her. The girl whined and gasped in pleasure, falling back into the furry chair. I watched as they began to suck on each other's tits, sending the guys crazy. Although I was relieved not to be stared at any more, I was also feeling a little left out. I shifted uncomfortably in my chains. Dixie – who had given me such a great climax – was soon coming herself. Her loud cries demonstrated that quite theatrically for the benefit of a lot of the men watching. I looked around, clocking their delighted reactions.

After a while I noticed a man come into the room and stand surveying the scene. When he finally spotted me, he took me in, swollen pussy and all, and approached me deliberately. He was wearing a tuxedo and a long black cloak. He had a black mask on that covered half his face and his hair. Everyone else seemed to be glued to the Alicia-Dixie floorshow and didn't notice him.

He stood before me and eyed my body so intently that I felt goose pimples spring up. He ran his hands gently up my legs, caressing me behind the knees, which made me tingle and shiver. I was too weary to struggle. Then he focused between my legs, inhaled and sighed. He opened me up with his tender fingers and kissed my pussy gently, carefully, little kisses at first, then longer, deeper French kisses. His mouth was sweet and unhurried on me, his tongue muscular and sensitive. He tasted me and moaned, licked me and groaned, cupped my bottom and held my cunt steady against his mouth as he worked his magic on it.

I saw across the room that Alicia and Dixie were naked and locked into each other's bodies, grinding their genitals together wantonly, crying out little orgasms for the satisfaction of their audience. Their little white bottoms humped frantically. I preferred my intimate stranger and his delicious slow tongue. My pussy was warm and wet still, my body bristling with arousal. I pushed myself nastily into the stranger's mouth and he responded by licking me harder and sucking greedily on my clit.

'Oh, yes,' I sighed as I melted into him. 'Like that.' He pulled me closer and his tongue fucked me, his face crushed against my slippery mound. 'Oh yes!' I began to tremble again, rocking against him, unable to cope with so much pleasure. 'Oh God!' He found my clit with the hard tip of his tongue and began to flick it fast. 'Oh Jesus!' I shuddered against my bondage, my body out of control. My lust poured out of me and my orgasm came rapidly, taking me by surprise. I came tenderly in his mouth. Afterwards he lapped me clean, unwilling to stop. His tongue was still curious inside me.

'Please, I can't take any more,' I sighed as he licked me harder. 'Please!' His tongue pushed into me and wriggled deliciously. 'Oh, please!' He stopped and brushed his soft cheek on me, dousing himself in my scent.

'God, I want you,' he murmured and hearing his voice I realised suddenly that it was Tom. I looked down at him and our eyes met. I would recognise that beautiful green anywhere. He noted my recognition and started to lick away again. Knowing it was him made it all the more erotic. At the other end of the room, his sister was sucking one of the porn actors' cocks while Mr Wootten fucked her hard from behind. She was squealing in delight. All around us other couples were fucking like animals. Tom ate away at me and I started to climax again, desperate to come in his mouth, urgently wanting his cock inside me. I started to cry out, whimpering with pleasure.

'Oh, Tom,' I sighed, and he stepped up a gear at the sound of his name. I wished he would take the mask off so I could see that handsome face buried between my legs. 'Oh, I want to fuck you,' I panted and he groaned into me. 'Please let me down so I can fuck you,' I pleaded. His tongue penetrated me deeply and I sighed. 'Please!' He pulled his head away and pushed the mask off. Lust was etched in his face, glowing in his eyes.

'Not here,' he said. 'Come to my room.' He started to release me, little keys turning to unhook my feet. His face was never far from my burning wet slit and he couldn't resist the occasional lick.

'Please hurry,' I whispered urgently as he fumbled with the rope to pull me down.

Suddenly he was pushed away and flung to the ground. I thought for a moment that Alicia had spotted us but was appalled when I saw Jerome's face staring up at me instead, his jaw tight with anger. He looked like he was about to hit me, his fists clenched with rage. His black hair was even more dishevelled than usual.

'What the fuck is this?' he spat, indicating my bondage and my craven nakedness. 'Who the fuck is that?' He hadn't recognised Tom, who was staggering to his feet. 'No wonder you haven't bloody returned my calls.'

'Jerome, calm down,' I said quietly and with as much dignity as I could muster, suspended from the wall with my pussy on show and steaming with desire. 'Don't make a scene.'

'Don't make a scene? Don't make a fucking scene?'

He laughed incredulously and indicated the orgy that was going on around us. People were fucking and sucking, sighing and coming, wanking and watching. Men with men, women with women. A naked Alicia was gyrating wantonly on a fully clothed Mr Wootten's face. I had to admit, it didn't look good.

'And what are you? Pin the tail on the pissing donkey?' He reached out and grabbed my cunt roughly, his fingers sliding easily into its unashamed wetness. 'Oh, you little tart,' he muttered, not sure whether to be aroused or livid, and began to finger me roughly.

'Hey,' Tom protested and pushed Jerome away. 'Who the hell are you? This is a private party, you know.' Tom started to let me down, unpinning my skirt to cover my modesty.

'I'm her fucking boyfriend, you moron,' Jerome said, turning his fists to Tom.

It was ironically the first time Jerome had ever deigned to call me his girlfriend, and it was too little too late.

'Not any more you're not,' I remarked sharply. 'I'm a free agent, Jerome. Ring any bells?' He glared at me in disbelief. 'That's right,' I said, as Tom finally released my wrists. 'You're chucked.'

9

In the north of Brazil, deep in the Amazon, they have spells and voodoo – *Umbanda* – that my mother would often say had the power to cure absolutely anything. But as I lay in bed the next morning I was sure that there wasn't a potion in the world that could cope with the hangover I was suffering. It was the mother of all hangovers. The sun slicing through my curtains was as piercing as an SAS interrogation beam, the sound of my own breathing like thunder in my ears. I would have groaned but knew the noise of it would split my head open. I turned my face creakily on my pillow and squinted at my bedside clock: 1 p.m. Sitting next to the clock was a glass of water, cool, tall, clear. Was it a mirage? The desert of my mouth longed for it, but my limbs were too heavy to reach out. How had it got there? My brain whirred painfully until it stumbled on an image: Tom, in his black cloak, laying me on the bed, kissing me on the cheek; Tom putting the water there and making me promise to drink it. Then a load of other memories flooded my mind – oh, my God, last night. The groan came then, involuntarily.

Jerome's anger had not abated easily, I recalled. At one point I thought he was going to knock Tom out, his fists clenched white with fury. But I had countered him with a candid, cocktail-fuelled speech on how badly he had treated me, quoting Ruby extensively on the subject of his general crapness. Ah, yes; then he had claimed that Ruby just had the hots for him. That was when I had started to lose it; half laughing and half shouting, not able to believe his arrogance. And all the time my body urging me to whisk Tom upstairs and finish what we had started, what had been brewing for days. Finally Alicia had come over and charmed Jerome into some kind of trance-like submission, her fluttering eyelashes dazzling like butterfly wings. He was practically drooling over her.

That had been the final straw, as I seemed to recall. That's when I saw red. I recollected having a handful of his hair in my fist and perhaps punching him across the cheekbone. Christ, I must have been drunk! I bravely reached for the water and took a tentative sip. I could feel it cleansing my insides and clarifying my mind. I recalled begging Tom to stay in my room with me, but sadly he had been a gentleman, insisting that I was too drunk. 'I don't want to take advantage,' he had said. Even in my drunken stupor I had found that ridiculous. He hadn't hesitated in taking advantage of my being suspended in bondage at the party. Oh no, the bondage! The memory of Alicia's little trick with the handcuffs was too much for me and I buried my face in the pillow.

Three hours later, hunger got the better of me. After a bath and some cleverly applied make-up, I looked presentable enough to venture downstairs in search of afternoon tea, although my craving was for a bacon sandwich with lots of ketchup. On the stairs I could hear Alicia's tinkling laugh and the hopeful clatter of crockery. Mouth watering and eyes bleary, I followed it through to the dining room. They didn't spot me immediately, so for a few seconds I had an uncensored vision of Alicia sitting astride my ex-boyfriend, feeding him strawberries. Jerome was lapping up the attention along with the whipped cream, his head hanging back. They giggled like kids as she wriggled around on his lap and teased him with the fruit, making him strain forward to catch it in his mouth, or holding it between her teeth and sneaking a kiss when he bit into it. It was all quite sickening and smug. Suddenly Jerome spotted me and flinched guiltily.

'Oh, relax,' I muttered wearily, my headache giving me a deadpan voice. 'Don't mind me, I'm just after food.'

Alicia got up and turned to me, looking more radiant than ever. How had she managed that?

'Do help yourself,' she said in her best wonderful-hostess voice. 'There's tea, coffee, scones, jam, toast, sandwiches . . .'

She trailed off as I sat silently at the table, unashamedly helping myself to everything. My appetite knew no bounds, and didn't seem to mind any combination of foods.

'My, you are hungry,' Alicia commented wryly as I took an enormous bite of a salmon and cream cheese bagel.

'Mhm.' Even if I had wanted to make conversation with the woman, my mouth was too full to speak. There was a stiff silence.

'Well, this is an awkward situation,' Jerome said tightly.

I let out an ironic guffaw, crumbs spraying across the table. I didn't care.

'I could think of worse,' I muttered, shooting a look at Alicia. She was a picture of disingenuous loveliness.

'Oh, you mean the silly game last night?' she smiled. 'Just a bit of fun, Jo. I knew you could take it.'

I grunted, slurping down a slug of hot sweet tea.

'Oh dear,' she laughed. 'I think someone overdid it on the pink cocktails. They're lethal.'

She leant over and whispered something in Jerome's ear. By the sleazy look on his face, I could guess it was something lascivious. He furtively put his arm around her narrow shoulders, tickling her neck. She stifled a giggle like a schoolgirl in front of her mother. I began to realise, appalled, that my presence was some kind of titillation to them. I represented the taboo in their relationship, and there was nothing either of them liked more than breaking taboos. I cleared my throat.

'Don't worry about me, you two,' I said breezily. 'You go ahead. I've dumped him. You can have him. Good luck to you.' I directed this at Alicia, but realised it applied just as much to Jerome. 'Good luck to you too, actually,' I smiled at him. 'You're going to need it.'

They looked at me nervously, unsure how to play the situation. I was surprised at how fine I was with the fact that they had obviously been shagging all night and were now enjoying rubbing my face in it. They glanced at each other. 'Are there any strawberries left or have you used them all up in your clichéd pseudo-erotic flirting?' I asked bluntly.

Jerome looked embarrassed.

'Jo!' he scolded.

'Oh, don't be such a girl.' He really was pathetic, I noticed for the first time. He seemed overawed by Alicia's class and breeding, chastising me as if we were having tea with the queen. Even his clothes had changed. Gone the leathers and rough 70s-style threads. Now he sported crisp chinos and a white linen shirt. I couldn't be bothered to look under the table, but fully expected him to be wearing deck shoes. I chuckled to myself as I tucked into a fruit scone piled with butter.

'So,' he said eventually. 'How's the article?'

'Great.' I was damned if I was going to sit there having a cosy work chat with him. Alicia leant forward, turning on the charm.

'Is there going to be a lot about me in it?' she beamed.

'No.' I reached across the table. 'Is this apricot jam? Yum, my favourite.'

Alicia's blue eyes went all steely, the smile fixed on her pretty face.

'I see,' she said. 'Then what *are* you going to write about?'

I looked at her with a steady gaze, unhurriedly swallowing my mouthful.

'Daphne, of course,' I said. 'And Tom. If he'll let me.' I knew that would hurt. She widened her eyes and let out a sharp, shrill laugh.

'Tom?!'

'Yes, Tom.' I poured myself more tea. 'You see, I don't know how much old Jezzer here has told you about our little operation. Probably not a lot, he isn't a great conversationalist.' He scowled at me. 'But *A Tempo* is really a magazine about talent. Musical talent.' I took a sip. 'I suggest – if you are desperate to get your face into a mag somewhere – that you try the society columns of *Harpers and Queen* or *Horse and Hound*. You can tell them about all your pretty dresses and stable-hands and things.' Her mouth fell open and she made a funny noise. She may even have muttered 'Cheek'. I don't know, I wasn't concentrating. I was just thinking how my headache had miraculously disappeared.

I found Tom sitting at the far end of the grounds, where a small brook snaked its way along the edge of the woods. He was perched on a log, throwing stones into the gushing water. As I approached him, I noticed how effortlessly handsome he looked in his simple cotton shirt and dark blue jeans. The sun was dappled in his blonde hair. He was deep in thought, not seeing me until I was very close by and the twigs cracked under my feet. He looked up and smiled warmly.

'Hey,' he said, 'how are you?'

I thought about this.

'Hung over,' I began. 'Embarrassed. Disappointed. But mostly hung over.'

'Me, too.'

I sat next to him on the log and tossed a couple of pebbles in for good measure.

'I was just thinking about you,' he said.

My heart did a little leap, although something in his tone told me it wasn't all going to be hearts and flowers.

'Anything in particular?'

He squinted into the sun.

'Well, for a start, I was wondering what you were ever doing with that prat.'

I laughed.

'I mean, the haircut for a start.'

'I know,' I said with a sigh. 'And now your sister has taken up with him.' I knew I sounded a little bitter at this and he looked at me sharply, wondering if I still had feelings for Jerome.

'It won't last,' he commented, either to comfort me or himself. I don't think he relished the idea of his sister embroiled with a has-been rock star.

'I don't care, Tom.'

'Good.' He took my hand. 'Then I was thinking of you last night, how you looked in that beautiful gold dress, like a vision.'

'Yeah, I bet.' I winced at the thought of myself hanging off the wall with my rude bits on show.

'Honestly. I've never seen anything sexier in my life.' He looked at me intently for a moment and bent over to kiss me, his warm lips melting onto mine like butter. I pulled away slightly.

'Really?' He nodded and kissed me again, sexily.

Things were looking up. He broke away and rested his forehead on mine, talking into my cheek.

'And then I was thinking, I don't want to botch this one up.'

I could feel a big letdown coming on.

'Meaning?' I prompted.

'Meaning, I obviously have to sort things out here. I don't want my sister or my situation to jeopardise what you and I could have.' He stroked my hair. 'I don't want to rush in and ruin it. And my sister needs to cool off a bit. So I've arranged to go and visit a mate in Paris for a week or so. To get my head around things.'

I thought about this. Was it just another little victory for Alicia?

'You're not just trying to chuck me in a really crap way are you?' I asked softly.

He pulled back and stared at me, his green eyes smiling.

'Chuck you?' he repeated. 'Does that mean we're "going out"?'

I laughed, his awkward terminology making me feel like an insecure teenager.

'I don't know,' I sniggered. 'Are we?'

'I hope so,' he replied seriously and kissed me again – very much like a grown-up, so that my knees trembled and my body longed to open up to him.

Oh God, I thought, I hope he sorts it out soon. His arms surrounded me and he pulled me against him.

'I don't want to go, but if I stay here we're just going to get caught up in the momentum,' he said.

'True.' I mused on how exciting the momentum could be. 'When are you leaving?'

'This afternoon.' He took my hand. 'Look, Jo, I know it's frustrating, but you know it's definitely going to be worth the wait.'

It was as if he had read my mind.

10

That evening we were treated to another of Alicia's ostentatious dinner invitations. I was sitting at my desk, ostensibly writing my article but actually day-dreaming about Tom, when the gilt paper slid under my door. I sighed and stomped over to get it, reading the script sullenly: 'Alicia Hathaway requests your company at dinner tonight. Dress: smart. 8 p.m., dining room.' I snorted with laughter at the preten-tiousness of it, realising the full extent of Alicia's sense of fantasy about herself. The role she was playing as the cultured, enchanting hostess – the dazzling slice of old England – had gone to her head. I wondered if she lived in the real world at all, or whether her whole life was a childlike game of dressing up and masks.

This time I knew better than to try to compete with Alicia in the clothing stakes. I had been tripped up by that before. I opted for a simple combination of tight jeans and a clingy white T-shirt; admittedly the kind that used to drive Jerome wild. I left my hair loose. I surveyed my reflection critically in my bedroom mir-ror. Even though I had no interest in Jerome now, I still wanted him to know what he was missing. I looked satisfyingly like a just-got-out-of-bed rock chick. Taking a deep breath I sauntered down the stairs, determined to be cool and witty tonight, and not let the meal reduce itself into a slanging match with my ex.

As I walked in to the room, I saw Ollie was the only

one there. He was sitting at the table, drumming out a rhythm with his knife and fork. When I came in, he looked up, startled. Then he laughed at his own jumpiness. I smiled and joined him reluctantly at the table. I had never had much to say to Ollie, and he made me vaguely uneasy. We avoided each other's eyes for a while as he continued his nervous drumming.

'Wonder where the others are,' I said eventually.

'Late,' he replied. 'I thought you English were sticklers for manners.'

'Ah, yes, but it's the lady's prerogative to be a little late,' I corrected him. 'I'm sure Alicia adheres very strictly to that rule.'

'Too busy giving it to her new man,' Ollie retorted charmlessly.

I saw from the narrowing of his beady little eyes that there was some resentment in that statement. Surely he hadn't picked our hostess out for himself? I was intrigued.

'Probably. I think she could do better,' I said leadingly.

'Of course she could,' he snapped. 'She's hot. Hot hot hot. And I know for a fact that she loves sex. I've seen them before – sex addicts. And she fits the bill. I don't think she needs a guy like him. I think she's compromising.' He was warming to his theme, his eyes darting round the room a little as he spoke. 'You know, she's come on to me so many times, I've lost count,' he said confidentially. 'I mean, she's insatiable.'

I nodded.

He suddenly leant forward and eyed me intently.

'You,' he said. 'You're a good-looking woman, you know that?'

'Thanks,' I replied flatly at his half-hearted compliment.

'But you've got your feet on the ground. Not like

her. You can take care of yourself.' He thought for a moment.

I wondered where this conversation was going.

'How would you like to be in a movie?'

I let out a laugh, more at his clichéd chat-up than the idea of me on the silver screen, but he misinterpreted my reaction.

'No, baby. I mean it. You've got what it takes.'

'Right.'

'I've got contacts,' he said. He was pathetic, I decided, the sweat gluing his hair to his forehead, churning out the kind of lines that only a teenage wannabe would fall for. 'I've got the brains, you've got the looks. And the breasts!' he sighed as he gawped at my tits. There was a silence as I contemplate hitting him.

'Look, babe, you don't have to make a decision now. But let me know, OK?'

I looked at him with an even gaze.

'Opportunities like this don't come along all the time,' he said emphatically. 'And you're not getting any younger. Soon you'll be thirty. Then you can forget about it.' He sat back in his chair with a smug smirk plastered on his chubby face, obviously satisfied that he had made a good argument.

Luckily at that moment Ray and Jerome came in, otherwise I would have definitely taken a swing for him.

I hadn't seen Ray since the party and he looked at me a little sheepishly. I remembered with a sudden twinge the melting sensation of his bristling moustache against my clit the night before. Now he was the perfect gentleman again, sitting beside me and kissing me lightly on the cheek. Jerome took a spot opposite and we scowled at each other a little.

'How are you, gorgeous?' Ray whispered.

'It's been an interesting twenty-four hours,' I replied.

'That's an understatement,' we heard Jerome mutter. 'Little tart.'

'I think I owe you an apology ...' Ray began.

'Forget it,' I said, desperate to get off the subject of the previous night. It was bad enough that a group of people had witnessed me suspended and naked and dripping with lust, but that it should be incorporated in our polite dinner chit-chat was too much. Ray got the hint and changed the subject.

'So, what were you and Ollie discussing?' he asked brusquely. 'I hope he wasn't leading you astray?'

It was jokingly meant, but I noted a glimmer of warning in Ray's cool eyes. Ollie shifted in his seat.

'No, he was just kindly informing me that when I hit thirty I'll be past it,' I smiled. 'Which is bad news for everyone else at this table,' I commented, looking at the trio of men before me. Ray was easily in his forties and Jerome and Ollie were getting there.

'It's different for men!' Ollie exclaimed and I gave him a wry smile. I saw he was devoid of irony. 'It's true. We get better looking as we get older.'

'Well, you must have started out pretty rough then,' I blurted out cruelly. Sometimes my sharp tongue got the better of me. Luckily Ray chuckled next to me.

'That's good,' he laughed, continuing the joke. 'By the time Ollie's seventy he might be a half-way decent-looking fella!'

Ollie looked less than amused and recommenced his incessant table drumming. Perhaps he was ready for his next fix, I pondered. I could see the rhythm driving Jerome mad.

'Ollie, if you want drumming lessons, Jez is your man,' I said in an attempt to shame him into silence. 'He plays the kit brilliantly, don't you? Have you heard of Black Heart?' Ollie looked blank but Ray made noises of recognition. 'Well, Jez here was their frontman.'

'I'm impressed,' Ray said.

'I also played the kit on two of our hit records,' Jerome continued. '*Angel Cake* and *In Deep Water*.'

I began to regret opening up the subject of Jerome's past as he proceeded to boast about his achievements, delighted to have a new audience for his endless anecdotes. When Alicia finally deigned to come down, I was actually quite pleased to see her.

'Darlings,' she said from the doorway. Tonight she had chosen to be sexy. She wore a layered antique lace dress, which hugged her figure down to the knee. Underneath she was absolutely naked. The layers of material were almost see-through and you could just make out the dark peaks of her nipples and the neat shape of her bush. She had scraped her hair up off her face in a severe style that accentuated her sharp bone structure and azure eyes. On her feet she wore soft camel leather knee-high boots with high-heels, which gave her movements a sassy edge. The men fell silent as she walked in.

'Oh, don't stop your conversation on my account,' she beamed. 'I love to hear about Jerome's rock and roll years!'

She came and sat next to him and I couldn't help but bristle as she ran her hand possessively over his neck.

'Oh yeah, wild times, wild times.' Jerome laid his hand on Alicia's lap under the table. I couldn't see from where I was, but by the delirious look on her face he was fondling her intimately as he spoke. 'Half the time we were so out of it we didn't know what we were doing. The parties were incredible.'

'I'll bet you had some female admirers,' Ray prompted.

'Oh, God, don't get him started on that,' I groaned. 'We'll be here all night.'

Jerome ignored me, eager to talk about his glory days.

'Shit, yes. We had girls throwing themselves at us, mate. The amazing thing was, they were wet even before you had time to take off their panties. They were all so excited just to be in the room with you.'

Ollie sighed at the idea of this. It was obviously something that was never going to happen with him.

'One girl came just because I whispered something in her ear once. I didn't even have a hand on her. It was just the vibration of my voice in her ear!' he vaunted. I had heard many versions of that story before and my reaction was jaded, but Alicia wriggled a little, her cheeks flushed. 'But I'm sure we've all got our sexy stories to tell,' Jerome continued generously.

He looked at me and I wondered if I did compare to the people at the table: two porn kings, a nymphomaniac and a rock star. Suddenly I longed for Tom to be there; a rock of sanity in this crazy collection of people.

'I've *only* got sexy stories,' Alicia declared. 'I just seem to attract people. I always have done. And I'm very ... open.' She said this word as if it was the dirtiest in the English language and Jerome grinned suggestively at her when she said it.

'So we saw with your little old tutor,' I commented, wondering if Jerome was aware of the extent of Alicia's conquests. 'Mr Wootten, wasn't it?' Alicia sighed as if remembering a fine wine.

'Ah yes, Rory,' she purred. 'He, of course, awakened my libido.'

'Quite a can of worms,' I muttered.

'Well, we were cooped up in that musty library all day talking about kings of England and Latin declensions. Of course a girl's mind was going to wander. And my body had long been ripe for the plucking, I can tell you. Tom had gone away to school, Papa was in South America and Mama had already passed away, so it was just Rory and me. Just the two of us stuck in this house all day. What red-blooded man wouldn't have taken the opportunity to teach me a few things about the facts of life as well as all that boring rubbish I've never even used?'

'Isn't that illegal?' I asked coldly.

'Oh, silly girl. I was sixteen!' Alicia exclaimed and then looked a little doubtful. 'I'm sure I was. Anyway, I was a very developed girl. And we didn't go all the way – not at first anyway. That came a little later, in the "special room".' She flashed me one of her teasing blue stares. 'You know the one, Jo. You've been seen "hanging around" there yourself!' She laughed uproariously at her own lame pun. I tutted and Ray squeezed my thigh good naturedly.

'What did you get up to?' he asked Alicia, taking the heat off me. Ray's eyes twinkled with aroused curiosity as he leant across the table. 'Tell us. Paint a picture.'

'Are you really interested?' Alicia looked around at our expectant faces. Even I was intrigued. 'Well, it all kicked off when we started reading literature with erotic content: *Wuthering Heights*, *Lady Chatterley's Lover*, that sort of thing. We would sit in that room all day, poring over these sexually charged stories and my girlish mind would simply wander naughtily. I think he caught me jigging around a few times, pressing my thighs together. I knew I was having an effect on him – girls of any age know how powerful they are, gentlemen, that's how we wrap our own daddies around our little fingers – so I started to wear my skirts a little shorter and my shirt buttons a little undone. He began to pay compliments to me. He told me I had lovely smooth skin, pretty pert breasts –'

'You still do,' murmured Jerome, clearly turned on by this schoolgirl image of Alicia.

I saw his arm move and knew he was still caressing Alicia intimately as she spoke.

'Then, one day, he brought the Nabokov book, *Lolita*, into class. Oh my word!' she cried, her cheeks getting rosier by the second. 'All the stuff about this little nymphet driving the older man to distraction almost made me wet myself. We read it aloud to each other and I would enact the poses described in the book. I used to lean back and let Mr Wootten have a full, frank view of my little white panties. Soon, he was so frustrated and desperate that it would have been cruel not to let him fondle me a little. To start with he just played with my little breasts. He would diddle my nipples so sweetly. He liked it best when I read out certain passages to him while he played with them. I would sit there with my shirt open – no bra – and let him feel me quite happily. Of course my panties were flooded, but I didn't know what to do about it at that age. Usually I got too aroused to continue, especially when Mr Wootten would lick my nipples – ooh, I loved that!' She wriggled at the memory and Jerome brushed his spare hand across her breasts, her nipples like bullets. 'The tingling drove me to distraction!'

'Go on,' Ray whispered hoarsely.

'Well, one day I told him how I always got a strange aching in my intimate place whenever he played with me like that. I said my panties were always gooey when I took them off at night after he had been teasing me in the day. Oh, his face! I think the idea of my slippery little slit was almost too much for him.'

I looked around the room. The guys were all listening open mouthed. The idea was obviously almost too much for them too. My own pussy was moistening at the story.

'He told me he could cure me of the aching, if I wanted him to. I pleaded with him to make it better. So, that day, after he had played with my nipples for a while – I was reading his favourite passage in the book – he let his hand crawl up my skirt and pressed his thumb against me through my underwear. Oh! I thought I had died and gone to heaven! I whined and panted and squirmed as he slipped his hands under the elastic of my knickers and discovered my virgin pussy. I tried to keep reading but my voice was getting higher and higher. I couldn't get my breath. I didn't know what he was doing to me but before long I had dropped the book to the floor and was crying out in ecstasy. All those weeks of being teased and aroused flooded out of me in one big orgasm. Oh!'

Jerome was massaging her faster now, I could see from the movement of his arm.

'Oh! Oh yes!'

We all watched as Alicia went beetroot red, her nipples straining through her dress. Her voice was trembling now.

'And then one day he licked me. It was such a shock. I was so excited. He pulled off my knickers and started to lap away at me like an eager Alsatian! Oh! I was so excited! Oh God!'

Her head fell back as she started to lose control. I saw Ray slowly stroke himself as he watched and I wanted to do the same.

'Oh, my poor little pussy didn't know what had hit

it! I was squealing and writhing on his face. I didn't care if he could breathe.' Alicia struggled on with her anecdote, panting for air. 'Then, every day, he would dive down there and lick me before lessons. Oh yes! Every day we would start with an amazing session. It was the only way I could concentrate for the rest of the day. Sometimes I would get so horny he would have to lick me three or four times a day. He couldn't get enough. I couldn't get enough. Oh! Oh God!' She leant right back now, her legs splayed. Jerome's hand was going wild in her lap. We could all hear the squelching evidence of her arousal.

'Then, when he taught me how to suck his cock, I thought that was the horniest thing I'd ever done. Oh! Oh the taste of it! Oh! I loved to suck it! Yes!'

Finally she came, her body stiffening and her breath caught in her ribcage. Jerome gazed at her until her body relaxed again. Her eyes were gleaming and her cheeks red as she came back to her senses. She smiled at us all.

'Sorry about that. I get quite carried away,' she said. 'Shall we eat?'

Over the next few days the relationship between my ex and Alicia grew more cloying and claustrophobic, and it became harder to avoid them. Alicia would always have him locked away in her chamber, or she would be openly riding him in the grounds. Occasionally I would come down for food and discover them feasting on each other in the dining room. Once I came into my own bedroom to discover them fucking doggy-style on my bed, with Alicia wearing one of my dresses. I bumped into Kieran who complained that his mistress was no longer interested in Harry and him except to make up a foursome with her new boyfriend.

'You know what they say,' he said. 'Three's a crowd but four's just downright ridiculous.'

'A logistical nightmare,' I agreed, secretly impressed by Alicia's sexual ambition. 'I mean, what would she do with you all?'

'Oh, she had it all worked out,' he explained. 'Me in her mouth, Harry in her cunt and the new guy up her arse. She's desperate to do it. Desperate! She even begged.'

He looked a little worried. After all, his job relied on him not rubbing Alicia up the wrong way. I assured him that I couldn't imagine Jerome indulging in sex games with two other men. He sighed with relief.

'I don't suppose you could be persuaded back into our bed?' he asked. 'We loved fucking you.'

I was tempted, but I decided to keep my nose (and other parts) clean. After all, I was in love with the master of the house.

Sometimes, when the article wasn't going too well, I would creep up to Tom's bedroom and roll in his sheets, basking in the sweet smell of him. I would sit at the piano and tinkle on the keys, daydreaming about his long fingers and imagining us in all kinds of lewd situations. One day, just as I was mastering 'Chopsticks', the door opened. I swung round, my heart in my mouth. Tom had come home! But the man who came in wasn't Tom – it was Jerome.

'Oh, it's you,' I said gracelessly. He gave me an awkward smile and edged his way into the room. He looked around a bit.

'Doesn't like clutter, does he?' he remarked, somehow making it sound like an insult.

I bashed away at the keys, hoping my ex would get the hint and leave. He didn't.

'A bit of a cold fish, is he?'

I finally turned round in exasperation.

'Do you have a point, Jerome?' I demanded. He raised an eyebrow at me and sat on the edge of Tom's bed. 'Shouldn't you be off sticking things into your little playmate? I'm sure she's missing you.'

He sighed smugly.

'Jealous, Josephina?'

'Ha!' I tried to sound as derisory as possible and returned to the piano, clunking away angrily. 'I don't think your socially crippled little friend would like you treating his prize instrument like that,' Jerome said snidely and I stopped.

I turned to Jerome, who was leaning back now, Tom's teddy crushed under his elbow. I got up and extricated the toy from him.

'Ah, sweet.' As I leant over he grabbed my arm, holding me close to him for a moment. 'Does he satisfy you?' he whispered. I yanked myself free. 'Does he make you come like I did?'

'Let's not get delusional,' I retorted. 'The sex was OK with us, but I've had better.'

I didn't want to let on that Tom and I hadn't got that far yet.

Jerome smirked.

'Oh, yeah? Well, Alicia says I'm the best,' he bragged. 'She can't keep her hands off me.'

'I'd noticed.'

The vain smile faded from his face slightly and he sat up. He put his head in his hands.

'She's quite ... demanding,' he said eventually.

I was confused. I thought he'd come up purely to rub my nose in it but, looking at him, I could now see that he actually wanted to talk.

'I know. I thought that's what you liked about her?' I said. 'A confident little nympho; what could be better?'

Jerome grimaced.

'Yeah, I'm not complaining ...' He trailed off.

I waited for the 'but'.

'It's just – and I never thought I'd hear myself say this but – sometimes you want straight sex, you know?'

'As opposed to gay sex?' I asked, bemused.

'No! As opposed to kinky sex.' He shrugged. 'I mean, I'm all for a bit of deviation. You know that.'

I nodded sagely.

'But she's got this unquenchable desire to make sex a bit pervy. She asked me if I'd have a foursome with her stable-hands, for fuck's sake!'

'I know.' I couldn't resist a smile.

'Then she wants me to star in a porno film Ray and Ollie are making. She loves to do it in front of a camera. I mean, I obliged. Of course, it was fucking sexy.' He got out a fag and lit up. I tutted and went over to open Tom's windows emphatically. 'But she's crazy. She doesn't know when to stop. She wants me to tie her up, to fuck her with this huge vibrator, to spank her. She wants me to chase her through the grounds and ravish her. She wants me to take her roughly up against a tree. She got me to do it with her while she was going down on one of those porno actresses. It was wonderful at first but now ...'

'You just want a good old-fashioned shag?'

'I guess.' He inhaled deeply on his cigarette. 'I'm a bit tired, that's all.' He looked at me with pleading puppy eyes. 'We used to have great sex, didn't we? We didn't need toys or shackles.'

I laughed at his deflated face.

'You've just had too much of a good thing,' I commented. 'And now I think you should go back down and see if Alicia needs sating again. It's been at least twenty minutes.'

He smiled and rose to his feet.

'You're a great chick, you know that?' he said and walked to the door. Suddenly he turned back to me. 'Don't suppose you'd be interested in a threesome, would you?'

I gasped at his cheek and threw the teddy at him in disgust.

'Oh, well. I had to try.'

After he'd gone I shut Tom's window and made his bed. The charged atmosphere at Hathaway Hall suddenly seemed stifling and unhealthy. I was finding it harder and harder to write without being consumed by daydreams or interrupted by sounds of compulsive sex coming from down the corridor. With Tom gone there was nothing left to keep me here. I needed a change of scenery. I decided it was time to leave.

I glanced around my room for the last time, feeling a tug of regret that I had never got to make love in my fantasy bed. My bags were packed and my taxi booked. The idea of going back to London filled me with relief. It was a crazy city at times, but at least you knew where you stood with the nutters shouting on the pavements. At Hathaway Hall it seemed the dangerous people came in the prettiest packages.

My research was pretty much done and I had decided on an angle for the piece. I was determined to showcase Tom Hathaway, using Daphne's newly discovered diaries as a lead in. I didn't think the general public really needed to know about Alicia's debauched lifestyle. I struggled through my door laden with a laptop, briefcase and suitcase and made my way along the corridor.

As I passed Alicia's room, I heard the familiar tones of Jerome in the throes of sexual passion. From the buzzing and clinking and whipping sounds echoing through the hall I guessed she was making full use of her Pandora's box of sex toys, and Jerome seemed to be enjoying it. Obviously he had got over his doubts about the sex. The floorboards creaked as I passed by and Alicia began to screech out a histrionic orgasm for my benefit. 'Yes! There! There!' she cried, chains clinking wildly. He grunted out a response. I shrugged and walked down the stairs, her cries ringing behind me. She was clearly enjoying her moment of triumph, but I suspected it would be short-lived. Jerome had never wanted to be one of many.

The taxi arrived and I watched the Hall disappear out of the back window, hoping that the next time I saw it life would be less complicated.

'You sure you've got everything, love?' the cab driver asked as we reached the end of the drive. 'Don't want to leave anything behind. Things tend to get lost in big old places like that.'

'That's true,' I replied absently, thinking of Tom. I wondered where he was now. He always struck me as a little lost. 'Well, if I have I'll just come back for it.'

11

'This is good.' Ruby put down the article and took a swig of her gin and tonic. 'Really good.' I let out a heavy sigh of relief and took the pages back before she dribbled salad dressing on them, slipping them carefully into a plastic wallet. Ruby was always a clever and honest judge of my work and, even though she knew little about the music scene, she had one of those minds that can adapt itself to anything. She was wasted in her PR company. 'I love the stuff about different kinds of inheritance: looks, talent, music. How it all mutates from generation to generation like Chinese whispers.'

'Not too cruel about Alicia?' I asked tentatively.

She snorted and flashed her black eyes.

'Girl, you could have *ripped* into her. I would have done.'

I had thought about it, but had opted for a subtler form of criticism, writing about how Alicia's obsession with her great-grandmother led her to emulate certain self-destructive traits, while Tom's had led him to write great music. 'Well, I suppose she's lumbered with Jerome,' Ruby continued, tearing off a hunk of bread and dipping it in her plate. 'That's punishment enough.'

I laughed, imagining the two of them together. I knew they would have a honeymoon period of constant and experimental shagging – after all, they both had a high sex drive – but beyond that I couldn't imagine a less compatible pairing. It had been nearly a week since I had left them, so I expected that the sheen was already fading from the relationship.

'Good,' I said. 'I'll submit it to Jerome when he can be bothered to tear himself away from the bitch and come back into the office. I bet things are chaotic there, he's been away for so long.'

'There's just one thing,' Ruby interrupted, leaning forward. 'It's just a niggle really.'

'Go on.'

'It's just ... you describe these new pieces by Tom so well, it makes me want to go out and buy them. I want to hear them. I want to get a real flavour of the music. But I can't.' She looked at me directly. 'It's going to piss people off.' I thought about this for a moment, feeling a little defensive but knowing she was right.

'I suppose,' I said eventually. 'Short of signing him up to a record company, what can I do, though?'

We sat thinking, Ruby glugging down her drink like a baby with a bottle, me gnawing on the bread.

'You say Jerome wants this article to be an attention-grabbing thing?' she said eventually.

'Yes. Sales are low. We need a boost.'

I could see her brain ticking away behind her sharp eyes as she slipped into work mode. This was executive Ruby: quick thinking, creative, fast.

'Well, when we want to get attention for a product or even a person, we always do it by giving away freebies,' she thought aloud. 'People love nothing more than a freebie. Something for nothing.'

'OK,' I pondered. 'But what could we give away? A free coaster set depicting Hathaway Hall? A free diary?'

She sucked her teeth at me and I felt like the dunce in class.

'No, the music, sweetheart,' she said. 'That's the whole point.'

'What, you mean record a CD to include in the

publication?' I could imagine Jerome's reaction to something so outrageously expensive.

'Yeah, just a mini one. A couple of tracks, or movements, or whatever they call them.' She read my dubious expression. 'Honey, you gotta give a little away to get a lot back. I can find you a studio, no probs. A couple of my clients owe me favours. And if this guy Tom is as talented as you make out, he'll be in and out in no time. No session musicians, just him and his piano.' She eyed me warmly, knowing how fond I had become of Tom. 'And who knows, Jo, he might get a contract out of it at the end of the day. It'd mean you get to be his knight in shining armour. Sorted.' She drained her glass triumphantly and grinned. 'Well, as I've been sitting here doing your job for you, I guess lunch is on you,' she winked.

The office was its usual hive of chaotic non-industry: Corinne speaking to some relative in New Zealand, Sven trying to change the toner in the photocopier. They both looked up at me with slightly desperate, claustrophobic expressions when I walked through the door, as if they were the last two survivors on *Big Brother* and I had come to release them. Sven's ash-blond locks were even more dishevelled than when I had left, and his pale eyes were heavily ringed with lack of sleep.

'Hi guys,' I said cheerfully, slapping my article down on my desk. 'I'm back. What's new?' Sven shrugged and lost control of his task, sending a sooty shower of toner down his khaki trousers.

'Typical,' he muttered, trying to smile. Corinne wrapped up her conversation with a cursory, 'Mum, I've got to go!' and turned to me accusingly, pointing a well-manicured nail in my direction.

'Where the hell have you been?' she snapped. 'It's been mad here, hasn't it, Sven?'

He nodded wearily.

'We're up against it. We desperately need that article you've been working on. And Jerome's disappeared off the face of the earth.'

'Yeah, he's kind of "in meetings" with Alicia Hathaway,' I replied pointedly, remembering Corinne's many fob-offs on the phone. She was obviously too thick-skinned to get the dig.

'Well, I wish he'd bloody come back. I've got the parent company on the phone from New York every two minutes wanting to speak to him, I've got deadlines, I've got advertising queries . . .' She pulled at her cropped hair. 'Who's this Alicia, anyway?' she continued. 'I thought you and Jerome were . . .?' she trailed off, realising that our relationship hadn't exactly been common knowledge.

Sven looked up, curious.

'What gave you that idea?' I asked.

She floundered.

'Well . . . I don't know. Just, he was always a bit odd around you. And . . .' She obviously had more to tell, her eyes darting around as if searching for an escape route.

'What?'

'While you were away he had a lot of appointments with someone and he asked me not to tell you.' She shrugged guiltily. 'Sorry, but I didn't know what to do. I was sort of hoping you'd suss it out anyway and come back.' That explained all her ultra-lame excuses, I thought, my anger with Jerome coming back to life.

'I see. And who were these appointments with?' I demanded as calmly as I could. Corinne swallowed before replying.

'His wife.' This was ridiculous. I let out a belly laugh

and came and sat on Corinne's desk. Jerome had told me all about his silly relationship with his ex-wife, a seventeen-year-old groupie he'd drunkenly agreed to marry ten years ago. It had lasted two years and she had gone back to America with a chip on her shoulder and a huge divorce settlement. That was why he was sometimes a bit tight with money, he'd told me. He was still recovering from that legal battle.

'No, you must be mistaken,' I smiled. 'He's divorced. She lives in Boston.'

Sven looked uncomfortable and pretended to be engrossed in changing the water on the cooler.

'Doesn't she?'

Corinne shook her head slowly.

'They're just separated,' she grimaced. 'And that's Boston, Lincolnshire. Not Massachusetts. Sorry Jo.'

I couldn't believe his cheek.

'If it's any consolation their reunion didn't last long, just on and off from the time you went to Brazil till last week or so.'

It was no consolation. I marched into his office and slammed the door, glaring at his things. His pens, his Dictaphone, his ridiculous gold discs covering the walls all angered me beyond belief. My blood started to race through my body and I found myself reaching out to smash everything in sight. That's when the phone rang, and I started out of my fury, staring at it. I picked it up.

'It's me,' came Corinne's voice. 'Just wanted to say – please don't break anything. A big cheese from the New York office is coming over next week to do an appraisal and they've frozen our funds until then. Can't afford any broken windows. Thanks, bye.'

I looked at her through Jerome's window and saw myself reflected, standing with one of his brass awards like a weapon in my clenched fist. We both smiled then laughed, wrenching, hard laughs. Only Sven looked a little scared, as if preparing to duck. I came back into the main office, still holding the statuette.

'Be warned, Sven. A woman scorned,' I joked. His face cracked into a relieved smile. He had an attractive face, I noticed, lined in all the right places. 'Right,' I said, getting my bags and waving the brass figure. 'I'm off to the pub. Anybody coming?' Sven and Corinne both dived happily for their coats. 'Then I'm going home to ring Jerome and tell him where he can stick this.'

12

Back at my flat my answerphone was blinking merrily with messages. I poured myself a large gin and tonic to keep the others in my tummy company and pressed play.

'Hey Jo, it's your friend and saviour, Ruby. Guess what? I'm fantastic. Studio's booked for the weekend, no charge. And they'll cut and package each CD for 30p. Bargain! So tell that gorgeous man to come to London and do some serious playing. You owe me. Ciao!'

'Jo, babe. It's me...' It was Jerome with his honey-voice on, full of longing and apology. I sat up. *'Look, I really miss you. A lot. I really do.'* He sounded surprised at his own emotion. *'So, what do you say? The thing with Alicia ... Some of the things she wants me to do are just crazy. It's got worse – much worse. And since those Americans left, she seems really edgy. I mean, I've got bruises, for Christ's sake. I think she's out of control. And at first I liked that. I mean it was great, so sexy, so alive...'* He checked himself. *'But it's crazy. No, it's you I want, Josephina. Call me. I love you. Honestly.'*

I was amazed but resisted listening to the message again. There was a time when I would have been delighted to hear those words. Now they rang very hollow indeed. I quickly erased his message, feeling a flush of liberation as I did so. Ruby would be proud of me.

'Jo, are you there? Pick up.' This was Tom's voice, urgent. *'Look, it's nearly ten o'clock. Um ... I didn't know who else to call. It's Alicia. She's disappeared. She had a blazing row with me when I got back from France this morning. About you. Then she had a horrible fight with Jerome – that was about you too, actually. She said some weird things, said she was going to make us all regret it. Said she had plans, had "offers". I don't know ... something tells me it's all really suspect. And now she's gone. Nobody's seen her for hours. And some of her stuff's gone, too. I've got a really bad feeling about this.'* There was a pause and when he spoke again his voice was calmer and more intimate. *'God knows what you could do about it, I just needed to talk to you, I suppose. She left a note – it's bizarre. It just says: "Today is the day we two become one. Today we do things we knew we should have done. Today we take the thorny path." I mean, do you get it? Please call me.'*

The machine clicked into silence. I suddenly wished I was sober. I tried Tom's number a few times but it was constantly engaged. The note Alicia had left seemed typically dramatic and attention seeking, but something about its whimsical, elliptical optimism alarmed me. She wasn't a subtle person, or a poetic one. The 'thorny path' was a phrase that echoed round my head like a snatch of a familiar tune. Was it from a famous poem, I wondered, pulling down my dictionary of quotations. I couldn't find it.

I heard the phrase in my head again, lubricated by the gin into a complete sentence. *'If only I had taken the thorny path,'* I remembered. I paced my small flat, taking books off my shelves. What followed that phrase, I wondered. I listened to Tom's message again. Alicia had written, 'we two become one'. Who was 'we'? She couldn't have meant Jerome, or Tom by all accounts. Perhaps there was another man, I thought. Did she mean marriage? Surely Harry and Kieran would have filled me in about that. And what were the things they 'should have done'? Suddenly the words resonated deep within my psyche and I ran into the bedroom. Daphne's diary lay on the bedside table. *'Today's the day'*, Alicia had said. The date today was 3 August. I flicked through the pages until I came to that corresponding date all those decades ago and absorbed the writing, looking for clues.

August third, despair of soul

How tawdry and shallow my life seems as I read back through these pages. Even my joys, my pleasures, are tainted with loss and lack. My moods have altered greatly from the girlish feelings I had at the beginning of the year, and it cannot only be my deflowering by the severe Rev Hartley that has precipitated this. Can it? Since then I have been deflowered many times, of course, each man believing fully that he was the first to enter my sacred chastity. Perhaps it is after all sacred; it has indeed been blessed by a man of the cloth.

I have been lodging in London some five weeks now, boarding with cousin Evelyn, who is so pre-occupied with her children and her suffrage that she does not notice my day-long absences from her rooms, nor my nightly escapes. London is a long way from Hathaway Hall, not in miles, you understand, but in temperament. If Hathaway Hall is a kindly uncle, then London is his evil brother, who likes to fondle one at dinner and spy on one when one is dressing. My despair is that I am fonder of the evil uncle than the kindly uncle.

They have these wonderful places here, deep in the heart of Soho: dark rooms lit by red candles, oriental cushions strewn along the floors. Opium dens. Such a variety of people! Old, young, rich, poor. But mostly intellectuals or artists, and I am an artist! In the dark of night, we suck in pleasure juiced from the poppy, and my veins are now black with its narcotic voluptuousness. Oh! How it slides into your blood and slows your heart! It makes the world seem like a shady, wonderful, lawless jungle of desires. Tonight one of my companions, a gentleman I know not, was stretched beside me as we delighted in the opium. We spoke of many things – politics, issues of art, nature – but all the time my eyelids were heavy and my sensitive parts were seeming to swell and open.

As we spoke I lay back slowly and he came up on his elbow. He was in a dress coat – I believe he had just been to the opera – and he was remarkably handsome in the dim, giddy light. His dark curly hair was thick and he had the most defined cheekbones. He looked like a Slavic prince. His black eyes were intense as he watched me. As I was talking I noticed that his mouth was on mine, my voice now merely a whimper of pleasure. How my body ached to be touched by him. He kissed me fulsomely. The yearning was shameless and decadent. I was not myself, you see, I was like an open poppy welcoming him in. Sensations were both heightened and numbed, but soon he was on me and inside me.

Others around us watched. Some conversations dried up and murmurs of approval filled the room. Some others engaged in their own forbidden pleasures. This stranger was as slow as I, as heady, as longing. Only the heat of our bodies' union seemed to be real, our grinding connection. How wonderful to have a strange man inside you, someone you may never see again. There is an exquisite, exciting darkness about a union like that, and we felt it both as he sank inside me feverishly. Oh, I gasped and moaned and sucked on opium as he filled me with lustful tremors, both of us fully clothed with just our undergarments tossed aside. I think we may have been there for hours, rolling in our bed of silky excitement. I remember reaching a frantic peak and feeling the hot essence of him fill me – Oh heaven!

As he lay there afterwards, sighing into my ear, he beckoned me to come back with him to Paris. Only then did I notice his French accent. He had many other opiates, he said, with which to tempt and titillate me. He was an artist and wished to sketch me frankly, every part of me. He had brothers who would like to enjoy me. I could live with them all on a wheel of titillation and satisfaction. He described a life of utter hedonistic pleasure, where my only degradation would be to fulfil the erotic desires of four young Parisian men. Four handsome brothers! How I longed to go with him, to meet his brothers, to be their shining toy. However, I have a cowardly spirit. I knew that escape from such a life would be impossible. I would emerge a black-lipped, diseased whore, even if I were in some way satisfied. So I said my goodbyes and fled, into the safe light of my chosen path, my class, my music, my family.

And now, as I sit here, my whole being aches for the touch of that stranger and for the wicked joys he promised. If only I had taken the thorny path, the shaded way, the unknown route. I shall never know what my life could have become. I am no better than Emily or Grace. I am even less than my father's new bride Julia, for at least they share their darker pleasures openly with each other. I have chosen to walk in the light, and my life illuminated seems dull and vacuous. Ah, nocturnal satisfaction! How I crave you again!

I think I shall go and compose a nocturne on this mood. Only my piano will chart the empty, regretful twists and turns of it.

I sat back and contemplated the entry. The desire for drugs, sex and attention – all traits Alicia had adopted wholeheartedly – shone through. I knew she and Tom had copies of the diary, and obviously the 'thorny path' reference came from Daphne. Had Alicia's desire to emulate her famous ancestor led her into trouble? She certainly wasn't au fait with the drug dens of Soho, although I was sure they still existed. The only supply of drugs I had seen her use was from Ollie. The thought of Ollie gave me an instinctive shudder, as I remembered his sweaty, furtive watchfulness. And even his pal Ray had warned me off him, had said he got 'carried away'. Then I remembered his film offer at the dining table. But I didn't believe even Alicia would enter into a life of compulsive sex with Ollie. Even she had standards, surely? I rummaged through the utter chaos of my bags, which I still hadn't unpacked properly. I was sure Ray had given me his card. I eventually located it, stuck under the lining. It just had his name and a US phone number, no mention of Ollie or the film company. I dialled hurriedly, sighing with relief when he answered. I wouldn't have mistaken that smooth drawl anywhere.

The moment I told him of Alicia's disappearance and of my suspicions I knew I was on to something. I heard Ray swear under his breath. He told me of Ollie's hopeless addictions and how he would finance them any way he knew how.

'This is ridiculous!' I exclaimed down the phone. 'Are you suggesting Alicia's got caught up in some white slave trade or something?' I didn't like the way Ray paused before he replied.

'Maybe not,' he said eventually. 'But as a filmmaker, Ollie doesn't have many scruples. I've heard a lot of bad things about him. I guess I just didn't want to believe them.'

'Hang on,' I interrupted. 'I didn't get the impression that you were exactly making educational videos at Hathaway Hall. It was pretty obvious they were sex films.'

'Sure,' Ray replied. 'And they're pretty hardcore. But what we're talking about with Ollie is something else ...' He trailed off. 'Shit, I sure hope Alicia hasn't fallen for his bullshit. I knew I should have dropped him the minute he started going astray again.' His voice was hard with annoyance.

'What are we talking about here?' I asked nervously. I sensed I was getting a little out of my depth.

'We're talking very hardcore pictures. S&M mostly, but where people really get hurt.' He cleared his throat. 'Let's just say there's no acting involved and I hear some girls have not come out unharmed.'

'What?' I gasped. My skin started to crawl.

'That's just the gossip. But there's no smoke without fire.' Ray's voice was grave and hesitant. 'There's a lot of money in it, I'm afraid, Jo. For the filmmaker, at least. And Ollie loves money.' He thought for a moment. 'Look, I've got some contacts. Give me your email address and I'll send you an address for Ollie when I can get it. I'll come and help you get her back. I feel real bad about this.' We exchanged details while I wondered what the hell I was going to tell Tom. Just before we rang off Ray said, 'But, hey, explain something to me. Why would a pretty little rich girl with everything want to ruin it all by taking a big risk like this?'

'God knows,' I sighed. 'But if it was attention seeking it's definitely worked.'

13

Tom was bent over the dining room table, his pale face drawn with sleepless worry. Opposite him Jerome was chain-smoking. They both digested everything I told them – slowly, incredulously. I read them the diary entry and the email Ray had sent me with a few ideas about how we could track down Ollie. Finally Tom looked up at me.

'This is a nightmare,' he stated blankly. 'Obviously I'll have to go and get her. But what if he's too difficult to find? What then?'

I couldn't imagine Tom on an undercover rescue mission in New York. He was so unworldly. He would just get himself hurt. Jerome, on the other hand, was more than familiar with the seedier side of life. I tried to catch his eye but he was staring at his cigarette.

'Tom, I think it'd be better if someone else went,' I said eventually.

'No, she's my sister,' he protested.

'Exactly,' I said. 'I don't want to lose both of you! Jerome – she's your … girlfriend.' The word stuck in my throat. 'Why don't you go?'

He snorted out a laugh.

'What's so funny?'

'Look.' He sat up finally and addressed Tom and me. 'She's a nice girl, but I've only known her a few weeks. I'm not going out there to risk my neck for some sex-crazed druggie who doesn't know better than to trust another junkie.'

Tom launched himself to his feet and punched

Jerome square on the jaw. Jerome flew back off his chair and landed against the far wall right under Daphne's portrait, fag still in his hand. Perhaps I was wrong, I thought, perhaps Tom could look after himself.

'For fuck's sake!' Jerome slurred as he staggered to his feet. 'It's fact, you stupid toff. Deal with it.' Any remainder of affection I had for my ex drained out of my body at that moment.

'Jesus, Jerome, you really are a coward,' I hissed. 'You can't face up to anything, can you? Not commitment, not telling me about your marriage,' – he look startled and teetered for a moment, – 'and not your responsibility to Alicia. Just piss off back to London. Tom and I will sort this out.' He swore, rubbing his face, and left the room in a haze of smoke.

'I'm sorry about him,' I said. Tom's green eyes filled with tears.

'I shouldn't have argued with her,' he began.

'Stop,' I ordered. 'Look, she needs to be argued with. Her problem is that nobody has ever stood up to her. And I'm glad you did.' I took his big hand in mine, enjoying the safety of its warmth. I couldn't quite believe what I was about to volunteer to do. 'Listen, I'm a journalist, I know how to find things and I know how to get out of situations when they go pear shaped,' I lied. 'Let me get your sister out of there. Anyway, I've got another job for you this weekend.' He eyed me with a mixture of incredulous admiration and curiosity.

'What's that?' he asked.

'You're going to cut a CD,' I smiled. 'And you'd better make it good.'

I had never seen anyone pack a bag like Ruby. Her suitcase bulged at the seams and her hand luggage comprised four different bags crammed with items. I was travelling light, hoping that a toothbrush and some spare knickers were all I would need, but Ruby insisted that everything she had brought was absolutely essential.

'Listen,' she had said emphatically. 'If I'm going to risk my life and waste my time looking for some dumb bitch in New York, you bet I'm going to do some partying as well.'

I could see her point. She had valiantly insisted on coming with me on my mission, ever the loyal friend, although she would rather have left Alicia to stew in her own juices. So I had a trusty companion with me on my journey – generously financed by Tom – and I was grateful for it. Ruby's positive presence beside me on the plane – downing Bloody Marys and cackling at the dreadful in-flight movie – took my mind off the job in hand and I relaxed. After all, I would need all my strength, both mental and physical, and I never worked best when I was tense.

When we finally trundled through the customs gates at JFK airport we soon spied Ray waiting for us on the other side. He smiled his broad, slow, Southern smile.

'Well, hello,' Ruby muttered appreciatively as we approached him. 'Who's this baby?'

He charmed her endlessly as we drove through Queens and across the bridge onto New York Island. Before us the crystalline peaks of skyscrapers glinted and twinkled in the night sky and Ray pointed them out for us like a solicitous host, never referring to the murky nature of our visit.

'That's the Chrysler Building. Pretty ain't it?' he said. 'And the Empire State, of course. Magnificent. Think you'll get any sightseeing done?'

'You bet,' Ruby grinned, just as I was about to say

that we really didn't have the time. 'Statue of Liberty, Central Park, shops, shops, shops!' She pulled a guide book from her pocket and started to flick through it. 'So much to do, so little time.'

'That's my girl,' Ray said and winked at me in the rear-view mirror, recognising the tension on my face. 'My ma always said, don't waste your energy on worrying about the bad things – they're gonna happen anyway.'

'Is that supposed to make me feel better?' I asked wryly.

'No, baby,' he smiled. 'Just something to think on.'

Ray had thoughtfully booked us into a hotel on the Upper West Side with beautiful views of the park. Ruby and I had a spacious suite on the twelfth floor with enormous beds and an endless mini-bar. Soon Ruby had extracted all her favourites and made herself a cocktail.

'This is the life,' she grinned, flinging herself back onto her bed and bouncing like a happy baby. Her luggage was strewn recklessly around the room. I went to the window and watched the tops of the trees sway in the balmy night air. A couple of die-hard joggers went past below us, tiny figures on the pavement, flanked by rows of yellow cabs. A siren wailed in the background. 'Well,' sighed Ruby, sitting up. 'I am ready for New York.'

'Yeah, but is New York ready for you?'

Two hours later, Ruby was sharing her trademark laugh over a tall martini with two very gorgeous men in a downtown jazz club. One of the guys was meant for me, obviously. When they had sidled over to us it had been clear that the short Italian one with the unfeasibly hairy chest was mine, but I was fidgety and preoccupied, knowing that somewhere in this town was Alicia, somewhere so close you could almost smell her, and my instincts told me she was in trouble. Ray was still waiting for some contacts to give him a list of addresses, so we were holding on till morning before staging a hunt. He had smiled and told me to enjoy my night in the Big Apple. But sitting in the neon lit, smoky bar, the Big Apple was tasting a little sour. I was having trouble getting drunk and my date was coming up with such cheesy lines that I nearly threatened to melt him down and serve him as a fondue. Soon he got the message and turned his attentions to Ruby, who looked stunning in a red handkerchief top and tiny suede miniskirt. Now she was happily entertaining both of them. She was telling stories about her escapades at college, where she had a reputation as a practical joker. She was recounting how she had trapped a notoriously pervy tutor in a lift and let him fondle her, knowing that the surveillance cameras would pick it all up. This man had been sexually harassing female students for months, but no one on the board had believed it. Until they saw the video footage of him with his hands up Ruby's skirt, that was.

'All in the name of women's lib!' she cried, toasting herself with her drink.

'You're crazy!' the Italian was saying, a hand on the smooth ebony skin of her thigh.

'No one told us you English girls are so much fun,' added his friend, obviously a little peeved that his girl was now to be shared. I knew that I was letting the side down by being no fun at all. I got up to make my excuses.

'You know what? I'm really jetlagged,' I said lamely. 'Ruby, do you mind if I go back to the hotel?' She flashed me a warm smile that said she could take care of herself and I left, stumbling out of the dark haze onto the bustling streets, whistling, New York style, to hail a cab.

I was in the shower when I heard a knock at the door. I thought Ruby must have grown tired of her two admirers and come back early. I draped a towel around my dripping body and opened up. Ray was standing there with a bottle of champagne. He took in the sight of my near nakedness with an appreciative smile.

'I was wondering if you ladies would like a drink?' he said as I dripped onto the carpet. 'Is it a bad time?' I let him in and he laughed at the mess we had already created. 'What is it with women? Don't you know how to put things away?'

'It's Ruby. She says life's too short for tidying, and I agree with her. So...'

Ray was looking for somewhere to sit, all the obviously places being covered with clothes and toiletries.

'You know what? I think you should come to my suite,' he said eventually. 'There are more ... surfaces.'

'I was just going to bed actually...'

'Oh come on, Miss Bell.' He chucked me a white shirt that was lying on a dresser and turned his back so I could pull it on. It skimmed the top of my thighs, but I was aware that I had no knickers on and that the dampness of my skin made it cling to me. He turned back to face me again.

'Wow, you look good in just about anything,' he complimented. 'Now come on before the booze gets warm.' He pulled me across the corridor and into his own suite, which was a little roomier than ours. The window looked out over New York, and you could clearly see into the other high-rise apartment blocks nearby. Ray pressed a champagne flute into my hand and toasted me.

'To a beautiful Brazilian princess,' he said.

I snorted with laughter.

'To a tall, handsome Southern gentleman,' I said, and we drank. The bubbles instantly detonated in my weary mind and I felt myself relax. He put on some music and I sat on the couch, carefully curling my legs up so as not to expose my naked crotch.

'You know, you never kept your promise,' he said, coming to sit by me.

'What promise?' I could smell his scent, a smoky, sweet cologne.

'You promised to pose for me, young lady. It's been playing on my mind.' His voice was soft and deep, the drawl of it almost hypnotic.

I drained my glass.

'I think you'll find that that was the pink cocktail talking,' I smiled, as he filled me up again.

'Well, alright. But, if you're curious, I've got some girls coming over to do a quick shoot tonight. You can see what the deal is.'

'Here?' He didn't waste a moment. 'Tonight?'

'Yeah, well, they're New York models and I don't come here much.' He grinned. 'And we always have a great time, if you know what I mean.'

'I can guess,' I said. The idea of watching Ray flirting with a load of blond bimbos didn't fill me with delight. 'I'm too worried about Alicia. I think I'll give it a miss.' I got up to go, but he took my wrist in his big hand and pulled me back down. As I toppled back, my shirt rode up a bit and I saw him take in a flash of my pussy.

'Don't be jealous,' he purred in my ear.

'Ha!' I cried indignantly. But his breath was heady on my neck and his hand was crawling up the still-wet brown skin of my thigh. 'Please, don't.' But my voice was barely a whisper. He nibbled at my ear, whispering how beautiful I was, how much he wanted me. I knew it was a line but still it made me melt and, as his hand cupped my sex, I felt myself cream into him.

'Baby, you're so sexy,' he murmured, 'so wet.' His hand massaged me gently and my legs fell open. 'Ever since I saw you dancing on that table, I've thought about you. Your sweet body...' his hand pressed harder now, 'your beautiful breasts. I could suck on them all day long. Oh, baby...' a stealthy long finger slipped inside me, then another. He curled them within me and vibrated them, hitting some secret hidden spot. The sensation of him inside me and the hard pressure of his knuckle on my melting slit made me abandon any resistance. Suddenly my cunt was burning with longing and I moaned. His hand vibrated faster, encouraged. I tried to wrap my legs around his wrist, to swallow up the pleasure.

'Oh, God,' I groaned, and he grabbed my long hair, tipping my face to his for a long, deep kiss. His tongue pushed into my mouth. I ached for him to unbutton my shirt to push me back and fuck me hard. I leaned back invitingly, but then there was a knock at the door and he pulled back.

'That'll be the girls,' he said, his eyes clouded with lust. His hand slipped from me with reluctance. As he walked to the door he made no attempt to hide his erection, and I was left on the couch pulling down my shirt. I was annoyed that we had been interrupted just when Ray had been taking my mind off things, and peeved that he had seen fit to invite other girls along to the party. I suddenly began to feel like one of Ray's harem and decided to get out as soon as possible. After all, I had a lovely sexy English guy waiting for me back home, who didn't need a gaggle of young naked girls to boost his ego.

I got up to go just as Ray opened the door. Two tall,

trim girls came in and kissed Ray enthusiastically, chirping out greetings and flicking their hair. One was in her late twenties with very long blond extensions right down to her hips. She was curvy and assured. The other was much younger – no more than nineteen – with a slightly shy, pretty smile. Her body was much less womanly and her honey blond ponytail gave her a preppy all-American look. When she opened her mouth her voice came in a chirpy New York accent. Ray greeted them both warmly, his hands all over them, and they obviously adored him, returning his kisses eagerly. Eventually, he turned to me.

'Hey, Jo, come and meet my sweethearts.'

I smiled tightly, wanting to feel aloof from them but knowing that my state of undress was letting me down. Ray perhaps sensed my discomfort and talked me up a bit.

'Jo's a music journalist.'

The girls' eyes widened in polite appreciation. 'From London!' This clinched it. The younger one gasped.

'Wow, London must be beautiful,' she enthused.

'Some of it is,' I said a little meanly, wondering how long I would have to leave it before I made my exit.

'Jo, this is Candi,' Ray stepped in, introducing the younger girl. 'She's a fabulous model, really natural. And this is Diondra.' The older woman smiled at me a little warily.

'Are we interrupting something?' she asked, sensing my hostility and seeing my clothes. Ray cleared his throat and made us all sit together in the lounge, pouring generous helpings of champagne all round. Stuck with the girls, I decided to make conversation. Besides, I was curious about them. They answered my questions about modelling frankly, insisting that it was a great job and they never felt exploited.

'Of course, you get arseholes, like you do in any

profession,' Diondra smiled. She had the most perfect teeth I had ever seen. 'Surely you've worked with a few?'

Jerome sprang to mind and I nodded.

'But Ray's the best, aren't you, honey? Always a gentleman when you want him to be.'

'And a tiger when you don't!' giggled Candi, much to Ray's delight. He sat next to her and squeezed her thigh. Her little skirt rode up. 'Anyway, when are we going to get to work? I can't wait,' she continued, leaning into him. 'Ray takes the best pictures.'

'Only with the best models,' he purred, caressing her bottom.

'Get your camera then,' said Diondra, also impatient. Ray dutifully got up and set up the equipment. 'I've been looking forward to this all day.'

'Really?' I was amazed. 'I thought you girls only did it for the money?'

They laughed.

'You must be kidding, honey,' Diondra replied. 'It's the biggest kick in the world. Knowing that all these men are going to be looking at your naked body, knowing that you're turning them on.'

'Some days, after a shoot, my pussy's so wet I don't know what to do with myself,' Candi agreed, smiling. 'It's so pleased with itself.'

'Really?'

'Of course.' Diondra was amused at my innocence. 'Don't knock it till you try it.'

'You're so beautiful, you'd be a great model,' Candi said, just as Ray was ready.

'That's what I keep telling her,' he called out and the girls sprang up to join him. He had set the camera up near the bed, but around him he also had the mini-bar, balcony and window as a backdrop. Even I could see the erotic possibilities.

'Do you want us separate or together?' Diondra asked, surely a question any man would relish. I leant against a wall watching as Ray got Candi to sit up on the mini-bar. Her little A-line skirt and simple white T-shirt gave her a schoolgirl look that he was obviously into. She even wore knee high socks. He took a few snaps of her fully clothed before asking her to lean back and give him a flash of her panties. His camera flashed and whirred.

'Ooh, you get all hot when it flashes right in your pussy,' she squirmed as he took a close-up. Soon her panties were off, revealing a tight, hairless, pink snatch. She pressed the cool metal cocktail shaker to her naked crotch. Candi seemed to be genuinely turned on, moaning quietly as Ray encouraged her to let ice drip on her nipples, pulling up her T-shirt so her firm little tits were on show. Ray was purring out compliments and giving directions. He obviously knew how to take a great photo. He got Diondra to shake a bottle of champagne hard and come into the shot, popping it open and spraying it against Candi's clit so that she screamed in delight, ending up drenched and flushed. The photos of the spray dousing her were going to be hot, I thought, feeling quite aroused. She pulled her lips open and started to massage herself, Ray's camera going crazy. She was dripping wet now, her clothes a sodden mess, and she slid about the counter top in a pool of champagne.

'Oh, they're going to love this,' Ray whispered to her as she slid the neck of a bottle into herself. 'Imagine all those guys out there jerking off to this picture of you.' Candi moaned. I could feel her excitement in my own body, my cheeks burning. Ray indicated for Diondra to join in. She had been gently caressing herself as she watched, obviously into this as much as I was. He continued to photograph as she pulled Candi's top and skirt off, leaving the girl naked except for her sweet socks. Then Diondra knelt in front of the mini-bar and began to take long, sensuous licks at her friend's pussy. Candi quivered and groaned, discarding the bottle and stroking Diondra's long blonde mane. I could clearly see the older girl's pink tongue exploring her friend's slit. I was mesmerised.

'Ladies, this is hot,' Ray sighed, his trousers straining against his stiff cock. Diondra was in a dark pink silk suit, perfectly immaculate in comparison with her writhing naked friend. The wet slurp of tongue on pussy turned me on. I absently stroked myself as I watched. 'You naughty girls,' Ray said. 'What would your daddies think?' Candi giggled, grabbing ice-cubes and sliding them across her chest. She popped a big one in her mouth and sucked on it deliriously as she started to come. 'Oh, baby, that's it,' Ray encouraged. 'Oh baby, come for me. That's right. Open your legs up, Candi, so I can see your pussy. That's it!' She sucked and moaned. 'Baby, pull Diondra's hair back so I get a good shot of her tongue on you. Oh, God, she's really licking you out good, isn't she?' The girls both sighed. 'She loves it, don't you, D?' Diondra was devouring her friend's pussy with frenzied tongue strokes, then pulled back a little and applied the sharp tip of her tongue to Candi's clit.

'Oh, yes! Oh, that's so good!' Candi cried, her thighs trembling uncontrollably. Diondra never faltered. Soon the young girl quavered and bucked until she finally pulsed out a noisy climax. Ray kept shooting all the while. After the girl had come he got some takes of her in the afterglow, leaning back crimson faced and wild haired, her splayed legs shamelessly showing off her mushy cunt. Diondra smiled, leaning back, too.

'Ray, I'm so hot,' she said in her deep voice. 'You gotta give me some relief.' She walked to him and pressed herself up against him. He left the camera on the tripod and kissed her deeply, his hand shooting up the silk skirt of her suit and rubbing her. He gyrated against her for a moment, his own prick in need of release, but pulled away.

'You know the rule, honey. We gotta keep horny till the end. Then we can fuck all night, I promise.' She nodded obediently and he asked her to get onto the bed. Diondra favoured the more traditional porn shots I was familiar with from magazines: slowly undressing and gradually opening herself to the camera. She had smooth vanilla skin and perfect if artificial breasts with small pink nipples. She was confident with the camera, eying it coolly, even when she opened her legs and Ray took frank shots of her trim dark blonde pussy. 'Beautiful,' he sighed as she opened herself up. 'The men of America are going to love you, baby.' Soon she was naked except for a pair of very high-heeled fuchsia shoes. She writhed in the cushions of the bed, moving like a big cat playing in the sun, ending up on all fours with her perfect bottom looming into the lens.

'I want you to fuck me like this,' she sighed to Ray. 'I want you to take me hard.' He snapped away.

'I know what you want, baby,' he said. 'You want all the horny men who jerk off over your pictures to come and fuck you like this. You want all those big cocks to fill you up. All the gas station attendants and the city workers. All the high-school boys and their frustrated daddies. All the teachers, politicians, janitors, jailbirds. You want them all to come and fuck you.' She groaned in agreement, falling onto her back again and masturbating. 'Remember that night when you fucked thirty guys in a row?' She groaned at the memory. 'All those cocks inside you. I still watch that video. It drives me wild.' Her long, manicured fingers danced over her clit and sank inside her, the pink nails disappearing. Soon Candi could take no more and dived on the bed with her and they engaged in a long, slow French kiss, the two naked women entwined with each other. Diondra wrapped her long legs around her friend and I saw them grind their crotches together, two wet pussies squelching away.

'Man, that's sexy,' Ray breathed, quickly reloading his film. 'Don't stop. It's gold dust.' Candi was sucking on Diondra's tits now, eagerly teasing out the nipples as the older woman sighed and whimpered. Then she slithered her hand between Diondra's legs and began to stimulate her.

'Yes, baby, that's good,' Diondra sighed. 'Higher, higher – ah, yes!' As Candi hit the spot, she started to climax, her excitement mounting in little cries. My hands were buried between my legs now, my wet pussy feeling quite neglected. Ray took his camera right into the action.

'Christ, they'll be spunking all over this shot,' he said, lining up the camera so it would take in both Candi's hand up her friend's snatch and her mouth over her nipple. 'They're all gonna want to come and fuck you. Good girls!' Diondra could take no more and her climax came to get her. She juddered and cried out in a high voice. Her face was contorted with ecstasy. Ray got a shot of that; I was sure that would be the sexiest picture of the lot.

Everyone had another round of champagne, the girls not bothering to dress again but sitting there in their unashamed nakedness, their inner thighs glistening with juice. Ray was teetering on the edge of constant arousal, occasionally fondling his guests' breasts or buttocks and enjoying their grateful kisses.

'You always show us such a good time,' Candi breathed, snuggling into his body.

'Likewise,' he said with a smile. I was still leaning against the wall, jealous of the uncensored intimacy the three of them enjoyed.

'Can't wait to see those pictures,' Diondra said. 'I'm getting all wet again just thinking about it.' Ray kissed her hard and dipped a finger inside her.

'You're not lying,' he growled. 'I can't wait any longer, I'm going to have to give you a good fucking, young lady.' She flushed with pleasure and pushed her breasts towards him.

'What about Jo?' Candi asked. Three pairs of eyes turned towards me. I coolly sipped on my champagne. 'We can't leave her out.'

'No, really,' I protested, 'I'm OK just watching.' Ray got off the bed and swaggered toward me.

'I don't believe you,' he said. He came very close so I had to look up at him. His body barred my vision of the girls and I felt suddenly intimate with him, as if we were alone. I felt singled out and my body started to relax. 'And anyway, I can't resist you any longer, Josephina Bell. You can't just stand there with those long brown legs and those full, gorgeous bosoms and not let me take a shot of you.'

The girls appeared behind him.

'He's right,' Diondra said, pulling me towards the bed. 'You can't knock it till you've tried it, honey.' She sat me down and slowly started to unbutton my shirt. I watched her painted fingernails, knowing that resistance would seem rude and uptight. And anyway, I wanted to have some fun. Candi opened up my shirt and stared appreciatively at my tits.

'My God, are they real?' she gasped. 'I can't see the scar.'

'Of course they're real!'

'But they're so big, Jo.' She ran her hands over them. 'And so upright. You're truly gifted, you know?' Her earnest tone made me smile. The girl was quite sweet, I decided, as her gentle fingers played with my nipples. Diondra pushed my legs apart and ran her fingers through the downy black hair on my mound.

'So silky,' she sighed. I caught Ray surreptitiously taking photos as she caressed me. 'It's been so long since I've been with a brunette. They're all blondes in my job.' As soft as a kitten, she parted my legs and began to kiss up my thighs. Candi took the shirt from my back and tossed it aside and tickled my breasts with her tongue.

'Mm, you're so soft,' she whispered. 'So fleshy.' She stroked my hair as she suckled me. 'She looks like a luscious caramel and tastes like a toffee,' she murmured to Diondra.

'Ladies, this is a dream come true,' Ray sighed as he clicked away. 'Isn't she a beauty?' My body began to warm up as Diondra's kisses rose to my pussy. She was clearly experienced. I lay back and surrendered myself to the pleasure, anticipating the electrifying moment when her sharp, soft tongue sank into me. The instant it did I arched my back and sucked in my breath. I heard Ray's camera frantically trying to capture the moment. She gave me a few gentle licks and caressed my buttocks. I felt the unfamiliar scratch of a woman's nails on my skin. Meanwhile Candi was sucking happily away. Diondra lifted her head to Ray.

'You know what I think Jo would like?' she said a little huskily. 'Black and white.' I thought for a moment that this was strange porn jargon for some bizarre erotic practice but, as Ray reloaded his camera, I realised she was talking about the film.

'Good idea, D. She's got class, she'd look great in black and white.'

'And I think she'd enjoy a little grooming,' Diondra smiled. 'I think she likes to be petted and pampered.'

The two of them shared a complicit look. 'Candi, go and get the stuff from the bathroom.' Candi dutifully pulled herself from my tingling nipple and hopped into the en suite.

'What's going on?' I asked, sitting up.

'Relax, honey,' Ray said, and he went around the room readjusting the lights. He swept open the vast curtain that led to his balconette and opened the glass door. The sounds of traffic and sirens swelled up into the room, and a balmy breeze billowed the curtains. I could see people in other apartment blocks going about their evenings, making drinks, playing guitars. I wondered if they could see me here, sitting naked on the bed with my hair all messed up. Soon Candi came back in with a little bowl of steaming water, a razor, some shaving cream and other items wrapped in a towel.

'Can I do it?' she asked with a smile, laying the towel on the bed and indicating for me to sit on it.

'Now, baby, you know how Ray loves to shave a pussy clean,' Diondra chastised. 'It means he gets to look at it longingly and imagine all the ways he's going to conquer it. Isn't that right, hon?'

'Too right,' he replied, kneeling before me. 'Lie back, baby, relax.' I obeyed and felt vividly naked as Ray parted my thighs and stroked my pubic hair. I shut my eyes. 'You're very pretty as you are, but I would love to see you with a bald little cunny,' he remarked. I heard the slosh of water and then a warm, moist flannel between my legs. He was tender and precise. I heard the squelch of the cream being squeezed out of the tube, then the cold surprise of it on my crotch. He lathered it up with a soft, wet brush. I parted my legs a little more as the brush circled my vulva and tickled my clit. The watery mixture trickled down my crack and I squirmed.

'Sit still now,' Diondra said. Ray's fingers explored me a little, opening me up as if to inspect the area he would be working on. I felt so exposed, feeling his breath on my inner thighs as he looked close into me. Then I felt the cool edge of the razor scrape across my mound, making a sharp scratching sound. My skin twitched.

'Easy, baby,' Ray whispered, shaving another strip. He was working outside in and, as he got close to my delicate lips, he held them in his gentle fingers, pressing on my clit. I couldn't move, scared of the razor, but how I wanted to press myself into his hand. As if reading my mind, he slipped a warm finger inside me as he continued his work. Soon he was done and I felt the soothing moisture of the flannel wiping me clean again. The fresh smell of shaving foam filled the air. It was a smell I associated with men and it made me feel very womanly. Candi and Diondra had been sweet and attentive partners, but what I wanted was a strong male to pleasure me. 'Beautiful,' Ray said. I opened my eyes and saw him examine me, his hand gently fondling my smooth pussy. He bent down and kissed it gently, then looked up at me.

'I want to get some shots of you by the window. Just you.' He helped me up and stood me by the open window. My hair was ruffled by the breeze. He went to his camera. I felt shy at first and wrapped myself in the long curtains like a toga. The girls giggled as he started to snap me.

'Good, good,' Ray encouraged, and I let the curtain drop a little, exposing my breasts. 'Stunning.' As he photographed me my inhibitions started to fade away and I pulled my shoulders back, making the most of the full swell of my bosoms. I let the curtain fall more, so the top of my shaven pussy was on view beneath the plain of my belly. I turned away from him a little to show the curve of my back and bottom. My skin felt alive with all the attention, my body finding the poses easy and liberating. My pussy started to moisten again at the thought of men looking at these pictures. I dropped the curtain and pushed the material between my legs like Salome doing a dance of seven veils. I pulled it tight and the silky material clung to my damp pussy.

'Oh, Jesus that's sexy,' I heard Ray say as I dropped my head back. 'Move to the balcony, darlin'.' I stood in the window frame, facing the twinkling lights of New York. I knew people in other blocks could see me now but I didn't care. I held on to the frame and widened my legs, standing in a star position, sticking my bottom up a little to show it to its greatest potential. 'Shit, it's true what they say about Brazilian girls,' Ray said. 'Best arses in the world. Lean forward, baby.' I obeyed, grasping the railings of the balconette for support. Now I was more outside than in, my heavy tits exposed to the world. I knew that the camera could see my pussy now, and I creamed at the thought of it. I leant forward more and presented my smooth sex to Ray. 'Oh, God, what are you doing to me,' he said. His voice was nearer now, and I felt him take a close-up of my pussy, the flash hot against my skin. The idea of the lens so close turned me on. I almost fantasised that he would press it inside me, fuck me with it.

'Turn around,' he ordered. I did and saw him kneeling before me. He took some photos working from the ground up. His face was so close to me. 'Open yourself up for me, sweetheart.' I tentatively pulled my lips apart and he got an eyeful of my clit and plump lips. 'Oh, man, you smell good. Oh, baby!' He momentarily dropped the camera and buried his face in my pussy, indulging in a few hungry licks. I was nearly thrown off balance and grabbed on to the window frame for support. My already tingling hole began to liquefy with excitement as his eager tongue worked its magic. I wanted to come so much I felt I would burst. I had wanted to come for about two hours now. I started to moan and grabbed his hair. He pulled away.

'No, no,' he breathed, his voice thick with lust. 'We have to wait just a little longer.' He slid the French window shut and turned me towards it again. I could see the reflection of our room clearly in the glass and across the way I spotted a man in an opposite apartment looking at me. He was in his late twenties, tall, sexy in a grungy way. He had been doing his dishes, I saw, and had noticed this naked girl in the apartment opposite. I met his eye and neither of us looked away. I pressed my body to the glass, my tits squashed up and my bald mound slippery on the cool surface.

'Ray, I want you to come here and fuck me,' I said quietly, hoping that the young man wouldn't lose his nerve and disappear. I wanted to give him a good show.

'But the pictures . . .' Ray replied weakly, obviously tempted.

'Fuck that. I need you to come here.' I heard him put the camera down and approach me. Still leaning on the glass with my hands, I pressed my body back against him. Now the man opposite could see the full swell of my hanging breasts; I could see them myself mirrored in the window. Ray stood behind me and ran his big hands down my body, cupping my bosoms and tantalising the nipples. I kept the young man's eye as Ray's fingers travelled downwards and eased into my pussy. 'Ah, yes,' I sighed as he sank into me. The man opposite reached hurriedly for his glasses and put them on. I saw him lick his lips as I came sharper into focus.

'You're so wet, baby,' Ray breathed into my ear. I watched our reflection as he began to masturbate me tenderly. I saw the young man's hands disappear downwards and hoped he would jerk himself off. Ray's fingers strummed my swollen sex and my legs began to quiver. I knew I was going to come soon.

'Please, Ray, fuck me,' I urged, pressing my bottom against his crotch. Through his trousers I could feel an achingly hard erection. He didn't need to be told twice. I heard him unzip himself and then his hands were on my hips. He steadied me as his prick played about at the entrance to my pussy. The photographic lights were candid and bright. I knew our neighbour could see everything. I reached down and guided Ray's impressive hard-on inside me, and he began to push gently, rising and rising.

'Oh, that's good,' I sighed, my whole body welcoming its new intruder. 'Don't stop.' Ray's hands tightened on my hips and he began to thrust. I jerked a little with each push. 'Oh, fuck me!' I moaned. The man opposite leant forward, taking it all in. Ray's cock inside me was burning as hot and hard as a rock. My pussy melted around it. I heard Ray grunting into my hair, his hands moving to my breasts. 'Oh, yes!'

'Oh, baby, I'm going to come real soon.' Ray's voice was tight with strain. 'Your little pussy turns me on so much.' His thrusts got harder. I sighed with pleasure as he buried his hand between my legs again and gently stimulated me as he fucked me. 'Oh, baby!' I could tell from the violent enthusiasm of his thrusts that he was on the edge, and so was I. My cheeks burned, my mouth was open and red. I could see the face of the man opposite contort a little as his own hand matched the faster rhythm of our fucking. 'Oh, man you're sexy. I could fuck you over and over again. I could eat your pussy till I'm eighty years old.' His hand vibrated hard across my clit and I felt the clutches of an orgasm start to tug at my body. Ray began to shoot off inside me, big, relieving, pumping strokes. As he doused me, I cried out in my own climax, his fingers never tiring against my clit. The man opposite was still jerking off. In my afterglow I pressed my cheek to the glass. Ray pulled out of me and I felt the hot mixture of our juices trickling down my legs. The room was silent except for our heavy, relieved breaths. Ray took my wrist and guided me back to the bed. He sat me on the edge. I could still see our neighbour and our own reflection as Ray parted my legs, kneeling before me.

'Baby, I just can't get enough of you,' he said with a sigh, and buried his head in my mound again. He started to lick my hot cunt clean, unsqueamishly lapping up both our mingled juices. His mouth slurped against me and my body ached to come again. I glanced over at the girls and saw that they had retired to the couch, lying in a languid sixty-nine position, Candi on top. Her ponytail bobbed up and down over Diondra's pussy. I could just see Diondra's face under her friend, her long blond tresses wound around Candi's leg. I pushed myself nastily into Ray's mouth as he feasted on me, and watched as our young neighbour grimaced as he came. In the glass I had a clear view of Ray's head moving around between my legs and of my own swelling breasts. I watched the reflection intently – it was so sexy! Ray was tickling my clit and moaning softly. I saw that his cock had recovered and was big again. I pulled him away from me and up onto the bed, unzipping him and mirroring the sixty-nine position the girls had adopted. He went back to licking me out as I sucked on his big prick, still tangy from our union. I kissed lightly around the base of his shaft and his balls, then lifted myself up and gobbled down on its bulbous head. It filled my mouth and I took it in as far as I could. I heard Ray groan into my muff and he lapped thirstily at me. His hips started to pump subtly and I fondled his balls as I sucked him off. I wanted to be filled from every orifice. I longed for Harry and Kieran to come in, to have three cocks filling me up. I sucked harder and swirled my tongue around Ray's cock as I fantasised that Harry, Kieran, Tom and Jerome were all lining up to get blowjobs from me, that I would be swallowing five lots of come, that they would all be nibbling on my clit as Ray was doing now. I wanted to be held down, tied up. I wanted to be fucked again.

I pushed Ray back and straddled him, lowering myself onto his erection. My sodden pussy swallowed it up hungrily and I started to pump my hips hard. Ray sensed that I needed a bit of roughhousing and rolled on top of me, pinning my arms above my head and thrusting inside me. After a few minutes, he pulled out and rolled me on to my tummy. He stuffed some pillows under my belly and entered me from behind, again holding my arms above my head. I lifted my buttocks to admit him deeper and he bounced on me fast, his hot breath tangled in my hair, his free hand frigging away at my clit. I moaned into the mattress, my tits burning as they rubbed against the sheets. I had never been fucked so hard, it felt as if I was being attacked, but I was loving it. My pussy was alive with pain and pleasure, pouring its lust all over the pillow and Ray's electric hand. His cock seemed huge inside me and I cried out, my voice muffled by the sheets. I heard him grunting and groaning into my ear as his fingers danced against my clit. I jerked out a wild, hard, screaming orgasm. Ray was nowhere near, though, and kept up his merciless pumping, his cock getting harder and bigger by the minute. His hand cupped my shaven, slippery sex and held me in place as he continued to thrust inside me.

'Stop, I can't take any more,' I urged, but he ignored me. I tried to struggle free but he held me still. I was pinned down, skewered by his relentless cock. 'Ray, stop!' I cried vainly. My cunt was aching and spent. He moved both hands under my body and held onto my breasts, kneading and pinching them. My whole body felt weary and used. 'Ray, I can't go any further,' I moaned as he stimulated my nipples. Amazingly they began to tingle in response and my pussy woke up again. The burning pain of his hard cock began to turn to burning pleasure again. 'Please Ray.' My own body confused me, responding again to the man inside it.

'Go with it, baby,' he insisted. 'Come for me. I want to feel you come again.'

'I can't,' I protested, but when he returned his hand to my clit and started to gently stimulate me again, I felt a new wave of pleasure come over me. His cock never stopped its insistent thrusts and now my body whorishly greeted them again.

'Be dirty, baby,' he whispered. 'Get fucked over and over again and love it every time. You know, some girls find that if they have a few orgasms, they just can't stop. They come and come and come, whoever's fucking them.' His tireless fingers vibrated against me harder now and I moaned. 'Yes, baby, that's it. That's it!' he whispered.

I began to tremble, to buck. This time my reactions felt purely physical, animal even. My greedy cunt couldn't get enough. My tired body geared itself up to climax again. 'Oh, you're a naughty girl, aren't you? You're a sexy little slut.' His words poured hotly into my ear. My own groans almost deafened me now as a hard, basic rapture gripped me. 'Open yourself up to me, baby. Come for me.' I yelled out as Ray's violent thrusts took me over the edge and I came. I felt him come, too, filling me up. He held me still as we both thrashed around on the bed, pouring every last drop inside me. Afterwards he lay on top of me and I was suddenly aware of his weight, his soaking body, his pungent scent. His penis began to wilt inside me and he gently pulled away. I lay motionless and exhausted. I didn't even look up when I heard the clicking of his camera. He was taking shots of my raw pussy brimming with his come.

'Turn over, Jo,' he said. I obeyed, lying splayed on my back. 'Shit, that's sexy.' He took more photos. I was too spent to care. 'There's nothing more arousing than a woman who's just had a good fucking. They're always my favourite shots.'

From the couch I heard the whimpering cries of Candi's climax. I had forgotten about the girls but they had obviously been at it all this time, spurred on by the sounds of Ray and me. Ray swung round and started snapping them in their happy duo. Candi's little rump was pulsing up and down on Diondra's face, her legs all a-tremble. I sat up and looked in the window at my dishevelled, disgraceful being. Naked, shaven, flushed and used. I decided it was time to go. Ray didn't even notice as I slipped out of the apartment, wearing my shirt, which was now crumpled and stained with champagne and semen. He was on to the next thing, engrossed in his models. I wasn't complaining; I had had my fair share.

When I got back to my room it was 4 a.m. and Ruby was safely tucked up in bed, snoring away. I eased myself into my own bed as quietly as possible and snuggled down. I could still feel the burning pleasure of what had gone before in my cunt, and Ray's spunk drizzled slowly out of me. I sighed, contented. That night, ironically, I slept the sleep of the innocent.

14

'It came in this morning. Got an email from a mutual acquaintance.' Ray tipped his laptop towards Ruby and me so we could see the screen. We squinted, both of us slightly hung over. A couple of other hotel guests looked at us curiously over their breakfasts.

'What are we looking at?' I asked. On the screen there was a grotty-looking porno site with a list of options.

'"Hardcore boot fetish, live action trios, taboo..."' Ruby read aloud. 'All looks pretty standard.'

'Yes, but look.' Ray clicked on the 'taboo' option and we were taken into a live web-cam site, with the heading 'Girls get hurt, live.'

'That's sick,' Ruby cried and an elderly couple shot us a sharp look. It obviously wasn't the done thing to be surfing porno sites over breakfast.

'It gets worse,' Ray replied, clicking us into the site. The screen changed and we were shown a grainy image of the inside of an airy warehouse. It was slightly run down and shabby. In the middle of the room was a bed with equipment – whips, chains, masks – hanging off the bedpost. At the foot of the bed, a skinny pale woman was shackled. Her heavy black-rimmed eyes and pale thin mouth looked dry and lifeless. She was wearing only a black PVC thong and her small tits sagged sadly. Her dark hair clung to the sweat of her brow. It looked like a still photo until she suddenly shifted her leg. At the side of the screen a chat-box appeared with the words, 'Greetings customer. What can we show you today?'

'This colleague found the site after Ollie boasted to him about it in a bar. It's the only lead we have,' Ray said. 'Not much to go on.'

'So that's Alicia?' Ruby demanded. Obviously the image on screen did not tally with the description of the sexy, man-eating beauty I had given her. In fact, I had only just realised it was Alicia myself. I was suddenly very glad that Tom had not come along to witness his sister in this state. Another message flashed up on screen: 'Welcome to the most dangerous, hardcore site on the internet. We will submit our girls completely to your will. Would you like to see Ali dance? Would you like her to strip? She has a lovely pussy. She likes it rough.' We watched the screen as Alicia's head dropped suddenly as if she had lost consciousness.

'Man, what drugs have they given the girl?' Ruby said. Looking at the room, I noticed that there was a wide window at the far end. Outside I could make out the bright shimmer of water.

'Ask him to get her to go to the window so we can see her tits better,' I said. Ray looked at me aghast. 'Just do it!' He typed in the command and sure enough Alicia hauled her weary body up. Ollie came into shot to unshackle her and she limped to the window. Bruises punctured the backs of her legs and there were welts on her back.

'Jesus,' Ray muttered. Alicia turned back to the camera and, obviously obeying some off-screen direction, pointed her breasts upwards. Just past her the outside world was more in focus now.

'Look,' I urged. 'Look through the window. There's water.'

'Oh yes,' Ray murmured and closely examined the screen.

'Can you make out any landmarks?' I asked, vainly

hoping that the Statue of Liberty would be there to guide us to Alicia. 'What's that ship there?' I could make out the edge of a huge deck.

'What ship?' Ray craned in to study the screen. Like me he could just make out the pale edge of a deck against the water.

'Shit, it's that thing! That aircraft carrier!' Ruby cried. The elderly couple moved to another table. 'I saw it in my guidebook. I was going to visit it.'

'What?'

'You know, it's a space museum now!'

'The Intrepid?' Ray looked harder. 'Shit, she's right. It's a World War II aircraft carrier on Pier 86. That's the corner of it.' Another message flashed up on screen: 'What would you like Ali to do for you, caller? You are paying – may as well get your money's worth.' I thought for a while, looking for words that would let her know we were going to rescue her but that would sound suitably lecherous for the porn site. I eventually replied: 'Ask her to lie on the bed. Tell her that her Kindly Uncle is coming.' Ray looked at me quizzically.

'It's a reference to one of Daphne Hathaway's diary entries,' I explained. 'She referred to Hathaway Hall as a kindly uncle. I hope she gets it.' Watching the screen I saw Alicia look up when she was told this and her eyes seemed to brighten. Maybe she did.

The theatre district traffic was impatient and congested, but we soon jolted our way past the garish neon lights of Broadway and arrived at the Pier at the end of W 46th Street. The air was cooler out here, the sharp light of the sun reflecting off the water. Tourist boats churned off from a nearby jetty and a few people were going to the Intrepid, a huge structure on the river, but the area had a deserted feel to it. There were no shops or residential blocks, just warehouses and garages and the odd bagel bar.

The three of us stood on the pavement planning our next move. We located the spot where we thought the window might have been and logged on again to check. On the screen Alicia was now on all fours and naked. A whip was slashing against her already sore rump. Through the window I noticed the tourist boat chugging past. We were so close! From the boat on screen we could calculate which building they were in. It was a shabby block of two stories. Looking up a it, I knew I could climb at least half the way; there were drainpipes and railings, loose bricks for footholds and the odd clay pipe to hang on to. Before I could change my mind I began my ascent.

'Wish me luck,' I muttered, launching myself onto a rubbish skip to get a head start.

'What the hell are you doing?' Ray protested as I scaled the wall. 'You'll kill yourself.' Ruby shushed him. She had seen me conquer quite a few walls in our time together at college, usually escaping from boys' bedrooms or breaking into campus after curfew. This was very high, though. My trusty trainers clung well to the brick, but my hands were cramping up at having to clutch so hard. I scraped my knees across the surface and swore. 'Keep going, girl. Nearly there,' I heard Ruby urge. I could see a window just above me. Its ledge jutted out a little, enough to stand on. I swung my foot up and levered myself onto it, quickly adjusting my position so I was not in full view of the people inside.

'Well?' I heard Ray call up. I peered in. It was a normal storage space – no sign of web cams or girls on beds. I shook my head. Like a cat, I suddenly realised there was no way of getting down. My only option was to break in.

'I'm going up another flight if I can,' I called down and heaved the window open. It was old and easy to lift, and I crawled inside. I ran quickly to the only visible door, which was ajar. The air was thick with dust and the stench of mould and damp. Boxes and crates were scattered around the place. Out on the landing, I could see a wooden staircase leading upwards and one leading down. Using my brain for once I went down, just to check out my exit route and to see if I could let the others in. Sure enough, I found a door which was easy to open and I called the others in.

'Jesus, you're crazy,' Ray said, admiringly, as he and Ruby quietly joined me.

'OK, now, let's go up. But silently – I think surprise is our best weapon,' I whispered, frankly enjoying the adventure of the situation. Ruby and Ray crept behind me up the stairs, which creaked and groaned under our weight. I heard Ruby stifling a sneezing fit as we walked through the dust and I tried not to giggle.

'It's not funny,' she hissed between muffled sneezes.

'Listen,' said Ray. The sounds of voices were just audible from the second floor. We climbed up and they became clearer. A woman sounded distressed. There was a heavy thud. Impulsively I ran up the remaining steps and burst into the room. Alicia lay in a crumpled naked heap with blood streaming from her nose. The room smelt of pee and drugs. I went to her and lifted her head. Her eyes turned on me slowly and listlessly. They had lost all their life. I could see track marks on her arms where she had been injected. Ray and Ruby thundered in behind me. I turned to see Ray grab Ollie's collar and shake him violently.

'You little snake,' he growled. 'Why, I ought to knock your block off!'

'Fuck that,' shouted Ruby and took a hard swing at him, punching him resoundingly in the stomach. She followed it up with a smart kick in the balls and Ollie folded over like a deckchair collapsing. We left him choking and spluttering on the floor and pulled Alicia away. Ray carried her down the stairs and out onto the street. Once outside, we dressed her in my denim jacket and tied Ruby's jumper around her hips. This was New York and nobody batted an eyelid. We hopped in a cab and took Alicia back to the hotel.

'Don't worry, we're going to clean you up,' I soothed, stroking her hair. She was so vulnerable now without her sheen of catty class. 'We'll give you a good meal and take you home.'

'She'll have withdrawal,' Ray warned. 'You might need professional help. I don't know what that bastard gave her.'

'I'll look after you,' I said and she leant on my shoulder, sobbing quietly.

Ruby took out her mobile and began to dial.

'Hi, is that the police?' she said. 'Good, there's a complete pervert on the corner of W 46th and 12th Avenue that you need to lock up. The warehouse with the green door. His name is Ollie –' she looked at me.

'Mangel,' I said.

'Ollie Mangel. You won't miss him. He's the one with the collapsed scrotum.' She giggled and hung up.

15

It was a week before I would let Tom visit Alicia. I kept putting him off with tales of her shame and embarrassment, but the truth was that she was sick, disoriented and disturbed by her ordeal. Her body gradually expelled the narcotics she had taken, but her mind found it harder to let go of the memories.

I never thought I would have the haughty Alicia sleeping on my sofa in Peckham with just a sleeping bag and a cup of tea for comfort, but she adapted surprisingly well. Every day she would bathe and listen to the radio, anointing her wounds and obediently eating the healthy meals I put before her, even though I was sure she had never eaten so simply.

Ruby's big sister Georgia was a nurse, and she popped by to keep an eye on my house guest, tutting disapprovingly as she did so, making it clear that she would never forgive me for dragging Ruby into such a murky world. Ruby herself was eager to come round and treat Alicia to some of her homespun wisdom. I looked forward to witnessing that conversation – when Alicia was up to it – but put my best friend off for the time being.

After a few days Alicia started to come round to reality again. I knew she was feeling a bit better when she began to make little digs about my flat.

'It's so very you, dear,' she sighed from her puffy arrangement of duvets and cushions on the sofa. 'A little ... chaotic.'

I smiled, relieved she seemed to be showing some

of her old character. I didn't like to point out that she had created more chaos than she could imagine with her escapade to the States.

'Chaotic, yes,' she repeated vaguely, perhaps having the same thought herself.

'I like it like this,' I said defensively, surveying the bookshelves heaving with books, papers, folders and ornaments.

'Of course! The mauve walls are a delight,' she said brightly, as if that had never been in question. 'Your little den to protect you from the outside world, eh?' She glanced out of my window. I saw my little corner of London through her eyes: lines of houses crammed together in terraces, backed by council estates and shopping centres. Quite a change from Hathaway Hall.

'Can't wait to get home?' I prompted, passing her a cup of tea. She held the mug as if it were a foreign object, clearly more accustomed to china cups. Her lack-lustre gaze sharpened for a moment and she shook her head.

'Christ, no,' she protested. 'I don't want to go back there. I don't have to, do I?' She looked distressed for a moment and I comforted her, sitting on the sofa and taking her hand.

'No, you don't have to,' I soothed.

'No, I crave life. Life. Human contact,' she insisted. 'In that place I could never really feel my life. It was always such a lonely place for me. That's why I . . .' She trailed off sheepishly. 'All that stuff with Mr Wootten. Harry and Kieran. All those men!' She looked at me frankly. 'That's why I couldn't bear to share my own brother, Jo darling. I was so afraid of being alone.'

I nodded, acknowledging this as some sort of apology. I saw that she was starting to get depressed again and I switched on the TV. She had never watched it at Hathaway Hall – it would have seemed incongruous and anachronistic in those creaky old rooms – but since staying with me she had grown quite obsessed with it. Her face lit up like a child's. 'Ooh, this is that wonderful soap opera!' she exclaimed. 'The one where everyone's always so dreadfully morose.'

I watched her as she became absorbed in the story, smiling at her naïve wonderment at other types of living. Thinking she would be happy for a while, I quietly got up to start making dinner. Just as I was in the doorway she called back to me.

'Jo?' I stopped in my tracks. She didn't look away from the screen. 'When do you think Jerome will come and visit me?' Her face was emotionless but the question hung heavily in the air.

I didn't know what to say. I knew him pretty well, and this was exactly the kind of situation he avoided like the plague: one emotionally traumatised, vulnerable ex in another ex's apartment.

'I'm not sure,' I faltered. 'He's very busy at the moment.'

Alicia nodded slowly and looked down. Her mask was cracked now and she couldn't hide her disappointment. I hurried to the phone in my bedroom and rang into the office. I wasn't going to let him wriggle out of this one. I got Sven, who stutteringly told me that the boss had gone off to have a meeting.

'Oh, come on!' I groaned. 'We all know Jerome never has meetings. Now, put him on!'

'Er, I can't.' Sven's voice was uneasy. 'Sorry, Jo. He expressly told me not to put you through. He told me to tell you he's too busy preparing for this visit from the parent company to talk to you.'

'What?'

'Sorry.'

My anger rekindled at Jerome's unerring cowardice. 'I don't believe this!' I cried and launched into a furious tirade, regaling Sven with details of Jerome's shoddy treatment of Alicia, of her brush with danger, of her extreme vulnerability. I didn't care how much people in the office knew, Jerome deserved no respect from anyone. When I had finished, there was a pregnant pause.

'Is that it?'

I detected a faint amusement in Sven's voice.

'I guess so.'

'Give me forty minutes and I'll be there,' he continued. 'Not all men are like Jerome, you know. Where I come from, you don't ignore a damsel in distress.'

After that, the tall Scandinavian became a regular visitor, bringing fortifying herbal teas and calming oils to Alicia. He was a patient man, and she clearly found him easy to talk to, easier than myself. Eventually I heard her tell him of the panic that had driven her to trust a man like Ollie. She admitted that Daphne's diaries had become an obsession, and that she was trying to rectify the regrets that had plagued her great grandmother by taking risks in life. Like Daphne, Alicia was strangely naïve about the world, although she liked to seem so sophisticated. Ollie had flattered her about her performance in Ray's softer films and had offered her a glamorous life in New York with lots of kinky pleasure and sexy parties. At first she had refused, she insisted to Sven, but her arguments with Jerome and Tom had tipped her over the edge. Here she shot me an accusing glance and I went off to make some of the root tea that Sven had brought. I knew the rest anyway; it was so predictable. The drugs, the manipulation, the exploitation. When I came back in, Sven was holding her in his long arms and I felt like a gooseberry. I slunk back into the kitchen and drank the root tea on my own. It was absolutely disgusting.

Eventually, Alicia had regained enough of her

former lustre to face her brother. I invited him up, half apprehensive about his reaction to Alicia's predicament and half overjoyed at the thought of seeing him again. Our week apart had made me realise how fond I had grown of him. Even though I had indulged in some sex-play with Ray, I was still frustrated and anxious to consummate my feelings for Tom.

When he finally arrived at my little flat it was all I could do to keep my hands off him but it didn't seem appropriate to jump him just as he came through the door. I realised he was here for sombre reasons and this prevented me from pursuing my feelings. Instead I kissed him briefly and led him straight through to Alicia, who was lying on the couch, chatting with Sven.

If Tom was shocked at the state his sister was in, he did a very good job of not showing it. He greeted her warmly, apologising for their row and telling her not to be such an idiot again. He did a worse job at hiding his surprise at my cramped flat, even laughing out loud at the half-sized bath and shower unit in my tiny bathroom.

'I like to think of it as *bijou*,' I scolded, slapping his arm. He wandered into my bedroom, where my clothes, books and paperwork were arranged in a chaotic mess all over the limited floor space.

'Well, lucky for you I'm good at tidying up. It seems you've found me just in time to rescue you from a life of complete squalor,' he teased. It wasn't the reaction I had wanted from him on first seeing my bed, but it made me laugh.

'We aren't all born with a silver spoon in our mouths, you know,' I complained. 'And I can tell you, I have everything in its place. I know where everything is in this room. Test me if you like.'

He looked down at me with those amazing green eyes and walked me backwards till I was leaning against the wall. In the next room I could hear Alicia and Sven laughing.

'Shouldn't you be tending to your sister?' I reprimanded as he leaned over me. I basked in the heat of his body.

'Oh, she's alright. She's got an admirer,' he said dismissively. 'It's you I've been missing.'

I melted a little.

'I'm glad you can be so blasé about it!' I exclaimed. He put his hand on my cheek. 'I was the one who risked my life to go and rescue her.'

'My hero,' he said and, with a smile, kissed me. His tender fingers played at the nape of my neck as his warm mouth covered mine. Time seemed to stand still and I forgot to breathe as the kiss grew deeper and more intimate. I wrapped my arms around him and he leant his weight onto me, my body welcoming its heavy pressure. I had forgotten what a great kisser he was. I felt suddenly a little guilty about my romps with Ray and his visitors, but this felt very different. This was gentle and loving and tantalising. I could hear Tom's breathing change as he became aroused and the kiss grew harder. His strong, inquisitive tongue pushed against mine and I sighed in pleasure. I longed for more, but was amply aware of Alicia's presence in the next room. If we couldn't shake her off at a stately home, we certainly wouldn't be able to in my little flat. Regretfully, I pulled away.

'Come on,' I whispered. 'Let's go and see your sister.'

He complained, pushing uncomfortably on his erection through his trousers to get rid of it. I stared at it longingly. The size was promising.

'God, Tom, I can't wait until we're finally alone together,' I said, resisting the urge to caress the burgeoning bulge.

'Me too.' He smiled. 'I've been thinking of little else.

It made the recording I did all the sweeter.' He kissed me. 'Thanks for that as well. It seems I have an awful lot to thank you for.'

'Well,' I said, and grinned naughtily. 'I'm sure I can think of lots of ways for you to show your gratitude.'

'Really?' His cock started to rise again and he held me to him. The throb of his body's energy against me was compelling. 'Like what?'

'You'll see,' I murmured. His hand wandered to my bottom and softly fondled me through my skirt. I remembered that I wasn't wearing any knickers and felt Tom stiffen.

'Jo, you minx,' he breathed, his hands gathering up my skirt until his fingers were touching my smooth bare bottom. 'Oh, God!' He crushed himself against me and slid his fingers between my legs. I was losing resistance now, wishing we had shut the door. I could hear Sven's deep voice in the next room.

'Tom,' I murmured as his fingertips slipped into me. I was still a little bristly from the shave that Ray had given me and as Tom's fingers explored he pulled back and eyed me questioningly.

'What's happened here?' he demanded playfully.

'What?' My face was all innocence but I wasn't sure how much to tell him. I wouldn't have liked it if he'd been having sex with other women, even if it was purely recreational. He walked away and pushed the door shut.

'Get on the bed, you little hussy,' he said. I did as he said and he came and lifted my skirt again. 'Lie back.' His hands trailed over the short bristly hairs that were just growing back. My mound twitched under his gentle touch and his scrutinising gaze. 'You weren't like this at Alicia's party, young lady,' he said.

'I know.' I squirmed.

'Have you been a bad girl?' His teasing tone encouraged me to admit to a little naughtiness.

'No. I've been a bit ... wayward, that's all,' I said as his fingers lovingly explored me with featherlight strokes.

'Wayward?' He leant down and kissed around my pussy a little.

'Yes. But it was all for you.' I decided a little white lie was in order. After all, I didn't want to spoil the moment. My legs opened instinctively to welcome his soft lips.

'Mm?' he said, still kissing me. Now he was exploring me with his tongue, still skirting around the area. I longed for him to lash me with it right in the centre of my sex.

'Yes,' I panted. 'Yes, I had some sexy photos taken. I was going to send them to you – oh God, that's lovely!' He cupped my buttocks in his hands and licked me over and over again with his curious tongue.

'Mm?' he said again, wanting more details.

'Ray took them in his hotel room,' I said breathlessly. 'He had two girls undress me and then he shaved my pussy. Oh!' Tom's tongue grew hungrier now as the image excited him. 'Then he made me pose like a slut and took photos of me.' Tom's face rose, smiling from its wet haven.

'Like a slut?' he said, crawling up my body. 'Well, that Ray's a bad man.' He unzipped his trousers and I reached down to release his cock. It was smooth and large, pressing insistently into my hand. I fondled it, running my hands over its satiny surface and feeling the impressive girth that I knew would give me the greatest of pleasure. At last I had my hands on it. Tom sighed as my hand curled around him and I felt a little drop of moisture forming at the head. 'Go on,' he whispered.

'Well ... when he'd taken lots of naked pictures of me – for you – we were both very excited,' I admitted. Tom was nuzzling my throat as he lay on me and I spoke very quietly into his ear. I opened my legs, aching for him to penetrate me. 'We were so excited that I asked him to fuck me,' I confessed. Tom groaned. I waited to see if he would be angry but he just levered himself over me and kissed me hard. This was a very different kiss: invasive and strong, almost overpowering. It was as if he was reclaiming me. Our bodies ground together as our mouths did battle. It turned me on to think that both of us were still fully clothed with just our private parts exposed.

'How did he fuck you?' he breathed, his cock waiting at the entrance of my desperate sex. 'Tell me.'

'Well, to start with he licked me,' I said huskily. Tom pushed into me a little and my body closed around him excitedly.

'Was it good?' he whispered.

'Yes, I loved it!' I sighed, longing for his thick cock to push further inside me. 'Then he took me from behind. I was leaning against a window.'

'Yes?' He sank deeper and began to thrust gently. My hands instinctively moved to his buttocks and I thrilled at the feel of his muscles tensing and releasing as he pumped me. He held himself up on his elbows so that we could look into each other's eyes. His green eyes were dark with desire and the veins were standing out on his neck and temple. He held my face in his hands. It was a tender gesture, but also slightly controlling.

'Then he fucked me on the bed, from behind.'

'Did you come?'

'Yes.'

He thrust harder.

'How many times?'

'I can't remember.'

'That many?' he looked momentarily worried.

'No more than three times,' I guessed.

He sighed and pushed into me, relaxing his neck and arms so that he lay flat on me now, his face next to mine on the pillow. I let my fingers wander into the crack of his behind and stimulated him gently. He obviously liked this, groaning softly at the sensation.

'Then I'm going to make you come four times,' he said, his hips picking up speed. He ground his pelvis against mine, my clit welcoming the gyrations.

'Promises, promises,' I teased and he chuckled into my ear.

'I didn't say they would all be today,' he joked. 'Give me a break.'

I giggled and turned to kiss him. The fabulous sensation of him inside me was overwhelming and as we kissed I crushed myself up against him more. He drew his manly big hands back down to my hips and held me against him as he pounded into me. I clasped his buttocks more firmly in response and moaned, excitement running through my veins like hot mercury. His cock felt so big and powerful inside my quivering little pussy! Suddenly I felt the tremors of a climax deep inside me. I cried out as the rapture mounted. Tom held me tight and pushed his body insistently against me, keeping up the pressure in all the right places. My cries were louder now. I knew that Alicia and Sven would hear me from the next room but I didn't care any more. I lost control, shuddering and sighing against him. 'Oh, Jo, you're so sexy,' he whispered as I shivered out my last ecstatic spasm.

'Likewise,' I replied as I came down from the euphoria. He continued to move inside me, slower again. Our eyes were locked together and I luxuriated in the warmth of his gaze, the chance to finally and frankly take in the greeny-gold detail of his iris, the long dark-blond lashes. I ran my finger over a little scar on his forehead.

'Chickenpox, aged four,' he explained. 'Don't worry, I'm not contagious.' I laughed and he jolted as his penis got an involuntary squeeze inside me.

'Sorry.'

'Please, don't apologise,' he whispered. 'That was nice.' I squeezed him again, pulling on my pelvic muscles so that they gently milked his cock. He caught his breath.

'Do you like that?'

He nodded, closing his eyes tight. I saw him swallow and knew that he was close to the edge. Soon he could hold on no longer and started to thrust again, kissing me messily, snaking his arms around me and pulling me into him. Our tongues collided and jousted. His hips were beating double time and I knew how excited he was. I wrapped my legs around him and he groaned into me, readjusting his position so he was higher over my body and my face was pressed against his firm chest. It was moist with sweat, furred with soft blond curls. I kissed him frantically, tasting his tangy skin, enjoying the male scent of him. Now the root of his cock was rubbing against my clit. I felt like a volcano about to blow, molten lava pouring from my frustrated pussy. I could hear the vibration of his groans through his ribcage and joined him with little cries of my own, my mouth crushed against his skin. His excitement turned me on more than anything else, knowing that his big cock was about to explode inside me, that I had done that to him. We were becoming helpless with lust, our bodies craving each other, needily pushing against each other. I heard him murmur my name over and over again. I felt it echo through his body. I was overwhelmed and pushed my groin harder against his. I began to come in rapturous waves, my cries louder and more desperate than before. His cock was pumping hard into me. I widened my legs and the pressure of his body on mine sent me over the edge. I held my breath and tightened my stomach. When my climax came I shuddered blissfully under him, the volcano finally erupting. He lifted his body slightly and looked down at my face.

'Christ, you're sexy,' he moaned. 'I could watch you come all day. Oh, Jo!'

As I kept on coming my orgasm massaged his already primed cock and he lost control, shooting off inside me in big, long thrusts.

We lay in a collapsed, trembling, wet heap for a while, our bodies rising and falling as we panted out our relief. He planted little kisses on my face and hair, his hand finding mine and holding it tenderly. Finally he rolled off and lay spent on his back, his fingers still laced with my own.

'I don't think they will have heard us,' he said with heavy irony.

'I just can't believe we finally did it,' I said deliriously. 'I finally got to make love to Tom Hathaway.'

He laughed softly.

'I know,' he replied. 'But I only made you come twice.'

I leaned over him, up on my elbow, my head resting on my palm.

'Sorry about that. Maybe Ray can give me a few tips.'

'Tom!' I chastised. 'Don't be silly.' I kissed him, my hand wandering down to lightly caress his sweet deflated penis nestling in his open trousers. I stroked it gratefully.

'You know what it's like?' I said. 'It's like chocolate.' He looked at me quizzically. 'You know, with cheap chocolates you can eat a whole box and somehow still not feel satisfied, just a little sick with yourself. But when you get the real thing – handmade Belgian chocolates made with seventy per cent cocoa and rolled in the most delicious things – you can only eat two. And afterwards you feel euphoric and satisfied and you'll never forget that wonderful taste.'

'Are you trying to tell me that I'm like the Belgian chocolates? And Ray and all the others were just cheap jobbies from the off-licence?' he asked smugly.

'Yes.'

'Good.' He smiled and pulled me down to kiss him again. When I pulled away he was laughing.

'What?' I demanded.

'I was just thinking, trust you to reduce everything to food,' he teased, and continued to laugh even while I was pummelling him with my pillow.

16

The office had never looked so much like a viable business venture. The carpets had been cleaned, appliances primed, paperwork filed; even Corinne had put on a trouser suit and stored away her nail file. Through the freshly scrubbed windows the generous sweep of the grey-green Thames rolled under the August sun. Jerome's office had been reorganised, gold-discs and awards now proudly displayed. He was particularly nervous, I noted, wringing his hands and occasionally dabbing at the sweat that clung to his upper lip. He had worn a blazer today and gelled his hair down to stop it flopping into his eye. We hadn't spoken much since I had retrieved Alicia.

'Obviously, we like to run a tight ship,' he was saying. The executive from New York was leaning back in his chair, surveying the office as Jerome spoke. His expensive suit and aroma of cigars made him seem deeply incongruous in our scruffy little space. 'And unlike other music magazines, we truly are cutting edge. We pride ourselves on encompassing the whole range of musical genres.'

'I am aware of the mission statement,' the American said. His name was Dirk Rosenberg, and none of us knew what to call him: Dirk? Mr Rosenberg? Sir? 'And also of the readership.' He raised a challenging eyebrow to Jerome, who faltered. The American pulled some of our back copies out of his briefcase and leafed through them. 'Quality variable, I would say.'

'Well . . .' Jerome blustered.

'You work best on a human angle; life experiences, well-written personal articles.'

'Yes.' Jerome smiled.

'But, this!' The executive pointed to an article that Jerome had written about the nature of the music business, a thinly veiled diatribe on how badly his band Black Heart had been treated. 'Subjective, unsubstantiated, weak. And I'm afraid there's more like that.' Jerome looked crestfallen. I almost felt sorry for him. Sven and I exchanged glances. This visit wasn't going well. Only Corinne managed to keep the smile plastered perkily on her face. 'So what is *A Tempo* magazine going to do about it?' There was a silence. The executive looked around the room like a schoolteacher waiting for someone to put up their hand. Sven coughed. 'Come on!' barked the man. I realised my job would be at stake if someone didn't pipe up soon.

'Well, Mr Rosenberg . . . er . . . Dirk,' I said. He turned his calm brown eyes on me slowly, looking me up and down. I too had dressed smart, wearing my lilac trouser suit. My hair was in a bun. But I still felt an air of disapproval in his gaze.

'Yes?' He looked as his papers. 'Josephina Bell, is it?' I nodded. 'Liked your Brazil piece. That's the kind of thing I'm talking about. When you write about music, I can almost hear it.'

I flushed at the compliment and felt spurred on by his words.

'Thanks. I think that's what we do best at *A Tempo*,' I replied loyally.

He leant back in his chair and gave me a cynical look. The man smelt of money, and I was quite aware that he had been paying my wages for the last year while our magazine had lost sales. Now we were all pandering to him like nervous servants.

'Continue.'

'Well, I was just going to say that we've had a great idea for the next edition,' I blurted out. Jerome looked at me sharply, a warning in his brown eyes. I realized that he didn't trust me. I hadn't had a chance to tell him about the free CD idea, or that I had single-handedly gone and authorised it (forging his signature with the help of Corinne). I decided I was on my own. 'OK, it was my idea. I'm afraid I went behind Jerome's back a little bit to get it underway. He was busy with other ... commitments.'

'Initiative or subversion?' Dirk Rosenberg said obscurely. He had a voice rich with cigars and good food. He looked at Jerome. 'Are you happy for your staff to be running the ship?'

Jerome shifted and narrowed his eyes at me.

'Not at all, sir,' he said. 'I will be reprimanding Miss Bell.' There was a time when those words would have filled me with erotic anticipation, but from his hard look I knew he meant the sack. This wasn't how I had wanted to broach the subject of my article and Tom's CD with Jerome; I had planned a subtle, persuasive approach. Now I knew I would just have to be honest.

'Before you judge me too harshly,' I said to both men, 'perhaps you would like to look at the article in question. The proof of the pudding is in the eating, as they say.'

'Yes, they do,' the executive purred, holding his hand out. 'Show me, then.' I hurriedly dived into my briefcase and pulled out my article on the Hathaways, along with a sample CD. He fingered the pages slowly as we sat and watched. Finally he held up the CD and looked at me questioningly.

'Yes, that's a free CD that would come with each copy,' I explained, avoiding Jerome's searing gaze. 'I felt that to secure a wider readership of *A Tempo* we had to invest a little in distinguishing ourselves in the market place. I consulted with my ... some people in marketing and PR.'

I heard Jerome snort. He obviously guessed I was referring to Ruby.

'And these people insisted that this was our best course of action. You have to put a little in to get a lot back and all that.'

'What are the costings?' the American asked coolly. My skin crawled. I hadn't had the time or inclination to produce any formal balance sheets or profit projections. I wasn't into all that stuff anyway. I was about to stutter out an excuse when Corinne produced a folder from her drawer.

'It's all in there,' she chirped in her clipped accent. 'The projections, the costs.'

I smiled at her gratefully. I had never quite known whether she ever did any work in the office – or indeed what her job really was – and now I was massively impressed. The room fell silent again and finally Mr Rosenberg leant forward and shook his head.

'The fact is, what you did was wrong,' he said to me. 'We can't have mavericks in the office spending all our money on their own schemes and dreams.'

I bit my lip, waiting to be given my marching orders. Jerome got up and paced over to me angrily.

'Too right!' he stormed. 'I cannot believe this, Jo. Your arrogance, your insubordination.' Clearly some of this display was to reassert his authority in the eyes of Mr Rosenberg, who watched with calm detachment. 'How dare you go behind my back? How dare you?' He glowered at me and I wondered whether he was actually waiting for a reply. He swung round to our visitor and his tone changed completely. 'I do apologise, sir. Obviously I would never have authorised such a hair-brained scheme as this. It's utterly ridiculous. I'm sorry to say that Miss Bell has been having some kind of sexual relationship with this young composer and was obviously using the magazine to win him round.'

I felt the blood rush to my face. I was embarrassed, furious and indignant. I was about to let rip at Jerome about his own dalliances when the executive interrupted, raising his hand.

'Let's not sling mud,' he said. 'I suggest you all leave the office while I have time to ruminate on what I've seen. Come back in an hour and I will pass judgement then.'

We all made uncertainly for the door.

'I will need a CD player, obviously,' he continued. 'To check this out.' Jerome looked stunned, as was I. I had assumed by Mr Rosenberg's tone that he had rejected my CD idea out of hand. 'Proof of the pudding, didn't you say, Miss Bell?'

'There's one in Jerome's office,' I said and smiled. 'Enjoy.'

We sat in silence, watching the slow passage of tourist boats across the water. Jerome was deep in thought, his ice-cream running down his hand. The breeze was trying to ruffle his heavily gelled hair. In this frank light he looked his age. Years of sex and drugs and rock 'n' roll coupled with the last hour in the office under the scrutinising gaze of Dirk Rosenberg had sent little lines across his pale skin. I almost felt sorry for him. A family of seagulls wheeled over us and broke him from his reverie.

'Where are the others?' he asked tiredly.

'Getting a pizza,' I said.

'Right.'

I leant back on the bench and tried to enjoy the afternoon sun. Jerome chuckled to himself.

'What?'

'Oh, nothing,' he sighed. 'I was just thinking of how pathetic we all were with that American.'

I laughed.

'I mean, it's only our jobs on the line.'

I stopped laughing. A large ship was edging its way under Tower Bridge. They were suspending the two halves of the bridge to let it through. It didn't seem possible.

'Jo, I've been an arse,' Jerome said sadly.

I tried to think of something positive to say, but I couldn't.

'No, I have,' he insisted.

'I'm not arguing with you, Jerome.'

'All that flirting with Alicia. It was all just ego stuff.'

'I know.'

'It meant nothing.'

'Obviously.'

He lapped at his ice-cream, deep in thought.

'It was just like those groupies in the 8os. I could get any teeny-bopper to suck my cock, and I went for it.'

I nodded. I'd heard it all before.

'All those little girlies wanting me to take their virginities; some of them were gorgeous, you know. It was like that with Alicia. I mean, a beautiful woman, throwing herself at me. It was meaningless and shallow.'

'But going back to your wife, that meant something,' I interrupted.

He smiled ruefully.

'We had a lot of history,' he explained.

I marvelled at his talent for cliché.

'She knows me so well. She doesn't expect too much of me.' He looked crumpled and defeated. 'So she doesn't get disappointed. I always felt you wanted more from me than I was able to give.'

I nodded. He was right there. Suddenly my mind settled on the lovely warm image of Tom and I realised how lucky I was to have found him.

'I've had an offer,' Jerome continued. 'They're doing one of those 80s revival tours. Got some good acts. They've approached Black Heart to come along on tour.'

I tried to look excited for him.

'Great! Where will you be going?' I asked.

'Oh, nowhere glam. Not like the old days,' he said, mocking himself. 'Stevenage, Dartford, Peterborough.' He bit into his cone and sighed. 'Of course, not all the old line-up will be available. Ron's running an accountancy firm now, and Jimmy was never really all there after all the drugs he took.' Jerome turned to me, his brown eyes imploring. 'I don't suppose I can persuade you to come with me? To give it another go?'

I stifled a laugh; he hadn't exactly sold it to me. 'You're such a fantastic girl. We had some good times, didn't we? We could be great again . . .'

'I don't think so, Jez.' He sighed sadly.

'I think I'll go back to the missus then,' he said eventually.

'You never know,' I smiled. 'We might not all be sacked. I think our friend Dirk secretly admires our little set-up.'

'No, I think my time is up.'

I took his hand and pulled him to his feet. It was time to go back. We walked slowly hand in hand along the river path to get the verdict.

Mr Rosenberg's face looked different when we came back into the office. He was standing by the window, smoking a cigar, with a satisfied glint in his eye. He gestured with his podgy brown hand for us all to come in and sit before him. When we were all in place he took a hearty suck of tobacco.

'You know, Mrs Rosenberg doesn't like me lighting up,' he began in his gravely voice. 'In fact, she hates it. She threatens to leave me. She threatens to sue.'

I exchanged looks with Sven; was this going anywhere?

'So, people, I am trained to limit my smoking habits to when it is really necessary. After all, I can't afford a divorce, know what I mean?' He grinned broadly for the first time. 'I only have a Cuban after a great meal, after great sex or with a fine cognac. That's it.'

We looked at him blankly. None of the above were freely available in our office.

'But today, people, I've made an exception. Because I feel like I've had all three rolled into one.' He walked over to me. 'Miss Josephina Bell, ladies and gentlemen.' I resisted the urge to giggle. 'This lady has just written the winning article, the one to turn this kooky little magazine of yours around. And on top of that, she has single-handedly, *single-handedly*' – that was aimed at Jerome who coughed nervously – 'come up with a simple marketing ploy that will boost sales and save *A Tempo*. Great CD. Not even available in the shops. We're talking cult here. This is the woman who has saved you your jobs.' There was a collective sigh of relief in the office. For the first time that day I saw the cheeky glint return to Jerome's eye. It didn't last long. Mr Rosenberg turned on him. 'Except you,' he continued remorselessly.

'What?' Corinne gasped, obviously believing Jerome to be invincible.

'That's business, folks,' Mr Rosenberg said. Jerome's ashen face was etched with resignation. Mr Rosenberg handed him a cigar. 'You will get a redundancy package, naturally. But we need to move on. Miss Bell?'

He passed me a cigar, too, and I took it, bemused. Perhaps I could experiment with it later, I thought,

White House style. I'm sure Tom would oblige. I wouldn't know where to start if I had to smoke the thing.

'How would you like to be editor? You've got ideas, wit, a spirit of adventure and, most of all, chutzpah! We need more like you, young lady.' I stared at him in stunned silence. He misinterpreted my reaction. 'Of course, there will be more money, better perks, more holiday, more resources. A great package for you.'

All eyes were on me. Finally Jerome came and hugged me, whispering congratulations in my ear. The shock started to crack and I screamed in excitement.

'When do I start?' I asked.

'Straightaway, if you like,' Mr Rosenberg smiled. 'Although I'm sure you'll want a few days off to celebrate?' I nodded wildly. 'And let me send a crate of champagne to the PR people who advised you,' he said generously. 'We owe them one.'

I laughed, imagining Ruby's face when she got it.

'We certainly do,' I said.

17

Tom and I were sitting cross-legged on the floor of the dining room at Hathaway Hall.

'Congratulations to the new editor of *A Tempo* magazine,' he said, holding his glass up to mine.

'Congratulations to the new – what was it again?' I rummaged around the messy chaos on the floor until I found the newspaper review of Tom's CD. 'Yes: "The new face of British jazz music". And a very endearing face it is, too.' We clinked and sipped our orange juice, allowing ourselves a smug moment of mutual admiration. I sighed happily. The house seemed so different now. Its veneer of well-ordered style was straining under the weight of my talent for getting things untidy. It was starting to look lived in again. And we were still getting used to the silence. Without Alicia there, it was a haven of tranquillity.

'It's been a mad few weeks,' Tom sighed. He looked tired, and it wasn't just my constant demands for sex that had got him that way. Neither of us had expected the amazing reaction to his free CD in *A Tempo*, nor the flood of offers it had provoked. He had quickly signed up with a manager – yet another of Ruby's contacts – and was preparing to record a full-length album. Classical and jazz artists were lining up to work with him.

'It's only just beginning,' I said, both in promise and warning. 'Anyway, it's about time you Hathaways did some work for a living.'

'Well, if Alicia can, I can.'

I couldn't help but smirk.

'Launching your own design label on family money is hardly work,' I commented wryly. Although my relationship with his sister had improved immeasurably over the past few weeks, I still thought she lived in cloud cuckoo land. But she had got the reality check of her life in New York, and now her decision to settle in London and try to pursue a career seemed to be grounding her even more. No more the affected speech, the glorious-hostess routine or the power games. The longer she lived away from her ancestral home, the more she was discovering her own style and personality. And the patient administrations of Sven weren't hurting either, I mused. The man was besotted with her.

'She's got talent.' Tom instinctively defended her. It was sweet really. He was a good person to have on your side.

'I know, I know.' I watched him sip his drink as he leant back against an armchair, finding a pool of morning sunlight to warm his face. He really was criminally good-looking, I noticed proudly, wondering if it was too early in the day to ravish him. He caught me watching him.

'What are you thinking?' he asked softly. He leaned forward and said with teasing deliberation: 'Are you anxious for your presents?' He flashed me a grin, knowing that this would get me going.

'Presents?!' I jerked out of my reverie. 'What presents?'

He reached behind him and pulled out a stack of untidily wrapped gifts. I squealed in delight, all thoughts of sex momentarily leaving my head.

'Your congratulation presents, of course,' he explained. 'Now that you're a hotshot magazine editor with her own office and a whopping salary, I guess

I'm just going to have to buy your love.' He pushed the pile towards me. The wrapping paper was pink and gold and he had inexpertly tied gold ribbon around it. It had obviously been a labour of love wrapping them up, each parcel as haphazardly assembled as the next.

'Well, I would argue with that, but I think this type of behaviour should only be encouraged.' I smiled, feeling one of the parcels. 'Bribery is a wonderful thing.'

'Of course, when I'm a world-famous composer with my face on the cover of *Time* magazine, you'll probably have to think of ways to bribe me, too,' he continued. 'Blowjobs. Strip shows. Blowjobs . . .'

'Yeah, we'll see. Just remember, *A Tempo* has first refusal on you, though.' I carefully unwrapped the top present, feeling his eyes on me as I did so and arching my back to make myself more attractive to him. I was still anxious for him to fancy me at all times. The present was hidden inside another layer of tissue paper, which I unfolded to reveal an expensive-looking black chiffon slip. It was entirely transparent in a baby-doll style and was so short I knew it would barely skim my buttocks. The bust was lined with lace. Tom grinned.

'More a present for me than you,' he conceded. I examined it. It was a little fussier and more froufrou than I would have chosen for myself, but I knew it would accentuate my figure well. It was truly a man's idea of sexiness and I creamed a little at the thought of Tom's reaction to it.

'I can't wait to try it on.' I smiled and dived happily into my next gift. This time I was less reverent with the paper and tore it off excitedly. Soon I pulled out a bottle of massage lotion and a sturdy black dildo. I clicked the base of it and it whirred into action. 'Tom!'

I was aghast. I hadn't had him down for a sex-toys type of guy.

'Just in case I ever fail to give you four orgasms,' he teased. I fiddled with the toy, seeing that it had three speeds and a rotating head that churned around. My hand numbed as it buzzed away. It was a marvellous creation. I stared at it wondrously and fingered its girth, putting it against my cheek. After a while Tom became exasperated.

'OK, enough of that.' He pulled it from my grasp. 'It's not supposed to be *instead* of me, it's just supplemental.'

I let go of it reluctantly and ripped open the final gift. It was a small box of luxury Belgian chocolates.

Tom grinned.

'As you like them so much,' he explained unnecessarily. I leaned forward on all fours and kissed him. He cupped my head in his hands as his yielding lips grazed against mine. I was all aglow with presents and erotic possibilities. The grandfather clock ticked away as our kiss unravelled and I sank between Tom's legs, our mouths never leaving each other. Whenever I kissed him, especially when his tongue played with mine, my panties became slick with moisture. He held me close, his hands moving over my body and finding my breasts. My nipples thrust through the tight fabric of my jumper, aching to be fondled.

'Aren't you going to try on your new present?' he asked throatily. 'I've been fantasising about you in it for days.'

'You've been fantasising about it in me, you mean?' I joked, clutching on to the vibrator.

'No, the dress, you little slut,' he said. 'Although I can't say the image of you playing with that big black dildo hasn't been playing on my mind.'

I liked that idea. I pulled away and stood before him, slowly unzipping my skirt and easing it over my hips. It sighed to the floor. I felt the heat of the morning sun warm my bare legs and moved slightly to illuminate more of my body in its light. Tom's eyes roamed over my body admiringly. I noticed with a tingling little ache that his trousers were tenting at the front. I longed to slip off my panties and lower myself onto him. I really had to learn to be more patient. I unhooked my bra and let it fall to the ground. My big tits bounced a little as they were released and Tom exhaled. My aroused nipples were erect and dark and ready to be sucked. They knew how well Tom did that. He had one of those hot mouths and a fast, solicitous tongue that telepathically knew where to lick and how much. It was all I could do to not fall onto my knees before him and press myself into his mouth. Finally I slipped my knickers down and kicked them off my ankles. Tom stared at the soft triangle between my legs, which had grown back now to its usual slight downy triangle. I basked in the warmth of his gaze, feeling utterly naked and exposed before him and enjoying the trust that went with that. He passed me up the slip and I wriggled into it. It was probably a size too small; the stretchy chiffon clung to my boobs and caught on my hips. My nipples and labia were clearly visible through the material. Tom reached up and touched me.

'It's even sexier than I imagined,' he whispered, his gentle hands exploring the feel of the fabric. His fingers landed on my pussy and caressed the inflamed lips, sliding around in my arousal. 'That's sweet,' he said. 'Your pussy lips are pouting at me.' He diddled them gently and then pulled me down on top of him. The hard shape of his erection pressed into my belly and I wriggled down his lap to unzip him and take him in my mouth. The air was cool on my upturned, naked bottom as I lovingly fondled his shaft with my tongue. I heard his breaths deepen with desire as I slid it in and out of my wet mouth, deliriously tasting his smooth, clean saltiness. 'Oh, Jo,' he murmured, 'yes.' His fingers curled in my hair and I swirled my tongue lightly around the fat head of his cock, flickering at the delicate underside until he quivered with frustration. I kissed lightly up the shaft and around his balls. When I finally took him all in again he groaned with relief and I felt his balls harden in anticipation. I glanced up at him. He was staring at my body as I went down on him, his eyes glued to the generous swell of my cleavage, which was accentuated by the baby-doll cut of the slip, and the pert roundness of my bare behind.

I sat up for a moment and unhooked the straps of the slip, pulling the top down a little so that my breasts were free. I grappled for the massage lotion he had given me and generously oiled my tits, trying not to get too much on my new slip. He groaned as I rubbed the oil into my skin. Then I sank back down and nestled his erection in the slippery haven of my cleavage. He watched intently as I slowly began to massage the shaft between my oily breasts, my whole body rocking over his to stimulate him. The sucking sounds of his cock rubbing up against my lubricated tits filled the air. I stuck my buttocks in the air, vainly fantasising that someone would come in and touch my smouldering pussy, and saw Tom take in the view of them with increasing arousal.

'God, that's good,' he murmured. 'If only I could make love to you at the same time. If only I could lick you.' I moaned in agreement, my neglected clit quivering at the idea. The cold air against my pussy accentuated how wet I had become. I wanted to make him come, but I wanted desperately to come myself. 'Oh, don't stop!' I returned my mouth to him with renewed vigour, milking him with my tongue. 'Oh, yes, yes.' I gobbled down the shaft with my wet mouth and gently wanked him at the same time. His body went rigid and I heard him hold his breath. I moaned, excitedly anticipating what was about to happen. My fingers curled around his balls and I felt them tighten and contract as he shot off in my mouth. He yelled out in climax and I drank down the salty mouthful with glee. By the time I had drunk the last drop my pussy was in a state of gushing overexcitement. I rolled onto my back like a cat inviting someone to caress her tummy. My legs fell open under their transparent canopy and my breasts were swollen with anticipation. Tom caressed my body and kissed me deeply, tasting his own come on my tongue.

'You're amazing,' he whispered, his finger slipping inside me. I sighed. 'Beautiful.' He reached over and poured some of the massage oil into his palm, rubbing it with his hands to make it warm, then smearing it on my legs. He sensuously massaged my calves and thighs, tickling my buttocks and inner thighs, which were already glistening with my own juices. I longed for him to press his fingers inside me again, or to lower his head between my legs and lick me. I raised my pelvis, pushing my groin in the air. My sodden pussy opened up in his face, demanding attention.

'Patience,' he said. I writhed in frustration as he oiled my tummy and let the mixture drip down into my navel and pubes. It tickled as it trickled over my skin and mingled with my own juices.

'Please Tom,' I pleaded, 'touch me there!' He tantalisingly kissed my throat and nibbled my breasts. 'Please!' I begged. He got the dildo and played it about the entrance of my sex. I felt the firm, intimidating size of it slowly sink into me and looked at Tom's rapt face as he watched it disappear into my wetness. Its head was wide and bulbous and I tensed up a little as I felt it shoulder its way inside me.

'Relax,' Tom soothed and pressed it into me. The oil eased its passage and soon I was crammed full, my pussy gratefully contracting around it. He looked closer, examining me intently, his eyes fixed on my ravenous cunt, which had swallowed up eight fat inches of cock. Then he clicked the vibrator on and I sighed as it jiggled inside me. He turned it up and it buzzed noisily. My whole body shook with its current and a slow fire ignited inside me. Tom groaned at the sight and bent down to gently lap at my clit as he manipulated the toy, moving it inside me like an insistent penis. As his tongue got faster, he clicked the toy onto full power and the pleasure of its vibrations filled my hungry hole.

'Oh, God,' I sighed. 'Oh, don't stop. Don't ever stop!' His tongue danced across my clit. The contrast between its hot, soft, malleable wetness stimulating me expertly and the unyielding cold plastic of the huge toy inside me was breathtaking. I had never been fucked and licked at the same time and it was almost too much excitement for my pussy to bear. I started to lose all control. I cried out and clutched Tom's head to me, vigorously riding the big black dildo until I had absorbed its entirety. The burning excitement in my pussy became more intense, hotter, wetter. The dildo was so big and Tom's tongue so fast that I worried that I would lose it completely and my bladder would release when I came. Sensing my excitement, Tom started to fuck me furiously with the toy, so hard it almost hurt. My whorish pussy welcomed the brutal thrusts and my feverish intoxication mounted. I surrendered myself, mashing my slippery sex against Tom's mouth. Rasping spasms shuddered through me and my body jerked up as I came. Tom's tongue tirelessly eased out the last of my orgasm and he looked up at me, still holding the huge vibrating object inside me. His hands and face were bathed in my slippery wetness.

'I can't wait to fuck you again,' he sighed.

'Please,' was all I could say. I writhed about on the hard plastic, longing for it to be his cock.

'God, it's good to be alone with you.' He gently eased the toy out of me and turned it off. I saw him sniff its sticky length and sigh. 'That's the most sexy smell on earth,' he breathed. I sat up and wriggled onto Tom's lap, straddling him needily. I took the dildo from him. It was smeared with the sticky evidence of my orgasm. As he watched I slowly fellated it, sucking it into my mouth and taking it in as far as I could. I lapped up my own tangy juices. Tom watched fascinated as I gave head to the big black toy.

'You're insatiable,' he teased, his hard penis pushing against my sex.

'You like to watch me, don't you?' I replied, noticing how his penis jumped enviously every time I sucked the dildo into my mouth. I did it again, just to check. Sure enough his cock strained at the sight of my lips wrapped around the pretend cock.

'I do,' he admitted huskily.

'Then I have a present for you,' I said. My heart was in my mouth.

'What's that?' he asked, eyes gleaming.

I hesitated. Was he really ready for what I was about to show him? All this sex talk was all well and good but I wondered whether he could take the reality of it. I faltered.

'You'll see,' I teased, buying time. He reached around him and opened up the chocolates. He chose one – a dark praline rolled in sugared almond pieces and bitter cocoa – and popped it into my mouth. It was so big that I couldn't talk any more.

'That's better,' he smiled. I nodded, loving the heady, creamy taste in my mouth. 'No more false promises of non-existent gifts.' Tom kissed me, stealing some of the flavour onto his own tongue. Our mouths became a messy, wrestling crush of melted chocolate. We broke away laughing.

'Who said you could have some of my chocolates?' I demanded.

'Ingrate.' He made to grab me and I got up and ran from him. I decided to make him work for it a little. I ran up the stairs, my black slip no protection against the draughts of the creaky old house. He followed me and soon we both ended up in his bedroom. I threw myself on the bed, the place of our first encounter, I remembered dreamily. His teddy was still there and I held it to my breast.

'Fancy a threesome?' I asked the bear. Tom pulled it away.

'Don't listen to that little slut,' he said, chucking it across the room so that it landed with a loud ping on the piano keys.

Tom slipped beside me and we nestled under the duvet, holding each other longingly. My body couldn't help but wrap itself around his. His mouth sought out mine and he kissed me profoundly. He still tasted of chocolate. I began to whimper as my arousal became unbearable again. I yanked his trousers and pants down so finally he was half naked, but I couldn't negotiate all the buttons of his shirt. His bare legs locked with mine, and his cock found my pussy like a heat-seeking missile. Soon he was inside me. He pulled my breasts free of the slip so that he could tenderly suckle as he moved inside me. The top of his blond head brushed my chin as he worshipped noisily at my breasts, sending quivers of pleasure all through me. The feel of his cock was warm and rubbery after the hard stabbing of the dildo and I melted around it. Soon, a heady, helpless intoxication overpowered me. He had whipped me up like cream into stiff peaks. Once again, my climax set him off and he tirelessly pumped inside me with the energy of a rocket, spilling his juices until they poured down my legs.

This time we had exhausted ourselves. My pussy was sore from its many invasions and my breasts ached from being sucked so much. Tom lay next to me, utterly spent. Somehow, though, I knew that we would soon recover and become compulsively glued to each other again. Our bodies had short memories and were constantly ready for more sex. We were like frantic teenagers who had just discovered the joys of fucking and couldn't stop doing it. Even after a few minutes my pussy started to twitch again, wanting another ride on the roller coaster. I heard Tom sigh and I imagined he was feeling the same thing.

'What?' I asked dreamily.

'I was just thinking, I hope nothing spoils this,' Tom replied. The idea of it stopped my heart for a moment. I had been in that smug honeymoon period where you never imagine the sheen of happiness getting tarnished. He must have felt me stiffen, because he rolled over and smiled warmly. 'I'm sure it won't,' he said. 'We've had all our impediments already. And anyway, we don't have any secrets from each other.'

I went quiet, thinking it really was time to hand over the present.

'Kind of,' I said.

Tom cleared his throat and sat up in bed. I sat up too.

'What do you mean, "kind of"?' He looked ever so serious all of a sudden, even under the comically tousled disarray of his bed-head.

I reached down under the bed and pulled out a wrapped present. I handed it over.

'What's this?'

'I haven't lied,' I said hurriedly. 'Not ever. Well, not to you.' He cautiously unwrapped the gift and saw that it contained the photos that Ray had taken of me. His face was staunch and unflinching as he slowly leafed through each shot. 'I just wanted you to see these. Although you knew about them, I was worried that they might upset you.' I gabbled, disturbed by his earnestness. He carried on his thorough examination in silence. I had been just as absorbed when I had first received them through the post from Ray. There were about twenty pictures, all flattering, frank and sexually charged. In each of them the explicit evidence of my arousal was clearly and beautifully depicted, my vulva as glistening and lush as a tropical flower. I hoped Tom would see it just as poetically.

'Are you upset?'

Tom got to the post-sex photo. I was splayed wantonly on the bed, my raw, puffy sex spewing Ray's come. Euphoric satisfaction was clear in my contented, exhausted expression and the sheen of sweat that covered my body. Beneath me the crumpled sheets were stained with semen. Not even the black and white film had taken the edge off the pornography of it. On seeing that photo my body had instantly ripened into an erotic state, but I imagined it could just as easily turn Tom off in absolute disgust. After all, another man had got me that way.

'Tom?' He was still silently poring over it, his eyes drawn to the frank openness of my labia. 'I just wanted you to see these. So there aren't any secrets.'

He finally put the photos down. The blood had gone from his ashen face.

'Are you angry?' I asked.

He turned to me gravely.

'I have never seen anything so...' he searched for the word, 'so *arousing* in my whole life.' I scoured his face for clues of his mood. 'You little hussy!' he cried and dived on top of me sending the photos flying across the room. 'What are we going to do with you, eh?' He yanked my dress off and I felt with amazement the stiff slap of his erection on my thigh. I laughed in relief. 'I can see I'm going to have to keep an eye on you,' he scolded, turning me onto my tummy and spanking my bottom. I had a giggling fit as he slapped away. I was thrown across his lap and with every strike I ground against the hardness of his cock. 'What if I go off on concert tours? What if I have to go and promote myself in America?' he said, still spanking.

'Tom!'

'Are you going to be a good girl?'

'Maybe.'

'Are you?' he spanked more sharply now and I felt my buttocks start to glow red under his palm.

'Yes.'

'Promise?'

'Ow! Yes!'

He slapped gently at my pussy and the blood rushed to my lips again.

'Even if I'm away for months on end?'

'Yes!' my voice was rising in excitement, my engorged clit loving the sensation of his little slaps.

'Good.' He pushed me onto my back and I laughed at his stern face. 'If you're going to be a naughty girl, I want to be there to see it. You understand?' he chastised.

'Yes.'

'Yes, what?'

'Yes, Mr Hathaway?' I said with a giggle.

'You can call me sir,' he reprimanded. 'If other men want to fuck you or lick you or feel you up – and I'm sure they will – you do nothing till I'm there. Get it?'

I looked at him, bemused.

'You mean, you want to watch?' I asked. 'You mean, I'm allowed to do anything I like so long as you get to see me do it?' I was incredulous. I knew the Hathaways were bohemian and open minded, but I had never expected Tom to be so indulgent of my wayward desires. He dipped his fingers between my legs and massaged me possessively.

'That's right, you little minx.' His fingers slid around in the gloopy warmth of me.

My mind began to race with possibilities. Kieran and Harry would be delighted. They could fuck me while Tom looked on. Or maybe I could persuade him to live out Alicia's fantasy and take all three of them on, one in each orifice. I trembled at the thought. Tom tickled my clit and I shut my eyes. Maybe I could ask Mr Wootten over and have him fuck me, I fantasised. Alicia had seemed to rate him as a lover. I could dress up as a schoolgirl; that would turn him on. I sighed, my imagination running riot as Tom slipped under the sheets and placed his tongue where his finger had just been. He licked away tenderly, butterfly strokes sending my nerves all aquiver. Or perhaps Ray could visit us and Tom could watch as the skilled American brought me to a climax. Ray could take photos of Tom fucking me on the piano! I pulled my lover's head into me as my fantasies reached fever pitch. And there was always that 'special room' with its whips and chains and furred chairs. That room was buzzing with erotic memories. It had witnessed my night of shame at Alicia's party. It had seen Alicia herself being deflowered by Mr Wootten. Most arousing of all, it had seen Daphne have her first sexual encounter, with a man of the cloth. As I remembered reading about that episode I creamed in Tom's face. He licked at me frantically, his deep voice rumbling as he became excited at the taste of me. I thought of all the men I could fuck, of all the adventures I could have, and my pussy was crazed with desire. Then I considered the handsome, talented, sexy guy who was at that moment whipping me up to a fantastic orgasm with his tongue. The man with his head buried between my shivering thighs. The one with my pussy mashed up against his mouth. The one who yelled out into my cunt as he felt me buck out a climax when the excitement got too much for me. The one who loved me so much that he was prepared to put up with my curiosity and desire for other men. After he had licked me dry, he crawled back up my body and held me. His face was hot in my hands.

'You'd really let me do all those other men?' I asked, amazed.

'Yes, Jo,' he sighed. 'I don't want to tie you down. I want you to feel free. But mostly I want you to myself,' he warned. His handsome face looked down on me earnestly. I loved his crown of blond hair, his mesmerising green eyes. His powerful body was lean and defined, and his cock seemed to be eternally hard for me. I was reminded of a passage in Daphne's diary, where she fantasised about one day finding a man who could 'fulfil all my passions'. I suddenly realised that I had found him. I knew I'd never need anyone else.

'You've got me. One hundred per cent,' I replied. 'I'm all yours.'